THE
OBSESSIONS
OF
HARVEY
USHER

THE OBSESSIONS OF HARVEY USHER

A NOVEL

DAVID PUTNAM

LEVEL
BEST BOOKS

First published by Level Best Books 2025

Author Photo Credit: Heather Putnam

First edition

ISBN: 978-1-68512-862-3

Cover art by Christian Storm

This book was professionally typeset on Reedsy.
Find out more at reedsy.com

To my wonderful grandchildren, Elliot, Penny, and Oliver (Tank).

Chapter One

Current Day: The Mission District of Riverside, California

Harvey Usher's gnarled and bunioned feet with minds of their own found the fur-lined slippers long past their prime. Tattered around the edges with smooth leather cracked and desiccated. A gift from Sylvia not easily discarded. He smiled and waved a hand at the bird, "Go find some worms, it might still be early enough."

He suddenly froze. The smile disappeared. A second sound came from the other side of the bedroom door.

He stopped breathing and waited for a recurrence, a clue to the disturbance. A creak from a settling house, the feral meow from a tom on the prowl, or what a staunch recluse feared most: a knock at the front door.

Clink.

Barely audible, yet the sound made it past the thick reinforced bedroom door and its fellow deadbolt.

The shuffle-step across the gold shag carpet to the door allowed time for him to ruminate on the sound's origin. A tired ear eased against the door and waited.

Someone moved around on the other side. In the living room…no farther. Beyond the living room, all the way into the kitchen.

Someone had entered the house without authorization.

How was that possible? Never in the last four decades had anything like that happened.

Over at the solid oak nightstand sat an old push-button Princess phone. Call the police?

No. Not even if the interloper came to rob and steal. Can't have them in the house under any circumstances.

From the other side of the door came: "Harvey? Come, my dearest. Breakfast is getting cold."

A woman?

How could that be?

No one else resided in the house and hadn't since Sylvia... Not since that morning with the tray and the roses—

A rat-a-tat-tat made it past the door. A noise that could only come from high heels. A sound that ignited stark imagery. A memory that harked back to a time decades past to women in long creamy dresses and black stockings with lines up the backs of wonderful gams. A time of pink angora sweaters and red lipstick. But more important, of flashing young eyes seeking a forbidden undertaking, lurid and discreet, created by a natural yearning.

The black stockings only visible when the women laughed and twirled on the dance floor to the musical harmony of a brand-new sound called rock and roll. A bruised and tired memory of an eighty-year-old man might have mixed up the clothing, the music. The decades.

A smile in the face of adversity crept out and quickly shifted to a sneer. An image came to mind of a burglar, a lowlife, back-alley dweller. An animal who made the choice to prey upon the elderly did not wear spiked heels or have luscious gams.

Or a kind and alluring voice.

What did that leave?

The mysterious question left an unquenchable desire to know the answer.

No woman had resided in the big home since Sylvia had passed. Right? Damn memory slipped the same as skin and muscle that all sagged in a race to the floor.

The double-key deadbolt clacked loudly when turned, the two slide bolts, one atop and one down low—both needing oil—came loose only after vulgar words, that all on their own, spewed forth. Paper-thin skin on a shaky right hand tore and bled when it slipped off the sticky bottom bolt. But the door finally came free with a creak loud enough to wake the dead. Loud enough for the woman with the wonderful gams to hear all the way over in the kitchen.

Spiked heels again clacked on the highly polished hardwood floors. The sound headed toward the hall and the bedroom door, now open a crack. The disabled locks a rising vulnerability not easily suppressed.

Based on the sound, she stopped midway, hesitated. "Harvey? Love, we're not going to play this same silly, ol' game again, are we?"

"I don't know what you are talking about. I don't know you. Quit pretending that you know me. What are you doing in my house?"

"Oh, my poor, poor darling Harvey. Please come out and let's have a nice talk."

The bedroom door eased open a bit farther. What dangers could a beautiful woman pose?

Loneliness played too large a factor when safety was concerned.

Without relatives or friends, who was there left to talk to?

Could this be the entirety of a full life coming to an unremarkable end? Through the last ten or fifteen years, how easy it had been to gradually, without fanfare, allow life's social aspect to slide away into quiet oblivion. All of those lost years leading up to this strange person on the other side of the door, trespassing and pretending to be a friend.

No, that wasn't right either. Sylvia had been there for all those decades. Five wonderful, sweet decades. More than a wife. A special friend.

Now this. "Ugh."

The bonehead counselor from the grief support group never missed a chance to remind everybody that the mind tended toward only remembering the good times. The reason grief weighed so heavy on a lost soul.

The woman appeared in the hall, ten feet from the bedroom door, held ajar, ready to slam shut and lock.

This aberration, this mirage, resembled Rita Hayworth in "Gilda." With perfect red hair and smooth, creamy skin. But most of all, mischievous yet inviting green eyes.

The door eased open even more in sync with a mouth agape in a full state of agog.

How could this be? A young man's dream come sixty years too late. Life wasn't fair that way.

Especially when it came to women.

Had the silly red robin from earlier been trying to warn him about this... this inexplicable Ms. Universe, burglarizing a tired old man's abode? All the while wearing a slinky black dress and black spiked heels? With hips and a bosom right out of the Hollywood Reporter?

Had to be a dream.

"Harvey, my love. Please, come eat your breakfast before it gets cold."

He stuck his head out between the door's edge and the jamb. "Who are you? What do you want? What is the meaning of this? You can't come into my house uninvited? Get out. Get out before I call the police." The tone lacked confidence.

Tears appeared under those luscious green eyes. She sniffled. "Baby, your vicious games have become tedious and more hurtful than you know. Come eat or don't. But you had better stop this..." She extended a hand and came slowly forward, mimicking someone in the wild approaching a timid baby doe.

The door wanted to close, to slam shut, but wouldn't obey.

She came on, step after step. Her hand rose and ever so gently touched the jowly cheek that had once been firm and handsome—so sayeth Sylvia, anyway.

The hand, warm and soft as a baby's bottom, mesmerized.

She whispered, "Come, my darling."

How could any warm-blooded male resist such an offer? Even for one far closer to the mortician table than the birthing bed.

In the formal dining room, at the long oak table, she had set a full breakfast; eggs scrambled easy, four rashers of bacon, and two flapjacks dotted with chocolate chips. Flapjacks that filled the entire plate. Orange juice and coffee, black. All told, an absolute perfect breakfast combination.

For a man of thirty, maybe.

CHAPTER ONE

A man of eighty ate no more than the silly red robin outside the bedroom window.

But how did she know this had been the meal of choice from way back when?

How did this vixen know about the eggs scrambled easy or the flapjacks with chocolate chips? Those particular ingredients had not been in this house for at least a decade. She must have brought them along, props in this insidious play of hers.

But what else could it be but a dream? One true even to the senses. Something not at all possible; the smells, the physical touches. The reality. Not a chance.

She pulled out the heavy dining room chair, sat, and watched. Her eyes trying hard to see into the unfavorable thoughts of a careless old man. An old man who desperately tried to shift away from her gaze and claw a path back to reality.

Her hypnotic trance could beguile the wisest of old fools. What geriatric gentleman with any hint of leftover testosterone, any whisper of a past memory of such, would not do anything this vixen asked?

"You have me at a disadvantage. You know my name and I don't know yours." The words wormed their way around the gnashing scrambled eggs and flapjacks.

She reached over and laid that same warm hand on the wrinkled jowl, a move that caused blood to flush warm up and down his back and into his face.

"Harvey dearest, you know my name. Please try and remember. You're hurting my feelings again."

"Hmm." Another bite of folded-over flapjack gave the pause needed to once again search every corner of his memory. No way could anyone forget such a...such a princess as this lovely woman.

But oh, she was a liar for the ages.

She sat back, those ruby red lips turning to a flatline. "Delores. My name is Delores. We met two years ago...no, two years, one month ago on the Santa Monica pier. I sat on a bench while my boyfriend Herb messed around

5

with two strange girls trying to get their car started out on the street. I was mad as a wet hen because they flirted with him and he flirted back. It was hot, a beautiful day. Bright blue with white clouds chasing each other across the sky. You remember any of this Harv?"

"Hmm, no."

"I was eating a pistachio ice cream cone, that was melting too fast for me to keep up with it. My tongue was really going to town."

Up until that moment, she had come off as a polite, genteel woman. But now made salacious movements with an overactive pink tongue miming licking an out of control cone in a delicate hand with bright red polished nails.

Absolutely captivating.

Who would've thought? Not in a million years. Waking to a slice of life, a burglar walking on spiked heels. A true beauty running a con game.

Any fool could see exactly what she was doing. The first rule of a con: delay and distract while employing sleight of hand to fleece the mark.

But what was the game? What could she possibly want from a doddering old fool who had to stand at the toilet every morning for fifteen minutes waiting for his pisser to cooperate?

Enough playing her game. Enough being batted around like a ball of yarn by Puss in Boots. Well, Puss in spiked heels.

The longer one allowed this type of praying mantis to run the game, the longer it would take, if at all, to extricate oneself from the perilous situation.

"Tell me your game or I'm calling the cops." The words were difficult to force out, obstinate, all of them trying too hard to be friends to the lovely woman.

Her eyes widened. "Seriously?"

"Come now, Delores. A pistachio ice cream cone in summertime? How trite. And I've never in my life visited the Santa Monica pier. Nice try, but a hit and a miss. Never work your mark unless you do your homework first."

The part about the pier was a lie. Sylvia loved visiting the ocean, the warmth, the salt air. But this was a game of wits, one where every inch of ground mattered. The give and the take.

She held out a hand and chuckled. "Go on then. This won't be the first time you've called them."

"What the hell?" The room turned hot, the air thick. Her response, not something expected or easily grasped. Advanced age, an evil mistress not to be trifled with. She'll snatch away memory cells when you aren't looking. Treat them to a meal before slicing their throats and laying them to waste. Had that been the case this time? Dead memory cells?

Rita Hayworth was good, no doubt about it.

Sylvia had been tried and true right to the end. The memory of her remained strong and indisputable. If that part were true, then where was the memory of Delores?

Delores had, simply put, appeared in the house with criminal intent. No other explanation made sense.

"Don't try and stop me, either. So, unless you get out right now, I'm calling the cops."

She again held out her hand. "Please, Harvey, just do it. Let's get this over with so we can start our day. We were going to the Getty, remember?"

The Getty, she said it as if she were cultured and not a throw-back to a fifties five and dime, pulp detective novel.

She got up, sauntered over to the counter, the black dress swished, the spiked heels clacked. She picked up the phone, gave it a little jerk to swing the long cord free. Her bountiful bosom jiggled.

Oh, dear Lord.

"Who dresses like that to go to the Getty?"

She didn't respond, returned and set the phone alongside the platter of flapjacks, barely touched, his appetite fleeing for higher ground.

Sweat ran and stung his eyes and tasted of salt.

Don't let her do this. Don't let her run the game. The distraction. She's winning with the distraction. Somehow, with her other metaphorical hand, she's fleecing you. Do something. Don't just bluff. Make the call.

With each number punched in, the phone beeped. Her expression never faltered and remained stalwart and unafraid.

What the hell was going on?

The nice woman on the other end of the line said, "Riverside Police Department. How may I help you?"

Chapter Two

Current Day

In the expensive part of any town, once the cops are called, they don't lollygag; they move their butts. Not seven minutes after hanging up the phone, a knock came at the front door.

Delores rose from the dining room chair as if nothing was amiss and clacked her way in spiked heels past the long entryway to the front door. The tight black cocktail dress rode the curves like a sports car on Mulholland Drive.

Red, blue, and orange shone through the stained-glass center of the door, lit Rita's legs and moved up a gorgeous body to wonderful, glistening red hair, creating an angelic aura. The sight gave pause. It would for anyone.

What the hell was going on? What was her game?

Was calling the cops on an angel a big mistake? After all, what did he have to lose? At eighty years old, was the last chapter in life coming to an unceremonious end? A life that roared in a like a lion and squeaked out like a mouse. How dangerous could it actually be to play her little con without involving the law? A woman right off the cover of Vogue magazine. In fact, something like this never happened. Maybe in a movie with Audrey Hepburn and George Peppard.

Why not wait at least an hour, maybe two, see how it all played out.

Too late now, though; the wolves already stood outside the front door.

"Wait. Don't."

She tossed that red hair over a delicate boned shoulder when she looked back. The grin of a victor in a game without rules crept across painted red lips. "Yes, Harvey? Would you like me to send them away, so we can dispense with this charade of yours?"

His charade?

She might have pulled it off had her tone not been laden with the syrupy sarcasm of a victor. She had not won, not by a long shot.

"No, let them in. When bright light shines on cockroaches, they scurry for cover."

"How droll. Harv, you used to be such a man of words. What's happened to you?"

Loneliness, that's what happened. It could kill the same as .38 dumb-dumb bullet to the gut. And for the last two years, since Sylvia passed, loneliness hung in the air thick as dust motes. Smothering all else.

The lock clacked open.

Seconds later, two officers in blue uniforms and shiny badges entered the dining room, their boots clunked, their black leather Sam Brown gun belts creaked. One stood six foot or better with wide shoulders. His partner a petite gal with brown hair cut short. Together they made a formidable and scary pair capable of taking down any thug who came their way. Delores wouldn't be a problem for them once they uncovered her devious intent.

Delores took a seat and waited.

The gal with "P. Sanchez," on a shiny nameplate, said, "How can we help you, sir? You called in a report of a burglary in progress?"

Delores held out a hand as if making an offering, "Go on, Harvey, tell them. Of all things, wasting these nice officers' time with this nonsense."

"Excuse me, Ma'am, please let him talk."

"I *will* tell them if you just give me a chance. This...this ah...woman came into my house today without permission. I've never seen her before. I want her taken away this instant. I have an appointment to keep, and I can't leave a stranger in the house when I leave. Take her to jail where she belongs. She's trying to gaslight an old fool, and it's not working. Not on me. Let her just see who the fool is now."

Delores sat, still displaying a smug expression as if this happened every day. A challenge that, if acted upon, would give her a prison record. The tall, black haired officer with "D. Donnelly" on his nameplate said, "Ma'am, can I please see some form of identification? Preferably with this house address."

"Seriously?"

Donnelly didn't reply to Delores' rhetorical question and stared at her. She again deployed those green eyes like a weapon, a tractor beam of sorts on the male gender.

"She doesn't have anything like that. She doesn't live here. Never has."

"Please, sir, take it easy. We'll get this all worked out."

"Damn straight you will."

Delores shifted to anger with a heated glare, one with enough sizzle to fry a silly old fool to ashes.

Delores finally got up, moved to the dining room counter, to a black patent leather purse with a gold colored clasp. She opened it and rummaged around for a couple of seconds. Enough time to locate and pull a gun. Slaughter a couple of foolish cops too stupid to believe Delores was a card-carrying burglar on the prowl.

She extracted a black leather cardholder and pulled out a California driver's license.

"Nice knowing you, Rita. C'est la vie."

Donnelly took the driver's license. "This says your name is Delores. Who's Rita?"

"Yes, that's correct. Rita is a new name Harvey just started using this morning. I'm sorry you had to come out here again, Officers."

"Ma'am, we haven't been out here before, and our call history for this address says no one from our department has ever been here."

"You see? You see. She's lying. Just like that, you've uncovered the despicable scam. Take her away, Officers. Book her for burglary…and…and elder abuse."

Donnelly said, "I'm sorry, sir, there is no evidence of elder abuse, and I can't take her from this residence. You'll have to evict her if you want her gone."

"What?" The room swirled as blood drained south toward toes and bunions.

"She says she lives here, and her driver's license confirms it."

"Say what? She doesn't live here. I'm telling you the truth. You have to believe me. She's never lived here."

He handed over the driver's license that read, "Delores Usher," with a date of birth that made her forty-one.

This couldn't be happening. How could it? What the—?

Rita-Delores made goo-goo eyes at Donnelly using a tool unavailable to others in a fight for control over the law, over the possession of a house that belonged to him and him alone for the last forty-odd years. Or was it fifty? When it came to counting gone-by-years, the mind played tricks.

Sanchez finally spoke. "Ma'am, what is your relationship to Mr. Usher?"

"Why, he's my husband and has been for two years now."

"I'm your what? No, no, no, officers. This is all wrong. She's running some kind of game. You can't allow her to do this. Look over here. This is my wife in *this* picture."

The floor underfoot shifted and wobbled as blood pressure rose and pulsed behind the eyes, not sending the correct information to the brain.

On the credenza, Sylvia's smiling face in a picture frame—who greeted everyone who entered the dining room—was gone. Replaced now with a studio-quality photo of Delores, burglar extraordinaire. The entire scam stunning right down to the minute details. Brilliantly executed.

Rita said, "Would you like me to dig up a marriage certificate. I can if you really need one."

Donnelly had followed Rita's eyes over to the photo on the credenza, then looked back at her and shared a knowing smile.

"She's lying. Can't you see she's lying? Anyone can get a driver's license now. You don't even need a birth certificate. Don't you two watch the news? She's committing some kind of brilliant fraud. Yes…yes, ask her to produce a marriage certificate. She won't be able to. Well, not unless it's forged. We're not married. Wait…wait, just give me a minute to think."

Donnelly, still absorbing Rita's goo-goo eyes, said, "Does your husband suffer from dementia?"

"No. Oh hell no. Of course, I don't. Ask me anything. Ask me the day of the week, the month. Who's the president? Better yet…wait…wait, ask her how much we have in our checking account? If we're actually married, she'll know. That'll resolve this entire mess."

Sanchez held up a hand but didn't move any closer. "Sir, please just calm down."

Donnelly said, "Is your husband a danger to himself or others?"

"No. No. Don't do this. Please don't do this. I was sleeping in my room. She woke me called me by name. I don't know her. I've never seen her before in my life. You have to believe me."

Rita smiled and said, "No, of course not. I can also call Dr. Goldfarb and have him increase Harvey's medication. This has happened before. I can handle Harvey just fine. Thank you, though."

"Dr. Goldfarb? Oh, dear lord, this woman deserves an Oscar. Can't you—"

To talk further would only raise the mud in the mire already knee-deep with lies. "Thank you, officers, for your time. I can handle this problem myself. She's only one burglar committing elder abuse. Good job, though, officers. Our tax dollars at work. Just go. Staying only exacerbates the entire issue."

Donnelly looked into Rita's entrancing green eyes and said, "You okay with this situation? I mean to leave you alone with him?"

"Yes, of course," she said. "But do you have a business card?"

He stepped forward, unbuttoning a uniform pocket and extracted a card.

"Dear lord, don't you know what you're doing? You are suckling at the teat of this succubus?" The words came out all on their own and couldn't be pulled back. Words of a crazy old man confirming everything Rita had said.

Rita, with the hair of a goddess, followed the two cops to the front door, their words low and indiscernible. She offered up a delicate hand to Donnelly, who took it, his eyes never leaving hers. Their simple physical contact lingered a moment longer than necessary, the sexual tension electric and witnessed by all present.

The woman was a champion of deceit.

With the door closed, she returned and sat at the table. "Now, will you please get out of those pajamas and get dressed so we can go to the Getty?"

"This whole thing would be comical if I only knew what you were after. There's nothing here that you could possibly want. I don't have but a few thousand dollars in the checking account. No CDs or savings. A shameless pittance for a life well-lived. I've made some mistakes, but nothing that deserves maltreatment on this herculean scale. Is that the kind of money you're after? A few thousand. A mere trifle for such an elaborate ruse."

Her eyes welled with tears. One escaped and rolled down unblemished, alabaster skin the sun never touched. She stood, picked up the platter of cold breakfast, and walked into the kitchen.

"If you really were my second wife, you'd know where I have to go this morning."

"No, Harvey, I won't encourage this fantasy any longer by engaging further in your demented and evil attempt to get me to leave. I won't do it."

"Rita, tell me where I'm going this morning."

In the kitchen, she let the plate and flatware drop into the sink. The plate shattered. The knife and fork clattered. She put her hands on the sink's edge. Her body shook as she wept alligator tears, the faked emotion missing its mark. Mostly. A woman in distress, no matter the circumstance, tugged at the heartstrings.

Chapter Three

Current Day

Two hours later, the doorbell rang. Esther, the elderly neighbor, right on time for the lift to the bi-monthly group meeting for grief. The only social outing on the schedule for a now dyed-in-the-wool recluse. He yelled from the master bedroom, "Rita, are you going to get that? I'm almost dressed." The words a common request between husband and wife. How easy to fall into a well-planned con game.

No response.

"Rita?"

She played coy, angry about the name Rita instead of using Delores. Good, one point for the home team.

A quick tour of the house found Rita conspicuous by her absence. Was it too soon to rejoice? Where could she have gone?

Esther would know something was afoot if Rita had answered the door. That's why Rita took a powder.

"Come in, it's open."

Rita hadn't bothered to lock the massive front door after the cops left, and Esther came inside on her own. She was a sixty-five-year-old woman who looked her age. Her demeanor and dress a throw-back to the sixties. "Harv, you ready to go? I'm sorry for running a little late." She had not entered the house since Sylvia passed. Much had changed, mostly the number of antiques, sold to stave off the tax man and a growling stomach.

"Hello, Esther. Thank you for donating your time driving this poor soul to the grief group. Please, have a seat. I've seemed to have lost something. I just need to check around one more time."

Esther wore an outdated tweed jacket over a plain dress, support hose, and black orthopedic shoes you might find on an obese mail carrier. The hairnet corralled pure white hair never before viewed unencumbered. A kind, gentle woman with perfect manners. A vulgar word never passed her lips. Lonely without much to do, she quietly waited for life to finish the game.

"Harv, do what you need to do. It's all up to you on the time. I'm only the driver. I see you have breakfast dishes. I'll just…oh my."

She found the broken plate in the sink.

With Rita nowhere to be found, had the entire morning been nothing more than a silly dream? The lonely machinations of an old fool?

One more tour through the house to be sure Rita fled, leaving behind a tiresome ruse to peter out all on its own.

The thought that she might be gone caused a stupid little ache of longing, an emotion conflicting with sanity. When relief should herald the day.

She had to know Esther would ruin the attempt to gaslight a tired old man.

In the master bedroom, the nightmare suddenly returned in full force. Steam roiled along the ceiling in a fleeting exit from the bathroom. The thickening humidity in the air confirmed someone was taking a *damn* bath.

"*Oh, dear Lord.* What next?"

Less than three hours ago, asleep in bed, life had been normal.

"Harv, is that you, dear? Could you be a doll and come wash my back?"

She had somehow slithered past unseen and gotten in the master bathroom.

The thought of a Rita Hayworth lookalike in the bathtub weakened the knees and made the air too thin to breathe. For a split second, a lurid idea joined with her intent. Maybe it wouldn't be so bad to give into the dream, go with it just this once.

For twenty minutes or so, maybe even—

What would twenty heavenly minutes cost in the big scheme of life? Climb in a warm, soapy tub with a redheaded vixen, one determined to...to do what?

Not a smart move. Not without knowing her motivation.

But maybe just step in, clothes and all, say something pithy like, "It may be normal, darling, but I'd rather be natural." What Holly Golightly said to the George Peppard character in *Breakfast at Tiffany's*.

Breath caught, lungs not cooperating as one foot, then the other stepped into the large bathroom, one tiled floor to ceiling in a floral mosaic. Only to find:

Bubbles.

Lots and lots of bubbles rose to an alpine height, concealing all but red hair and a beautiful countenance flushed rosy from the humid heat.

"Oh, there you are, Baby." She held up a large natural sponge that appeared out of the bubbles like an aberration. A sponge that never graced any bathroom in the house. She brought the thing along in her black bag of tricks. Every possible detail was covered in this long con that continued to blossom, like a delicate flower blooming in spring.

But why?

The blurred-over mirror that ran the length of the twin sinks added to the fog effect. Warm, wet steam hung three feet down from the ceiling. That same sink acted as a support, the closed toilet a flop-seat as a groan slipped out all on its own.

Her face and that damn sponge sticking out of those bubbles beckoned. A sponge, a face, and a request no red-blooded man could deny, no matter what age.

"Harv?" The sponge moved from side to side within the white background, her smile bright and clean.

Innocent.

"Come on, Baby, you know what I like."

Had she kept her mouth shut, the setup might've worked, the urge undeniable and unable to suppress. But that last request brought the situation back to stark reality. "Tell me. Please tell me what it is you want of me? Why are you doing this?"

From the other room, in the hall just outside the master bedroom, Esther raised her voice in order to travel the distance, "Harvey? Are we leaving soon? Harvey?"

"Who's that Harv, the neighbor lady you've been seeing behind my back? Yes, I know all about her. I'm not a fool."

"She's been out of town for two years. What are you talking about? You again just avoided my question. What you are doing here in my house is criminal trespass."

The bubbles continued to ebb. The accumulated pile, pop, pop, popped, creating a whisper of a hiss. With each passing moment, her camouflage diminished a little more.

Out of those bubbles, like Nessie in a Loch, rose the most wonderful sight, a creamy white thigh and gam with a delicate boned foot and red-painted toenails. A lurid red against all that wonderful white.

Another groan slipped out.

She smiled. "Harv, my love. You know this little blank spot in your memory, the one in between me and your beloved Sylvia, will all of a sudden slam you back to reality, and you'll later kick yourself for missing this perfect opportunity. You know how you like water sports, you kinky little perv. In the tub, you're like a playful little otter."

"This isn't working. I'm not falling for it. A blank spot in my memory, my aching ass. There, now you've done it, you've gone and elicited a vulgar response. I hope you're happy." Sweat beaded on his forehead from the heat and...and the near-nude situation. It rolled down stingy both eyes. "Okay. Okay. Prove it. If we've been together, talk to me. Tell me something about myself no one else knows."

The sponge moved up and down that long leg. "I don't think that'll work, baby doll, not this time. This is the longest you've ever treated me like a stranger in a strange land. See what I did there, layering in one of your favorite novel titles?"

"Talk. Tell me what's happening here."

"Okay," Her bottom lip came out with a Marilyn Monroe pout. "You're a retired certified public accountant. You owned, at one time, three Ethan Allen franchise furniture stores that you sold, for a good chunk of change, and have since been living off the proceeds."

"Ah ha, that's it. You think I'm rolling in the dough and you're out to get some."

"Oh, poo. You and I both know you lost everything in the 2008 stock market crash. You're down to bare bones financially. I stay with you because I love you, baby."

"Anyone could come up with that much information on the Internet. You still have not said anything in this…this master acting clinic that says otherwise. You're trying and failing to perpetuate this faux Alzheimer's disease used as an explanation, and think everyone will believe you. A sham that includes someone of…of your magnitude having gone missing from my memory. I say, horse feathers."

She smiled and made a cute tsk, tsk, tsk sound in her lovely throat. The water swirled as the one leg went down and the second one rose. The sponge routine started on an equally perfect leg. The woman must be a dancer when not trying to gaslight an old man in a large empty house.

The bubble mounds continued to decline and caused his Adam's apple to rise and fall in a long swallow. Quick, flee now before…before all is lost. If you climb into that warm, soapy water with the siren calling from the rocks, all will be lost.

Time for the big guns. "All right then." The words about to be uttered clogged coming up and out. Words rarely said, if ever, outside the support group. "Ahem, tell me then…tell me about the morning that—"

"Which morning is that, Harv? We've had many great mornings in this very tub. We call it rub-a-dub dub two—"

"Stop that. Tell me about *the* morning, the one…with Sylvia. With what happened to Sylvia."

The tub water rolled in a gentle slosh. "Harvey, my gentle little lamb. Doc Goldfarb said that in situations like these I should try something with a little memory shock-value to jog that obstinate mind of yours. Hold on to that toilet seat, Baby."

"No. No. Don't."

Rita Hayworth slowly rose out of bubbly cover, her skin slick and wet. A copse of bubbles sloughed off, leaving nothing else to hide her...to hide that—

My God, maybe it was a dream after all, one that came around full circle.

A robin red breast of a different sort just appeared and stared back. Mesmerizing. This one wasn't tapping a warning on the bedroom window.

"There, now do you remember me, Baby?"

From the bathroom door, Esther let out an "eek." Then, "Oh, my dear Lord. Harvey, I'll wait out by the front. You don't come in five minutes, I'll know you're otherwise indisposed."

Chapter Four

Current Day

E sther sat behind the large steering wheel, hands high, chin up, eyes peering through the windshield of the big four-door Lincoln Continental. An ant trying to maneuver an Abrams tank. Each time she turned her head, the cat-eye prescription glasses caught and reflected the late morning sun. The thick lens enlarged her eyes. "Harv, you don't have to tell me if you don't want to."

"Oh, for Pete's sake."

The first words spoken since the start of the trip downtown.

To explain away the entire morning suddenly became too overwhelming. Each segment grew more unbelievable, culminating in the grand finale in the bathroom scene.

The utterance, "Sweet baby Jesus," slipped out.

"You okay, Harv?"

"Yes, of course. Thank you for the ride, I'm most appreciative. I'm sorry you had to see something of that... ah...nature."

"You going to tell me about it or just let my imagination run full-tilt into a wall. Because I have to tell you, my friend, that was really something I would never have expected. I mean—"

"I'd rather we not discuss the matter.

"That's fine, Harv, you know you have a consoling ear if you need one."

"Thank you."

Esther and Sylvia had been close friends, even with the sixteen-year age difference. They took tea together on Mondays and Fridays and then attended a mahjong game in the park, weather permitting. They had recently started going to the mall that opened early to allow folks who like to walk to get out of the heat.

Esther retired with forty years as a kindergarten teacher and had always been a vivacious, outgoing sort, dispelling the school teacher, spinster image. By anyone's standard—back in the day—she was too pretty to be a spinster.

She nodded, maneuvering the beast of a car through the narrow city street. "My best guess is that you...you just accidentally walked in on her taking a bath. It happens."

"Esther, please."

Esther had lost her grip on life, "Just a tad." This, according to Sylvia. Even if Esther *had* been around for the last two years, asking her to be a witness to Rita not living in the house wouldn't end well.

The big debt owed to Esther now rose up and begged compensation.

What happened the morning Sylvia passed was too painful to deal with in words or on paper. Too painful to bring out into the light of day. That kind of grief remained hidden in the dark recesses of the mind. Insidious in the way it lurked.

Esther had not come right out and asked what happened that horrible morning, two years ago. Esther lived in that ever-diminishing generation where manners still remained sacrosanct.

She never asked about the details of Sylvia's passing.

But Esther was owed that story. For no other reason than being Sylvia's closest friend. Also, for being kind to Sylvia's sometimes obstinate, and often rude husband, by taking up the chauffeur's cap. Doing it without complaint and driving said husband to the group session to appease a black-hearted grief that hung on refusing to let go.

"After you drop me off...instead of going for coffee this morning...if you want, you can stay for the meeting. It's my turn to share today. I mean to talk."

If she said yes, she would hear all about the awful morning where one life ended and the other…well, it might as well have.

Her hands jerked the wheel to the right, almost sideswiping several cars before she got the big Lincoln back under control. She slowed and pulled to the curb on Willow, three blocks from the Evergreen Assisted Living Facility that had great programs, one of which was for the grief-stricken.

Sylvia referred to it as "The old timer's home," never believing she would ever be of an age where she'd need *assistance* in living. She'd said it with a lilt and mirth in her voice instead of disdain. *"Besides, who would ever want to live in a place with such a cold, hard name like, 'Facility?' There isn't one iota of warmth in the word, is there, Harv?"*

"No, my love. There isn't."

"That's right. Please, don't ever entertain the thought of putting me there. If given the option, I much prefer the fate of fair Juliet. What do you think about that, Harv?"

"I think it's crazy talk, my love."

"Quite right, let's put our heads in the sand and not contemplate such drivel until the need arises."

The need never arose.

Those probably weren't exactly the words she used. Memory worked on the brain like a boxer on a heavy bag throwing lefts, jabs, uppercuts, reshaping an opponent's life strategy, and most important the way things used to be. Important because the foundation of the future is based on history. From her absence two years hence, with each passing day, Sylvia continued to grow in iconic stature, growing larger than life.

Back in the big Lincoln, Esther's eyes filled with tears. "Are you sure? I mean I'd love to hear you speak about her. You never talk about her."

"Yes, I'm sure. It's time."

Under the circumstances, the idea had sounded so appropriate. Now, though, with the offer out there, unable to retract, a dark cloud settled in. A foolish thing to have said. Never would have if not otherwise distracted with what awaited back at the house. A problem of monumental proportions. One with red hair and black spiked heels.

Esther pulled back out into the road. "Are you sure you're all right? You look awful pale and the way you're acting, you might've come down with a fever. You know, a simple ague is dangerous for those of our age."

"I'm fine. I just need to talk this thing out in group. Relieve some of the pressure."

Her hand, riddled with age spots, snaked its way over and rested on an antsy leg that wouldn't quiet. "I'll take care of you, Harv. Sylvia was my best friend, and I owe her that much."

"Oh, dear Lord."

"Here we are." She took her hand away and used it on the big steering wheel to guide the Lincoln into the public parking section of the "Facility."

Unable to entirely see over the long hood, she parked cattywampus across two slots.

In the walk from the Lincoln to the clubhouse, the memory of what happened back in the bathroom all of a sudden struck hard and caused feet and breath to fail. This failure due to the obvious violations of Father's self-proscribed, *Moral Dilemma*.

How had Father known? How could he foresee and predict what would happen in the bathroom with red rob—with Rita Hayworth, seventy odd years later.

With one of Father's many rules on how a man must comport himself. The most important one was honor. Then integrity, loyalty, and truth, in that order. His words were still emblazoned in memory, the same as if put there with a fiery brand. Simple words, really. But weighty and filled with deep meaning.

"The truest test of a man is if he looks away."

The full impact of those words now came home to roost that very morning. Back then, Father went on to explain:

"For example, a man standing in his own house on a dark night, espies a woman across the way. Her curtains are open and she's backlit in a soft yellow light from her dressing table.

She doesn't know anyone is watching and has no reason to think otherwise. She unbuttons her blouse. With each button, the man has the opportunity to look away. Seven buttons, seven opportunities. The blouse slides off.

24

Last chance.

The woman reaches back to unhook her black lace brassiere.

When no one else is watching, if the man doesn't look away, he is not a man of honor and integrity. If he continues to look, he's the kind of man destined to wander lost in a world of moral turpitude. So, Harvey, my boy, you have to ask yourself, are you the kind of man who, when no one else is looking, will look away?"

The clunk, clunk, clunk of Esther's orthopedic shoes on the sidewalk sounded loud enough to spook the murder of crows roosting above in the big, leafless elm. They watched with their black eyes—little moving orbs that judged.

"Esther, I'm lost in a world of moral turpitude."

"Don't be ridiculous. You're the most upright man I know. But Harvey dear, you don't look so good. Let me take you home."

"What? Ah...yes. Yes, that might be best. Please take me home. Wait."

"What?"

"You were going to hear about what happened to Sylvia. I...I found I can't talk about it outside of group. But you're right, I do need to lie down and—"

She took an unwilling arm in hers, "You'll talk about it when you're ready." She made the U-turn under the large elm, still beneath the crowded audience of crows, headed back toward the Lincoln in the public parking lot.

Just as a white gob of bird excrement dropped from the tree to splat on the sidewalk not two feet ahead. A tacit comment from those above judging the decision to abscond from the group session. And probably for taking a big bite of the moral turpitude sandwich, when offered up back in the master bathroom.

Esther's grip tightened as she side-stepped the bird turd.

In the car and on the road, the anxiety over returning home rose to a jittery high and thinned out the air. The very reaction Rita was hoping for. Confusion in the face of distraction, phase one of the long con. Perfect. Even hyper-aware with fore-knowledge of the in-progress fraud, the conclusion to the con seemed inevitable.

Unless the woman could be permanently extricated from the house.

"Esther?"

"Yes, Harv."

"Didn't you say your nephew or some sort of shirt-tail relative worked...as a...ah private—" The sentence faded off, the idea too wild to consider. Hiring an unknown person to snoop around. What about the other secrets the investigator might uncover?

But what if...just to play the devil's advocate, what if what Rita had said turned out to be true? And that memory actually is capable of having a sort of blank spot that comes and goes. Was that too far out of the realm of possibility? Would the things this person dug up not be something aired out to one and all?

"What?" Esther said, "Oh, you mean Eddie Gurski? He's not a blood relation. Nothing like that. Just...ah...a good friend. That's all."

Esther had often talked to Sylvia about Gurski, a kid from Esther's past. One from her first year teaching the kindergarten classes. Gurski had returned twenty years later to scratch an itch, a childhood infatuation. Every kid had them with any teacher who took an interest and cared. Only none of the kids ever returned and fired-up weird and unhealthy relationships like Gurski.

Gurski came back into Esther's life at twenty or twenty-one years old. That meant he had to be close to forty-five now.

Sylvia always said Esther talked too fondly of Gurski, as if he were an errant Golden Lab who continued to *make* on the carpet. Sylvia had once commented on the relationship in a conversation on the way to visit the Getty. *"He's an untrainable scruff of a man, whom I don't think should come sniffing around, Esther."*

"Hmm."

"That's right. You know I don't like to disparage anyone, but that Gurski's no good. He's a leach, a parasite preying off the goodwill of our sweet neighbor. Our good friend, Harv."

"Let it be, Esther's a grown woman. If she wants to donate time, and energy to the likes of this fellow, it's her life."

Her head whipped around. "I said nothing of the kind. Nothing of 'energy,' or anything so lurid."

"Lurid? How do you get lurid out of a word like energy?"

"She...she gives him money. That's the gist of it."

"Like I said—"

"I know what you said. Harv, where you come from, you know how to read these kinds of people. In the past, that hyena sense of yours has saved lives. Please, when you get a chance, go next door and take a look at Eddie, talk to him. If he's a deadbeat with dark designs, run him off. Do it for me, Pumpkin?"

This also took place twenty-odd years ago, and truthfully, in memory, Sylvia using the name Pumpkin didn't sound right. A kind of word or endearment that clanged in the ear and rattled around in the brain. She never used, dear, hon, snookums', or any other idiotic term like Snuggle Muffin. She stuck to just plain Harv. But used intonation in a wide range of 'Harvs' to describe: anger, sadness, elation, and being coy. The best, though, was the one of passion. "Haaaaaarv!"

The use of "Pumpkin" was that prize fighter again boxing memory around like a heavy bag.

Back in the Lincoln, Esther said, "It's that woman, isn't it, Harv? The redhead? She's causing you all this undo heartache? We can call the police, sic them on that little doxy."

"No, the police won't do any good. I already tried that approach, and they gave me the high-hat routine. Esther, this bloodsucking gal's burrowed in under the skin like a tick."

Esther said nothing about Rita's misinformation of her possible wife status.

One possible and unwanted answer might reveal a tired old fool who didn't recognize a second wife of two years.

Esther nodded. "Sure, no need to worry. Eddie's a good egg. He knows his business. He'll sort all of this out in a jiffy. I'll call him as soon as we get home."

"Above all else, and I mean it, Esther, he needs to be discreet."

She looked from the road, her eyes as large as two angel fish in individual aquariums. Above those aquariums, the net pulling the mob of gray down tight miniaturized her head and made her eyes even larger. When she blinked, time took a pause, (at least that's the way it seemed), until they reopened. "He's a pillar of discretion, I promise you. He's a good kid."

"Kid?"

"He'll always be a kid to me. He hit a rough patch there a while back, just like most teenagers, but he straightened up. You won't be sorry you hired him. I'll give you my personal guarantee that if he screws up, I'll cover any fiduciary loss."

"You won't be putting money toward my problems, Esther. I can handle that part. But I'd ask you one favor."

"Anything."

"I don't want to tell Gurski what's going on. It's better if he finds out on his own without any prompting. Have him start fresh and let the cards fall where they may."

"Wait, the kid has to have a starting point. At least a scenario to work with. Haven't you read any true crime novels?"

"How can I tell him what's going on when *I* don't even know for sure?"

"Seriously, Harv? I don't know how Sylvia put up with you the way you keep everything so bottled up. A naked and obstinate redhead covered in bubbles standing in your bathtub seems like a good enough place to start."

She again did not declare Rita's status as wife, girlfriend, or interloper. That one last question, the one needed to verify the conundrum, fled for cover, afraid to come out and reveal the truth.

"I would prefer to tell Gurski as little as possible. Ask him to just look into my background. Look into what's going on at my house. I'll invite him over, let him look around, see what he sees, and write a report on it. A complete report on the backgrounds of all involved."

"I understand. I don't agree, but I understand. Do you want to stay at my place until Eddie extricates you from the sharpened claws of this doxy?"

"No one said anything about her being a doxy. And that's exactly what I'm talking about. I want him to make his own assessment, so please say nothing about the doxy, or otherwise."

"No problem, we'll play it your way."

Esther made the last turn back onto College Avenue and pulled up in front of her house, one half the size of the others on the street, and put it in park. She no longer attempted to park in her free-standing garage. Not after banging into the back wall, not once, but twice. She wouldn't be driving on public streets much longer.

The idea of a blank spot in the memory burbled up yet again. Could that spot be like a scratch on a 78 LP, the way the needle can keep coming around and hitting that same blivit. Blurp. Blurp. Blurp. What if Rita, by some strange circumstance, did actually belong there? And buried deep under a pile of bills and correspondence on the roll-top desk, there resided a marriage certificate?

Naw.

Not a chance.

She had done her job well, though, planting that insipid seed of indecisiveness. The details of her con, nothing short of fiendish.

"Yes, that might be a good idea. I mean, staying at your place until I have a chance to discuss this matter with Gurski."

"From what you're saying, you really mean *not* discussing it with Eddie. And that's a great idea, Harv, you can stretch out on my bed and take a nap. You look like ten miles of bad road."

Again, with the oddity, Esther had never participated in trite clichés.

"A nap sounds good, but the divan will be satisfactory. If you could call Gurski and have him come as soon as possible, I'd greatly appreciate it."

Chapter Five

L ace from a tatted antimacassar stuck to Harvey's face. He rolled to the side on the divan. Rays of sunlight speared through the elm branches in the yard and then the front room window, illuminating a trillion motes all vying for positions in a race to nowhere.

The nap helped immensely. This time, a talking red robin didn't populate a dream, nor did the red robin of the other sort reappear covered in a white bubbly beard sloughing down a perfect white thigh.

Father's question, though: *"Are you the kind of man who, when no one else is looking, will look away?"* The words left a gaping chasm in the "shame" category, along with an emptiness in the chest that begged for resolution.

Across the room, black combat boots came into view. Denim pants with a ragged hem, at the leg bottoms, the material worn thin. Above the pants, the man sported a black hoodie sweatshirt, popular and stylish for the time. When in actuality, a drab display to hide a personality rather than letting one out to breathe.

Gurski's face revealed a great deal about his past; the lines, the dark tan and sun damaged skin, the jagged scar that started above his right brow and ran down across the eye to the cheek below. How such a violent injury didn't turn the cerulean blue eye opaque was a story for another time. Black unruly hair matched his unshaven jaw. The rugged, "Don't-mess-with-me, look," came across loud and clear. Perfect for the task at hand.

Good. Just his appearance next door would be enough to scare off the likes of Rita, who goes by the moniker Delores.

"Bout time." Gurski's gravelly voice matched the overall package. "Been sittin' here watchin' your dumbass sleep for two hours." He checked his watch, "Two hours and twenty-one minutes. Es said I couldn't wake you."

"Sorry. I didn't sleep well last night."

"I charge five hundred a day plus expenses."

"You don't mince words and get right down to business."

No response, just the harsh glare disrupted only by the galaxy of wandering motes.

"Three hundred and you eat the expenses."

He rose into a tower of a man at least six foot. But skinny. Maybe too skinny. Somehow, he seemed more formidable sitting down.

"Catch ya later, pal."

"Wait."

He paused and looked back.

"This isn't fair, you're dickering from a position of advantage."

"I'm not the one with a squatter next door. And don't call me a dick."

So, Esther had told him. Darn her.

And again, like the earlier reference to "Doxy," "Squatter" could also be another misinterpretation, a slur for "wife."

"I didn't call you any such thing. Okay, five hundred a day, no expenses with a three-day maximum, unless approved ahead of time."

He extended his hand palm up. "That'll be five hundred dollars, cash on the barrelhead. I don't take checks. I don't need to work chasin' down deadbeat welshers."

"You haven't done anything yet. And I'm not a welsher. Never have been. I pay my debts."

"It won't take me two minutes to boot the broad out on her ass."

"No, wait. That's not what I want. Well, it is, but...I want you...I want you to be a casual observer. I don't want her to know what you're up to. That you're even investigating. You'll just be a friend who comes over for a visit and stays for a few hours each day. More than anything else, I need to find out what she's up to. If I don't she'll just return like a bad penny."

He came back to the chair and eased down. "Three days at five hundred a pop." The words came out like a guy sitting in front of a dollar-slot machine that just paid off triple sevens. He didn't care to ask about the background investigation versus booting her out on the onset.

"You seem to be more focused on the money going in your pocket, than the job at hand."

"I can handle the job, don't you worry about that."

"I want you to follow the leads wherever they take you."

"What are you talking about now?"

"I want to know if…no. I made up my mind. I'm not going to give you any information.

For this kind of money, I want you to look into everything. I mean everything…even me. I want a complete report. Backgrounds, motivations, whatever you find next door. Follow those backgrounds right to the end. I want to know who she is and why she's doing this."

"Heh. Heh. It's your nickel." He brought his foot up, rested it on his knee, exposing a white athletic sock with a red stripe and something else. A black band with a small black rectangle attached. Above that a colorful tattoo of Yosemite Sam with his bushy red mustache, floppy hat and two six-guns.

Esther appeared in the formal living room carrying a complete tea service atop a tarnished silver tray; porcelain cups, and plates with plain vanilla cookies. The load strained her delicate shoulders. Gurski jumped up. "Here, Es. What are you doing? Lemme get that." He took the tray and set it on the low maple wood table in front of the divan. Gurski dropped the tough-guy veneer when she walked in, showing a soft side that further supported an ability to handle an aberrant redhead. Use a delicate hand rather than a sledgehammer.

"Thank you, Eddie." She stayed busy pouring tea, adding cream and cubed sugar to order. "Don't worry about me," she said, "continue on as if I weren't here." She handed over the teacup.

The cup gave off a light rattle in old hands. The concoction warmed the stomach and went a long way to restore the world to its rightful place.

Esther took a seat with her saucer and cup in a chair across from Gurski. "Please go on." Shameless in her belief that the conversation wasn't of the utmost personal nature and that proper manners dictated she excuse herself.

"I don't need much else." Gurski said, "I think I got the lay of the land. I'm ready to get started."

"See, Harv, this is going to work out just fine."

The thought of returning to the house, a lair containing an unscrupulous fiery redhead, made the tea rise from the stomach into the throat. "I want you to spend the night. For that kind of money, I want a little protection as well."

Gurski jumped forward, spilling a little tea. "Bullsh—" the obstreperous language caught before the word finished. He looked over at Esther, his former kindergarten teacher and lowered his tone. "I am not spending the night in that ancient mansion. Not gonna happen."

"I won't argue with you. Let's get started. We can discuss it later. And it's not an ancient mansion."

Everyone stood. Esther followed along to the door and said goodbye.

Outside, a craven orange orb pretending to be the sun sat on the horizon, anxious for the day's demise and cast weak yellow rays on a world turning dark.

Gurski stayed close in stride.

A moment passed.

Esther called Gurski back. He hurried to her beckoning.

In a two-person huddle, her whisper carried. Old folks with deafness sneaking in the back door tended to overmodulate. "Eddie, I don't think it's a good idea for you to sleep over. With that…that woman there."

"Don't worry about me, Es, I'll be just fine. I can handle myself."

"You sure?"

"Positive. If this old bird here can stay in that place, so can I. Guaranteed"

"You're not afraid of a thing, are you, Eddie?"

"I wouldn't say that, I love your apricot cobbler, but your fish soup is—"

"Oh, Eddie, you're the worst." She blushed and play-slapped his shoulder.

Gurski caught up and again matched stride for stride.

"The law won't allow you to stay the night. That's the true reason you won't."

He stopped, straightened his back. "You saw the ankle bracelet? You're smart for an old dude. Yeah, I got a curfew at the halfway house. I'm on parole. I...ah, would appreciate it if you didn't tell Esther about the state bracelet or the curfew."

"How can you be a private eye and be an ex-convict? Your ankle jewelry will, of course, remain a private matter."

"Thank you. For the record, I never said I was a PI, you assumed it." He took off heading across the street.

"Hey, where are you going?"

He hesitated mid-street, said nothing, and waited. When no further words came his way, he said, "I'm assuming you don't want a con for this kind of job."

"You want the five hundred or not?"

He returned. "I'm not a heavy. I won't put the hurt on anyone, especially a woman. I won't do anything illegal. I'm not going back to prison."

"Can you do the background research like I asked?"

"Damn straight, I can."

"I don't appreciate the loutish language. Come and meet Delores, see what you think. Do some verbal bantering. Establish a baseline for the lies and then use it to uncover the truth. I want to know exactly what's going on in this game of hers. Who she really is. Catch her in lie after lie. That's all you need to do to earn your money. Then go back to your roost and come back tomorrow. Once you show up tomorrow, that's when you get the first five hundred. Tomorrow you can do all the background work. Deal?"

"Sounds good."

Gurski accepted the extended hand and shook. His grip was rough and solid. One finger on the left hand, he sported a silver colored ring in the form of an ugly skull with two red stones for eyes. A ring large enough that when punched in the face, the skull would leave an indelible imprint in flesh and bone. On his left, the wedding ring finger, he wore a gold ring with a tiger's eye stone. Was he married?

Two minutes later, after traversing the long, shrub-shrouded walkway up to the house, and before the key could be used, the wide wooden front door swung open.

Delores stood, door in hand. "Baby, where have you been. Group got over hours ago. I was worried sick. It's almost dark for crying out loud. You're never out after dark. You get so disoriented."

"I've been at Esther's if it's any of your business. This is Edward, a friend who I've asked to stay for dinner."

"Harv, Honey, I...I haven't planned anything for dinner. I planned on making sandwiches because—" Her eyes, all at once, locked with Eddie's. Even a novice victim could spot one predator recognizing another, paying silent homage to the laws of the jungle.

Delores wore a long black faux satin dress that hugged every curve and accentuated the important ones. The kind of curves a highway sign would caution, "Danger. Slippery When Wet." A hard-earned lesson learned earlier in the master bathroom. Crude words from a known origin. Stolen, maybe from an obstreperous associate whose face dissolved in memory like so many people from the past. The name suddenly bubbled up, Jackie Morano. Sure, he'd had that kind of mouth.

Delores didn't release Gurski's hand, her eyes still on his. "Edward? Are you a friend from Harv's group?"

Gurski didn't have time to answer.

Harvey moved forward. "Ah, hah. Got you. If you really were my wif—"

She let a smug little grin creep out. "Eddie Gurski, of course, Esther's friend. I haven't seen you in an age. Please come in. "You've let your hair grow, and that five o'clock shadow is very becoming. You've been away for a while, right?"

She stepped aside.

With his back to Rita, Gurski shrugged when he passed as if saying he'd never met her before.

No one could meet Rita and not remember.

"Nice recovery, Rita."

"Darling Harv, there was nothing to recover from."

On the way down the long hall, past the formal living room and into the formal dining room, Gurski's head never stopped moving from side to side, taking in everything, the crystal chandelier, the furniture carefully hand-picked by Sylvia. Piece by piece, she chose over decades what she called "antique store crawling." What was left of it. The really good pieces are gone. Gurski didn't so much send out a sense of a private eye, but more a petty criminal casing for a roll-back burglary.

The urge to blurt out an apology for not looking away in the bathroom rose to the tip of Harvey's tongue. "Look away," hell. Apologize for gawking at her guileless and lewd presentation. One put out there for no other reason than to distract and enthrall the prey before pouncing and eating the same.

Even so, the restrained apology ricocheted around in an already muddled brain, making logical thought difficult. Focus. Watch how Gurski interacts with her. Note the clues, the cracks in her story. Five hundred a day was a good bit of money, but well worth it if the house fell on the Red witch like in the movie, leaving only her feet exposed.

In the dining room, Rita stepped out ahead, her arm extended, "Harv, Edward, this is Andrew Johnson, he's a contractor here to give us an estimate on what it would cost to update the kitchen. Top-of-the-line stove, refrigerator, granite countertops, and backsplash. That sort of thing."

"Update the kitchen? There's nothing wrong with the kitchen."

"Hush, Harv. Don't you dare embarrass me. This morning with the police was bad enough."

Gurski surreptitiously moved over to the little business alcove just off the formal dining area and sat in the chair in front of the old oak roll-top desk. He kept his expression neutral and watched the way a disinterested bystander might.

Andrew Johnson leaned against the China hutch, clad in a black leather jacket, arms crossed. For just a fleeting second, his eyes locked onto Rita's. A smile started to slide out at the corner of Andrew's mouth. He caught it, wrestled it back into its cage. But not before exposing it to the world for what it really was: a male's flirtation with a voluptuous woman. Or could it have been a nod of sorts from a comrade in a conspiracy?

Had Gurski seen it? He couldn't have, not from his position in the business alcove.

"Now, Harv, I'm warning you. Be nice."

"Contractor? Where's your clipboard, Andy? Your tape measure? How can you work up an estimate without paper and pencil?"

"Harv, don't do this."

Andrew moved toward the hall. He wore black pleated slacks over black penny loafers, sans socks. "Maybe I'll let you folks discuss this first. I'll come back another time. Delores, I'll be waiting for your call."

He made haste for the door.

Rita's fists clenched down at hip level, face flushed red, and she shook with anger. "Harvey, let's talk in the living room. We don't want to air our dirty laundry to Esther's man."

"Nah, don't think so. You won't answer any of my questions. So, I'm done answering yours."

"Answer any of your questions? I've answered all of them. You're just not getting the answers your addled little brain wants. That's all. And you're blaming me for the missing blank spots in your memory."

Liar. A memory burned bright from mere hours ago in the bathroom, the white bubbles mixed with wet red. A heavenly vision never to be forgotten.

How was that for memory?

"If you don't mind, please entertain Eddie. I'm going to retire to my room with a good book. Call me when dinner is ready."

"Don't you dare." She rushed over, lowering her voice. "You can't just dump this guy on me and go to your room and read a book. I won't stand for it."

"Well, chickee baby, then maybe you better take a sit."

"Harv! Harv! I'm going to call Doctor Goldfarb, and you won't like what he'll have me do. He'll want you back for another long-term visit." Her vicious little words followed along into the master bedroom, the same as an ankle-biting little mutt with tiny teeth locked on the cuff of a pant leg.

In no place in any part of memory resided a long-term visit to—

Lies atop more lies. Of all things, a visit to the funny farm, the booby hatch, the cuckoo's nest. That had never happened and wouldn't. Those kinds of jabs now started to lose their sting as she began to overplay her hand.

Crossing over the threshold into the master bedroom gave some solace, some sense of security. The three locks on the door could hold back any green-eyed devil. Keep her from—

Dear Lord.

The two slide bolts, one high and one down low, had been removed. She had entered a place where she did not belong and stole what little security remained. Did it on purpose to spark a heated emotional response. The evil red-headed witch.

Closer examination of the deadbolt lock revealed brighter brass colored metal. That, too, had been changed. Now, nothing remained to keep her from entering at will.

Sweet baby Jesus.

Weak, rickety legs barely made it over to the chair to sit.

From the other room, the distant words drifted in, too soft to decipher. The intonation depicted a common conversation lacking anger as Gurski plied his trade searching for the truth.

What next? What would the witch bring about next?

The tone level rose. They laughed and continued to talk. She had worked her claws into poor Eddie Gurski. He'd fallen for her feminine wiles. Bewitched. The woman had an answer for everything.

Thirty minutes passed as slow as molasses on a cold day while fear and its partnered emotions clogged and choked all logical thought. Without the locks, she could skulk and slither in, put a pillow over a sleeping face, and snuff out a life. Then simply call the police and say…say what? That the grumpy old cuss died of natural causes.

Would that work?

Would the police delve deeper and discover this witch's dark design? Throw her in the joint where she belongs.

The heavy clump of work boots headed for the master bedroom. Gurski on his way in to talk before he left for the night. He had better have gleaned some tidbit to sink Rita in her quest to…to what? That was truly the issue at hand. What in the world was she after?

Gurski entered with a huge smile, one quickly snuffed and replaced with what passed as professional.

Why wouldn't he fall prey, once confronted with a more competent operator? Rita wielded that red hair, those dangerous curves, the red lipstick on luscious lips, and most off all, those mischievous green eyes, wielded them like a weapon. The entire package lethal enough to take a man—no an entire country to its knees.

Gurski turned and closed the door. A hand moved to where the top slide bolt used to be, the exposed wood lighter than the rest of the door. Fingers touched the spot as a blind man would, trying to read what had happened.

"That's right. She removed the two slide bolts and changed out the deadbolt. I'm vulnerable here. What are you going to do about it? I need help. Are you sure you can't spend the night?"

"This isn't good."

"Not good. You're damn straight it's not good."

The situation blossomed and brought out the worst in a person, the use of distasteful language.

Gurski wandered over to the other chair in the large sitting area of the master bedroom and sat down. "I can't stay over. I just came in to tell you I have to leave. In fact, it's already late. I might not make it back to the house before curfew."

"Did she say anything? Did you get anywhere with her at all?"

"I found some documents that I'll confirm as either real or frauds tomorrow." His gaze diffused as if his mind flitted across the top of a pond.

"What documents?"

"You said you wanted a report at the end of three days. Give me a little time to look into all this. Something's not right, I can tell you that much." He stood, his heavy boots clunking toward the door.

"What? Tell me what's not right."

He stopped and turned back, his face void of emotion. "What's a woman like her doing with someone…"

"Go on, say it. Like me. I know. That's exactly the crux of the problem. Until this morning I never laid eyes on her." A long sigh escaped.

Finally, some vindication, no matter how small. At least someone had now taken note of the outrageous situation.

"Are you bucks-up?"

"What?"

"Cash, you gotta a lot of cash?"

"That's an awful personal…no. Nothing even close to warranting the detail deployed on this scam."

"Yeah, that's what I thought. But there's a bigger problem."

"What's that?"

Gurski reached inside his zipped-up black hoodie and pulled out a sheaf of papers folded in half. "In the desk. Right there, close to the top, in a pile of bills. I found this. Not something usually mixed in with the bills. Put there almost as if someone wanted it found."

"Come on, don't leave me hanging. What? What did you find?"

"A marriage certificate dated two years ago."

Chapter Six

Current Day

The bedroom door closed after Gurski.

The ominous silence left behind rang in the ears. A lonesome fear never reared an ugly head, not with Sylvia around. A man always rose above that weak emotion to protect a loved one. Loneliness, though, had a way of creeping in and arousing a sleeping Mr. Fear, calling him to arms and turning the owner cowardly. That was exactly what happened now. Fear sauntered in, bold and fearless, taking full control of a weary old man in need of help.

The large clawfoot easy chair resisted being dragged over to the door. It too feared the evil redhead.

On the other side of the door, the clackity-clack of high heels on hardwood floors hurried toward the bedroom. The chair top reached just under the doorknob before the knob twisted.

"Harv? What's going on in there? What's that noise? What are you doing? Open the door this instant."

"You changed the lock? Why did you change the lock and remove the two slide bolts?"

A light bump against the door. Easily imagined as her forehead touching in mock frustration, all a part of her role in the long con. Her voice came low and muffled through solid wood. "Harvey? Honey, open the door. Come on, I'll run you a warm bath with those effervescent bath salts you like so much. You'll feel much better after a good warm soak."

Angry words rose to the tip of his brain and were snuffed out. *"Why, so you can push my head down and drown me? Make it look like an accident?"* But the question from the cop earlier in the day—in the morning when the nightmare first began—had asked the dangerous question, "Is he a danger to himself or others?" Or something on that order. Words that came right out of the Welfare and Institutions Code under section 5150. The kind of words that got a tired and discouraged old man put in the booby hatch for a seventy-two-hour hold. No, sir, the game had to be played better. Dodge and weave. Evade until Gurski worked some sort of magic and pry the two-bit chiseler out of the house.

Where did the words Welfare and Institution's Code and section 5150 come from?

Esther. Yes. Yes, Esther. Sylvia had been worried about Esther and had completed her due diligence, researching what could happen if Esther's eccentric behavior worsened.

What was happening on the other side of the door made Esther's occasional loopy behavior look normal.

"Harv, I'll leave you alone tonight. Let you continue to pretend to be this... this other person. Just for tonight. If you're not better in the morning...Well, I'll be forced to do something neither of us will like."

Play a better game.

To go against the tide was senseless and, at the moment, a losing hand. "Yes, I'll be better in the morning." The words all but gagged coming out. The very idea of playing nice went against the grain. But when in Rome...at least until the mystery of what she was after came to light.

"I love you, Harv."

No. To respond in kind was a bridge too far. "Thank you. I'll see you in the morning...Dear."

Silence. Seconds passed.

Finally, the click-clack slowly receded. The quick red fox returning to the lair.

To sleep in the bed left too wide a chasm of vulnerability, the one between the bed and the unlocked door. The deep, cushioned chair blocking the door made for a perfect alternative. If she tried to sneak in, the scrape of clawfoot legs against the floor would make noise enough. The sheer movement as effective as rattling tin cans.

Once nestled in the chair, sleep evaded him like a boxer with brilliant footwork. A swift trip to the Italian antique bureau and the return with a shoebox full of Sylvia's letters occurred without incident. The chair unmoved and still firmly under the knob.

Sylvia picked out the bureau at an estate sale down the street, paid just under nine thousand for it. According to her, it was a steal. This happened years back when the checking account, hale and health, still, "Bucks-up." That pop-culture saying used by Gurski.

Sylvia's written words in the letters always acted like a salve on an open emotional wound. A sedative. When separated by daily regimes, in a romantic gesture she would periodically write a note, a full-length letter and leave it in obvious places. Finding the little missives on the counter, the credenza or bathroom sink, brightened any day no matter how dim.

The envelopes, some five and six decades old were yellowed and brittle. The chronological order to the missives told the tale of two lovers. The slow relationship dance getting to know each other, to trust and believe in a future together. Both afraid to put oneself out there, afraid to offer up a vulnerable heart only to have it stomped on. But that hadn't happened.

In the past, the mere holding of any one of the letters (without opening it), brought back each and every word written in a loving scroll by a delicate-boned hand. The recently befouled memory that came natural with age, ruined all the cursive images. And now had to be opened and reread word for word to incite the sought-after comfort.

Letters toward the top, the latest in the bundle revealed a solid relationship with anecdotes that brought laughter and tears. She said words from the heart that shone better on paper. Words whispered in a lover's ear quickly dissipated in the air, lost for an eternity.

All except the top one. The top letter shouldn't be there. It should've been thrown away...no burned. But what octogenarian would have the nerve, the intestinal fortitude to burn the last words from a woman loved for five decades? A letter left unopened. Unread from fear of a truth as yet unrevealed. Written mere hours before she—

The bottom of the bundle, the first letters sent, spoke of the start of a boy-girl relationship dance. The all-too-common sparring needed when getting to know each other. The multitudes of heated emotions caught up in words when a couple embarks on a long-term relationship. The first decisions are the most crucial.

First up, at the very bottom, was an unposted note left taped to the door of a long-ago house in Hoboken, New Jersey:

Dear Mr. Harvey

I refer to you as "Mr. Harvey," because we have not formally met, and as of yet, I haven't heard your surname spoken by any of the neighbors. You and I have now and again merely exchanged a wave, "hello," in passing. The physical act of the wave (Minus the verbal hello). And maybe the lack of that actual "Hello" is, in part, causing the conflict between us.

You seem like a nice enough person, and I would hope that someday we could be friends.

But if you continue to throw large rocks on my roof while I'm entertaining friends, albeit somewhat raucous meetings among college classmates, I fear we may become quite contentious in every way.

Please stop in this Friday night for a mixer, seven-ish. An informal affair with wine and light hors d'oeuvres. I make the most wicked rumaki. For the too-shy Cro-Magnon Man who prefers to meet women using large rocks, rumaki is a delightful treat consisting of water chestnut and chicken liver wrapped in bacon.

Hope to see you Friday

Your favorite neighbor to be

Lois DeFrank

The words, the writing, harked back to a simpler time when things weren't so complicated and could easily allow a person to slip into a wonderful memory of the past.

* * *

By eight-ish that Friday night, another wild party was in full swing with bongos and a washtub bass. Loud boisterous folks who really let their hair down. Not the kind of thing a semi-recluse, five years senior to the college scene wanted to attend. Instead, a note was left in a small rock pyramid stacked on the front porch.

> *Dear Lois*
>
> *Thank you for the invite. But this Cro-Magnon is a traditional sort who still prefers to go out in the wild, and while evading the random Tyrannosaurs, bonk a woman on the head and drag her back to the cave by the hair, (that last part about the hair sounds crude and violent but in truth it's just an innocuous part needed to finish out the tired old cliché').*
>
> *Breakfast Saturday, nine-ish at the cave. I'll be preparing simple scrambled eggs and delightfully fluffy pancakes with chocolate chips. For East Fifth Avenue folks, that's pancakes from scratch with flour and the like.*
>
> *Hope to see you there*
> *Mr. Magnon.*

On Saturday morning, nine-forty-three, the knock came at the door right after all hope was lost that she would attend. The scrambled eggs had dried out beyond salvage.

Lois (she'd not yet had to change her name to Sylvia) stood on the stoop clad in a yellow sun dress, white gloves to the elbows, and a matching yellow pillbox hat.

"Good morning, Mr. Magnon. I'm afraid a lone girl can't be seen going into a strange neighbor's house unchaperoned. Not and still maintain a chaste reputation. I would suggest we take that big, nice car of yours into town and brunch at the country club."

The sight of her dressed to kill snatched his breath away and tamped down any and all logical words. Why had she not...looked like this before? Was it the way the sun reflected off all the yellow and illuminated her lovely countenance?

Not entirely. The attire may have had something to do with it, but the real reason was her note had been so revealing; terse yet informative of the person behind the pen. Creative, full of verve, combined with a sense of boldness, enough to take on the world. Could a person fall for someone based on a simple missive?

What was it that Oscar Wilde said?

"You don't love someone for their looks, or their clothes, or for their fancy car, but because they sing a song only you can hear."

"Yes, that's a wonderful idea, but I have to warn you, I've never been there before and am not a member." A small lie, in a feeble attempt at a diversion to a different location.

"I am. Please come along, it's hot standing out here." She pivoted, stopped, and looked back. "Mr. Magnon, please lose the ruffled apron and put on a sports jacket. I'll wait by the car."

The drive to the country club in the new '68 convertible Cadillac Deville happened too quickly. She broke the ice first. "I feel the undeniable urge to inform you of an error you made in your correspondence. It's like an itch I can't quite reach. I hope you won't think me droll?"

Her words, the vibrancy in her eyes, a person could listen to her speak all day and never tire.

"Please, tell me, I can't wait."

She opened her clutch and took out the note he had left. She leaned across the Caddie's long bench seat. The wonderful scent of White Shoulders perfume wafted over, further enchanting, mesmerizing. "See, right here, your reference to the tyrannosaurs. Dinosaurs were long dead by the time man came on the scene. It's a scientific certainty."

"I'm not entirely sure you're aware of our age difference."

Her sudden burst of laughter struck a bone deep inside, causing a yearning to hear that carefree mirth again and again.

Under the wide porte cochere, the valet dressed like a penguin opened the door and accepted the car. Lois unpretentiously took hold of a proffered arm and walked into the joint like she owned it.

The male host recognized her and immediately found a table, leaving others already present to wait. At the table, she gently tugged off white gloves, watching for a Cro-Magnon's reaction to the snobbish surroundings, and wasn't disappointed when she didn't get one.

The breakfast passed famously with casual small talk and little note given to the top-drawer food. The presentation, the flavor, none of it mattered. Only her beautiful eyes across the white linen tablecloth.

Had she been present on other occasions at the club and been overlooked? How was that even possible? The woman lit up the room.

"Sorry, I have to ask, did your folks name you after Lois Lane?"

"Hmm, I've never heard that one before." She let a little smile squeak out.

She finished half the food on the plate before pushing it aside to daub her lips in search of an errant crumb that wasn't there. "Do you have brothers and sisters?"

The easy-going, non-personal banter over, now came the soft-shoe to get around the damning pitfall questions with damning pitfalls. One in particular. "I'm an only child. I grew up in a small Southern California town, came here to attend the university, found work, and stayed. Been here eight years. Your turn."

"No siblings. An only child. Daddy jumped into plastics early, and now he's diversified. Do your folks still live in this small Southern California town?"

"It's called Ontario. Not the one in Canada."

"I figured as much. What kind of work do you do?"

"This is a little one-sided. What are you taking in college? What's your major?"

"Psychology with a minor in Russian literature. You side-stepped my question."

"Ouch, you're a real brainiac. So, Tolstoy, Anna Karenina, War and Peace? Are you psychoanalyzing me now? Am I the topic of your thesis? I can only imagine the title: The Socialization and Urban Impact of Cro Magnon on a young Rebecca of Sunnybrook Farm."

She laughed, reached across the table, and laid a hand on one damp with sweat from nerves.

"You're funny and keep me on my toes. I like that. For the record, I'm not Rebecca, though my family does own interest in a farm. Sheep, I believe."

"Baaa."

"Nice. Say, not to be too forward, but I noticed you're home most nights. Do you do any reading?"

That wasn't what she really wanted to know. She'd homed in on the diversion, the three-card monte trick, dodging the one question. The dodge to keep from lying.

"Have you read Desert Solitaire by Edward Abbey?"

Her eyes grew large. "Yes, I have. That's an amazing book. Now I want to go see that desert. You didn't say what kind of work you do?"

"My parents died in a car accident and I was raised by foster parents."

"Oh, I'm so sorry." Her eyes shifted to sympathy.

Never had there been a more wondrous afternoon.

Until a tap came at his shoulder.

All at once, Lois' expression shifted to confusion.

The man belonging to the fingers doing the tapping said, "Mr. LaBruzzo would like a word." The man stood by waiting for compliance with the request that in reality was a demand.

Lois leaned in close. "How do you know this, Mr. LaBruzzo? He's a pirate, a parasite that's weaseled a membership into this club. Some say, through arm-twisting and...and blackmail."

To answer in the negative would automatically get back to LaBruzzo via the thug in the nice suit standing too close with his hands crossed at the waist. What she had said already walked a dangerous line that would cause serious repercussions for all involved.

"It'll be fine. I'll only be a minute. Mr. LaBruzzo just wants to say hello.

I didn't know he was a member of this club." Another blatant lie. Not the best way to start a relationship.

What were the odds that Mr. LaBruzzo would breakfast on the same day?

Upon returning from talking with Mr. LaBruzzo, the table was empty, the beautiful girl had fled.

Who could blame her?

* * *

Harvey opened his eyes and found he no longer sat in the chair. Morning light filtered in through the eight-foot-tall bedroom windows. The chair had been moved back where it belonged. The covers were warm and comfortable, the pajamas...wait, how had that happened? Who could pick up a sleeping body, carry it over to the bed, and change clothes? Not Rita. Certainly not Rita.

Across the room in the same chair that had been wedged under the doorknob, sat Rita with cheater reading glasses perched on her little button nose, one that turned up just enough at the end to make it cute. She read from a sheaf of papers and abruptly signed with a flourish using an engraved Montblanc pen, a gift from Sylvia. Pilfered from the roll-top desk. Using Sylvia's pen on purpose to rub salt in an already inflamed wound. The pen engraved: *"To Harv, my wonderful dinosaur slayer, with love."*

Rita's hyena sense apparently told her someone stared. She looked up. "Good. You're awake. I have to leave on business for a couple of hours. While I'm gone, I don't want you to leave the house." She took off the cheater glasses. "I say that for your own good, Harv. You might forget where you live and wander aimlessly until someone finds you and brings you back. I don't want to call the police and report you missing. Please, I'm asking nicely this time."

"If I go anywhere, it will be over to Esther's."

"Fine. Can you get yourself dressed, or do you require assistance?"

"In my entire life, I have never required assistance! The very nerve to suggest such an outrageous undertaking. If you're anxious to be helpful, tell

49

me what on earth you are doing in my house? What is it you're after?"

She slowly stood. She wore another open-shouldered black cocktail-type dress with a thin black belt that brought attention to a narrow waist. The low heels this time, more conservative and comfortable, didn't make a sound on the area rug as she walked over to the bed with hips that banged from side to side. Eye-catching. Entrancing.

She slowly leaned down, the ruby lipstick lips moving closer. Closer. Until she whispered in his ear with warm, minty breath. "Harv darling, you're testing my patience. If you're playing some sort of game, stop it. Because a fool and his money are easily parted. Don't be a fool, Harv." She punctuated the last with a kiss to his ear.

The reaction: a full body shudder.

Her lips moved around, her eyes coming even. Deep green eyes that could beguile the most stalwart of men. Her faux pearl necklace gently caressed neck and chin while her soft lips kissed the tip of his nose.

All part of the game. She knew exactly the effect she wrought on the male gender.

She stood from bending over and walked to the bedroom door without looking back and disappeared. The heavier click-clonk of heels moved down the long hall to the front door that opened and closed.

And just like that, she was gone.

But for how long?

She always wore black, and even with all that perfect beauty, she still resembled the black crows in the tree. Scavengers that picked over the remains of dead bodies.

Well, this body wasn't dead yet. Not by a long shot.

Too bad Gurski wasn't present to follow her to a lair and uncover clues to this treacherous conspiracy. No matter, plenty to do while the witch has fled the roost.

Across the room, the push buttons on the Princess phone were difficult to punch with shaky old fingers and required three attempts, while the cold floor, without slippers, made his arthritic feet ache. Gurski's number came to mind without pause. The nerve of the woman to gaslight everyone involved into believing a devious tale of dementia. But numbers had never been a problem. At least not a latter-day problem. Not for The Ledger Man.

A woman with a rasp in her tone answered. "Paradise Lost, Group Home. How may I help you?"

"Eddie Gurski, please."

On the other end came the whisper and a crackle from burning tobacco in a cigarette too close to the receiver, and then the pause while the woman exhaled. "Listen pal, I don't run up those stairs for no one. I take messages because that's part of my job. You wanna leave a message for Gurski?"

"Yes, please tell him—"

The doorbell rang.

"Never mind." The receiver clacked down too hard. The woman would think the caller rude, but she probably got a lot of that with her demeanor.

A stop at the bed to step into slippers immediately warmed aching feet and tempered the long trudge to the front door.

The large door swung open with ease on well-oiled hinges.

Gurski walked in wearing a well-worn green army surplus field jacket, Levi's, and black polished combat boots. "Hey, man, I called you twice this morning, and now it's almost noon. I gave up calling you after the broad threatened to call the police, said she'd get a restraining order. I can't afford anything like that."

"Welcome to my world."

"Really? You don't have it so bad. You got red lipstick on your nose." Gurski moved on into the house, down the hall into the dining room, and sat at the table. He chuckled. "Bro, you got lipstick on your ear, too. Had yourself a night, huh?"

"Never mind about that, you talked to her last night for thirty minutes before you had to run back to the group home or violate curfew. What'd you find out about her in your follow-up to that conversation?"

"Not much. Hey, I need that five hundred, though."

"Are you kidding? You have to earn it."

"That wasn't the deal. You said come over, meet the broad, then come back in the morning, and you'd give me the five. I'll get after it today, I promise I'll dig into it. I just need the green. I got a few people on my ass, and the five will go a long way toward cooling their jets."

What choice was there?

"Okay, okay. What did you think about what you saw yesterday in the brief moment you were here?"

"Like I said last night, a blind man could see something's up."

"Good. Good. Go on. What do you mean?"

"That guy Andrew Johnson, he's got eyes for your woman."

"She's not my woman!"

"She seems to know an awful lot about you for only being here a few hours. If this...whatever it is ever goes to court, well, she'd be very convincing to the judge and jury."

"Did you look into the phony marriage certificate?"

"I'll get to that today. I was locked down without access to any computer or phone."

"How are you going to get anything done if you have to go in every night?"

He took a small spiral notebook from his pocket and flipped it open. "At 945 this am, she came out of the house dressed to the nines, black outfit, black shoes, pearl necklace. She had some papers in her hand. She got into a dark gray Mercedes sedan license, personalized plate REALMAN."

"That's good. Did you see who was driving it? Why didn't you follow them?"

He held out his hand for the money.

"All right, damn you. Stay here."

The trip into the master bedroom and into the expansive walk-in closet only took a minute or so. The safe embedded under the hidden floor panel took longer to get open with uncooperative old and gnarled fingers.

Five minutes later, "Here, the first installment, five hundred as agreed."

"I didn't forget the combination, now did I?" The words came out in an utter meant for no one.

Gurski looked confused. "What?"

"She's trying to get everyone to believe I'm old and feeble, that I'm losing my mind. I'm not. My memory's still sharp as a tack. Now get on with it.

Who was driving the Mercedes?"

"Andrew Johnson, the construction contractor from yesterday."

Chapter Seven

Current Day

In the dining room, Gurski held up the fake marriage certificate, "With this, you can't really get the cops on your side. This is a golden bullet shot through your heart."

"Pshaw, to your golden bullet. Dig into the certificate, you'll find the county registrar doesn't have a record of anyone taking out a marriage license. Delores has not planned this caper for two years. It's a forgery. The lack of public record will bear witness."

"What kind of caper are we talking about?"

"Gurski, that's why I'm paying *you*. I'm pulling my hair out trying to figure her angle. If I knew, I could counter her move, and we'd be done."

"Take it easy, you're getting all red in the face. You're gonna stroke out. I'll go by the Hall of Records and check on this. But like I said, she's—"

"She's what?"

"Right now, she's holding all the cards, aces to our deuces. When it comes to that redhead, God gave with three hands. If you know what I mean."

"Exactly, none of this makes any sense. A criminal with her looks and cool demeanor under pressure could run any multi-million-dollar major scam in the country. Yet she's here fleecing a tired, broken-down old man without any money to speak of. Do you have the resources to run the plate on that car?"

"Of course. My sister's got a connection. She'll help me out."

"You didn't answer the earlier question. Why didn't you follow Rita?"

"Rita?"

"I mean Delores. And you just did it again, avoided the issue by *asking* a question. Answer my question!"

"I don't have a car."

"What? How do you get around?"

"I use the bus."

"And for this, I pay five hundred dollars a day? For a PI who gets around by bus?"

Gurski's ludicrous expression didn't lend itself to confidence. "You do believe me when I say, before yesterday, that woman had never set foot in this house? That I have never laid eyes on her before."

He squirmed a little, a product of not having enough backbone. "Es said for sure she hasn't seen anyone over here. No one, not even you. But she was gone for a while. Out of town."

"There, you see?"

"A negative doesn't prove a positive."

For the most part, Gurski presented as a rube who barely got by in life, and then he'd say something profound. An attribute of a true chameleon, someone who survives on the street by instinct. The question, though, was whether he was that chameleon or merely a mimic deriving information from the crook's university, the state prison system.

"But Es also said, since your wife passed, she hasn't set foot in this house. In fact, she said yesterday was the first time."

"I'm not in the mood to discuss a neighbor's useless observations. It's not pertinent to the situation unless she witnessed something of note."

"She said some furniture and home decorations are missing, but otherwise nothing's changed. Is that true?"

"That Esther, she knows how to run her mouth."

"Watch what you say about my friend."

"Take it easy, I didn't mean to denigrate sweet Esther. Did she say anything else that pertains to the problem at hand?"

"She said you've turned into a recluse."

"Wait. That's exactly right! Hey. I haven't gone anywhere in two years. How did this woman target me? Tell me how? That's an angle you can exploit. Find out where she's been in the last two years. This may be the angle we can work. Talking through this conundrum really helps. Excellent. Truly excellent. More than ever I need you to dig into her background, where she's from, where she grew up. Pull her criminal record. You do have the ability to pull a criminal record, right?"

"Yeah, yeah. I'll get right on it. But if what you say is true—"

"Gurski, if you don't believe in my truth, I don't want you working for me."

He stood. "We're not going back to that again. She took the locks off the bedroom door. Why would she do that? I don't think it's safe for you to stay here alone. Why don't you go over and stay with Es while I run a few things down?"

"I won't be bullied from my own house. I've lived here forty years. Fleeing is exactly what she wants. I'll be fine. Just get on with it. Find out who the heck she is, and while you're at it, do a background on Andrew Johnson."

"Don't tell me how to do my job." He walked toward the hall that led to the front door. Over his shoulder, he said, "Keep your head down, old man. I'll be back this afternoon with good news."

"Thank you. Yes, some good news would be most welcome."

The front door opened and closed.

Silence.

Ominous silence.

To shuffle over and lock the front door would do no good. Rita would've circumvented that easy method to stop her. When the locksmith came and changed the deadbolt on the bedroom door, she would've had the lock on the front re-keyed. No refuge remained in the large, forlorn abode, nothing but silence and loneliness.

The only thing that gave any solace came from Sylvia's letters.

In the kitchen, in the refrigerator, Rita left a plate stacked with diagonal-cut corned beef sandwiches on Wonder Bread. Yet another favorite. How did she know so much?

Thirty minutes later, hunger sated, the chair back under the doorknob in the master bedroom, and the shoebox of letters open on the lap, waiting for a tired old man to disappear into the words. Disappear into the past's safe haven.

The next two letters came free from the bottom of the bundle. The first had been found taped to the front door.

Harvey

Thank you for the lovely time. I am sorry I left without explanation. I hope you don't think me uncouth for such boorish behavior. I do find you kind and gentle and interesting. I would like you to know that the four years age difference between us is not at issue. What is at issue; I fear you have fallen in with the wrong element and because of this I would prefer that we simply remain good neighbors.

Sincerely,

Ms. Lois DeFrank

Reading that short missive did nothing to squash the ever-rising anxiety over Rita.

1968

That night, finding the note, Lois' words taped to the front door, came as a gut punch. Words that begged for an immediate response. A chance to correct the misperception of the real Harvey Dortmund.

But was it really a misperception or merely a misguided wish that it wasn't.

Lois' house sat dark. No one answered the repeated knock at the door.

With sleep nowhere on the horizon to grant relief, the only alternative left was to sit on her front steps. Sit until late-night dew settled, dampening hair and clothes and cold concrete steps worked on bone and flesh that caused a physical pain melding with the emotional ache.

All the while, obstinate words for a note in response to hers, circled and circled, birds looking for a perch and finding none.

What was there left to say?

What she said about the *wrong element* was true. The morally correct thing was to walk away. To further involve her would be life-changing. Only in the wrong direction. The conundrum could tear a person apart. But the answer was as plain as a nose on a face.

The only way it could be.

Walk away.

* * *

The morning after finding Lois' note, the knock at the door startled at first. Until the idea that the visitor might be Lois there to recant her words. Maybe she'd come to say a picnic in the country would be a delight. She'd mentioned a picnic over lunch at the country club moments before the ruinous tap on the shoulder.

"Hold on. Coming?"

Expensive clothes flew from the closet and fluttered to the floor until the right combination, a long-sleeved dress shirt and slacks in proper fall colors for an outdoor picnic, clicked in. Moments later, still barefoot, shoes in hand, the front door swung open.

A wonderful smile prepared for a wonderful girl next door disappeared, replaced with a vehement scowl.

On the front porch stood the hooligan, John "Jackie the Nose" Morano. He wore an expensive golf shirt tucked into pants with an expandable waist to accommodate the "lo stomaco," a vast belly that matched the glutinous neck and jowls. His nose had been broken too many times. The top of his septum wide and flat, blended in with the cheekbones. He had Johnny Carson hair and oatmeal for a face.

"Mr. LaBruzzo requests your presence, forthwith." Not Jackie's words, but repeated from a LaBruzzo mina bird meant to set the ground rules right up front.

Out at the curb sat a black Cadillac limo with tinted windows, the back door open. Waiting. The driver, a similar-looking thug but svelte by comparison, stood with his hands crossed at the waist, ready to assist if the need arose.

But Jackie the Nose didn't need help. His slovenliness a cover for a sadistic violence that simmered just below the surface, ready at a moment's notice to boil-over. He always carried an equalizer, a beavertail sap in his back pocket. He lovingly referred to the weapon as "Baby Bertha." On one occasion, while taking lunch at a hot dog cart in Manhattan, he pulled it out, slapped it against his palm, and spoke with his mouth open, displaying a gnashed chili dog. "Last night, you shoulda seen ol' Bertha here eat this guy's lunch. Knocked the livin' bejesus outta 'em."

Sammy Cohen, also there eating a mustard dog, extra onions, chuckled a response, "Yeah, but ol' Bertha got too excited and bashed in the guy's skull. We had ta run him out to Meadowlands for an unscheduled dirt nap. Mr. LaBruzzo about lost his cannoli over that one."

"Hey, look, there's a bit of the guy's hair stuck to Bertha. Ain't that sumthin? Huh?"

* * *

Back on the front porch: "Please inform Mr. LaBruzzo I'm indisposed and will contact him at a later—"

Jackie the Nose reached, grabbed a handful of shirt, and yanked. The shoes flung willy-nilly in the yard. He walked backward to the limo.

"Hey, hey. My shoes. I need my shoes."

"You mouth off like you *are* somebody. Count yoself lucky Baby Bertha doesn't come out and have a talk wit ya."

The limo ride took forty-five minutes. Jackie the Nose sat sprawled on the seat facing front, leaving only the back window to view passing landmarks. The driver took a circuitous route to shake off possible tails.

Jackie's eyelids tented, exposing slits of white, his breathing slowed. He passed gas, a horrid reek for which he made no excuses.

59

The Limo finally pulled down a long, gravel, tree-lined drive with a white, two-rail fence on each side.

The behemoth house, a gray slate Tudor, sat surrounded by hundred-year-old trees and acres of emerald green lawn. If owned by someone else, it might be found in Oz.

Jackie the Nose came back to life, scooted on his butt, grunting as he exited the car. He led the way into the house, straight through to the back French doors and outside again into the pool area. The concrete, hot on bare feet. The only relief, dancing the jig like some kind of fool.

Mr. LaBruzzo sat in a fluffy terry cloth robe under a CinZano umbrella with sunglasses hiding his expression. He raised his hand, offering a chair, and then said nothing for a long stretch, leaving the black mirror sunglasses to do all the communicating.

A tray of iced tea arrived, and still nothing, not a flicker of movement. The sun beat down, the glare off the pool intense. Jackie the Nose lounged out of hearing range on a chaise in the shade of the eight-foot slump-stone wall, fanning himself with the Daily Racing Form and sipping red Campari.

Finally, Mr. LaBruzzo spoke, his voice too high for a man of rank in his business, head of the family in New Jersey. "You know, Harvey, your work is important. That brain of yours understands numbers like no one I've ever seen. You can spot errors with just a glance at a column of numbers. That makes you worth your weight in gold. Quite literally. Another tick to the positive is that you're honest to a fault and...and naïve."

He paused, reached over to the table, picked up a tall glass of tea, the ice now melted, the wilted sprig of mint floundering. He took a long draught, downing half. He picked up a white linen table napkin and daubed his lips. "But. And this is a big but, you are not indispensable. Do you understand?"

"Yes, sir, we've had this same discussion on two prior occasions. I can give you the dates and times if you wish. If your point is for me to understand the pitfalls that come with this employment, I do, and I will never 'get sideways' with you." Words Mr. LaBruzzo liked to use during those two prior conversations. Fed them right back to him, a trainer tossing a sardine to a seal. Only in reality, it was more like a rib roast to a lion.

60

"Fine. I only wanted to remind you because I'm about to tell you to do something important. I'm not asking, I want to make that crystal clear. I'm telling you."

This never happened before, a harsh admonishment before the issuance of a work assignment. What came next would be nothing short of dire.

"Don't say anything until I finish what I'm about to say."

"Yes, sir."

He tipped his sunglasses down, exposing rheumy eyes, trying to evaluate the mistaken remark as innocent or a challenge to his authority. Satisfied, he continued. "I have two lives. The one I have here in this house, in this town. This one I keep separate from the other one in the city. The one you're a part of. That's what makes this situation very delicate. I don't want any slip-ups." He interlocked the fingers of both hands like a woven basket and pulled. "I don't want these two lives to collide."

He paused again, waiting for an answer that would never come.

A better demonstration would be two fists bumping together, but he'd said not to say a word until he finished.

He continued. "In the years to come, I don't want my son and daughter to deal with my world in town. I want them completely separate, living a normal life here in this world. Now this might sound strange, but I'm coming to the point. I wouldn't under normal circumstances explain my decisions. This time is different. It's important for all concerned to understand what's at stake.

What it comes down to is integration. For my plan to work, I need to integrate my family with these...these high-brow, tight-ass, chicken shits. It's not for me, you understand. It's for my family."

"I'm not sure I understand what this has to do with me." The warning bell sounded too late, words that slipped pasted the failsafe that violated a direct order. A panicked mind now alerting to a danger of the highest level.

His finger shot out, the elbow knocking over the second glass of tea that shattered on the pool deck, darkening the sun-white concrete. "I said let me finish before you toss in your worthless two cents."

"Yes, sir. Sorry, sir." The shards of broken green glass landed all around bare feet, creating a minefield.

Mr. LaBruzzo sat back, adjusted the sunglasses, and soft fluffy terry cloth that now appeared incongruent, ensconcing the volatile, overly tanned occupant. He took a moment longer to prove who controlled the conversation.

"When I saw you with that young lady in the country club, and after I took a day to think about it, I realized you had already integrated yourself in these circles. Ones I've been banging my head against a wall trying to break into. I asked myself, how could this be?" He raised his voice. "Jackie, how could this be?"

Jackie the Nose let the paper droop; he shrugged indifference and went back to reading.

"Nooo." The single word slipped out the instant the reason for the meeting finally clicked into place. The answer too terrible to abide.

Mr. LaBruzzo leaned forward, the mirrored glasses coming too close, his sour body odor wafting in. "That little bit of fluff you took to lunch is the daughter of the biggest, high-brow, tight-ass, chickenshit of this whole straight-laced community. And you...you somehow caught her eye. So, here's what you're gonna do. I want you to set her up with my son. Not just set him up, but whisper in her ear what a great guy he is. Are you getting my meaning here, Harvey Dortmund?"

No words could weasel past dry lips, not with a mind working high at speed between two issues; first, had Lois, merely enjoying an innocuous lunch with a low-level CPA, sealed her own fate. A Godawful fate? And two, the big one; what to do next? Never in all the years of college, not with the complicated word problems, the statistics, the calculus, nothing compared to anything close to a problem so intricate and convoluted. All the variables swirled round and round, one main factor, the only one that truly mattered; there was nowhere on earth to hide from a man like Mr. LaBruzzo. Once that variable was added to the equation, the solution became impossible.

That variable was the entire basis for the preamble laying down the law. He wanted the rules of this new game clear to all involved.

Forfeit Lois, or take a short ride out to Meadowlands, brace for a violent kiss from Baby Bertha, and then take a long, cold dirt nap.

Mr. LaBruzzo raised his arm. "Jackie? Get our favorite propeller-head the hell outta here and tell Naomi to shag her cute little ass out here with my lunch. And kid, watch the glass, only a dumbass'll leave the house barefoot."

The ride home in the limo happened in a couple of seconds. Without even a montage of passing landscape. A tightly wrapped mind spun out of control, the problem accelerating to the highest level in the definition of chaos.

* * *

That night called for another vigil on Lois' front steps. Most college co-eds shared a place with other co-eds, but Lois's father footed the bill with only one stipulation: that she live alone. His assumption being other girls would have an undue influence and lead Lois down the wrong path.

Lois must have stayed at her parents' house the last couple of days. Or she came home, kept the lights off, and hoped a wayward neighbor would tire and go away.

Mr. LaBruzzo expected results and, without exception, gathered them like a rapacious man raking in the pot at a high-stakes poker game.

Time now became the enemy. And time was inexplicably linked hand in hand with anxiety and insomnia.

Chapter Eight

1968

After giving in to the fruitless vigil waiting for Lois, and mere seconds after the head hit the pillow, a knock sounded at the door. Instant fear smacked the heart into high gear with enough electric shock to propel a person into the air. Could it be Jackie the Nose yet again? Two days in a row? Before all else, an ungentlemanly thought arose; jump out the back window, run like hell, and never look back.

Wait. The sun had risen without fanfare and filled the bedroom with yellow light.

How many hours had passed?

To flee, left poor Lois to fend for herself, left her standing in a pool filled with piranha.

This time, the shoes went on right after the pants and shirt.

The doorbell rang instead of another knock. An insistent ring from a pEsthering finger.

Only cowards ran.

Another one of Father's many bromides, *"The brave and cowardly are both fearful. However, the brave man faces his fear and does what needs to be done no matter the cost."*

Father never stood face to face with Jackie the Nose and Baby Bertha. Never looked into those piggish eyes and saw an emptiness as broad and desolate as the Gobi.

A cowardly peek out the window revealed a harried Lois standing on the stoop. It took a second look to ensure sleep-filled eyes had not made a mistake.

A shaky hand on the latch. The door swung open.

She barged in. "Come along, Harvey, we are going to take a motorboat ride on the lake."

"What? Ah, no. I don't think that's such a good-"

She quick-stepped over. "Harvey, please, don't make a lady beg. I've already stepped into your house unescorted. That has to account for something."

"What's happened? Did Giorgio…ah, do something?" Giorgio LaBruzzo, son of Mr. LaBruzzo.

"Who? I don't know anyone by that name. You're not awake yet and talking gibberish. Come along." She took hold of an elbow and tugged. "Grab that door and pull it closed. We'll be gone all day."

"I have to work. I can't—"

She spun on low, comfortable heels and glared. Said not one word. But those green eyes said a million at the speed of light and at the same time burrowed in and took control.

"Ahem." The only thing left to utter.

"It's settled then, come along. Over there, please get that picnic basket at the curb and put it in your car."

"I wanted to talk to you. I've waited at your house for two nights now."

She opened the door for herself and got in the passenger seat, another clue for the necessity to hurry. "That's fine, my dear, we can discuss it on the drive to the lake. Do you have swim trunks?"

"How can I have swim trunks? You just kidnapped me out of the house."

This time she flashed a smile that could melt an adult male into a puddle of quicksilver on the hot asphalt. "Oh, how droll. Kidnapping? You are a wag, Harvey Dortmund."

Minutes later, in the Caddie—traveling to Tomahawk Lake, an hour from Hoboken—Lois sat staring out the windshield with a blank expression.

"You going to tell me what's going on?"

"I've told you. I don't know why you don't believe me. We are going to the lake to swim and motor around."

A mile or two passed under the tires that whined on the warm asphalt still heating up with the rising sun. "You're quiet today. You're nothing like the person I took to lunch."

She turned and smiled. "Sir, I do believe I took *you* to lunch."

"Maybe you don't understand men. You see, they prefer to pay for the meals when accompanying a lady. But more importantly, they like to be the one to ask the lady out."

"Are you saying you would rather not go to the lake with me?"

"No. Not at all." The desire to go trumped all else...the need to eat...even to breathe.

"Why did you wait for me to come home? Isn't that what you said a little while ago?"

To look at her eyes would extract the truth, the same as a wily dentist's pliers. And at that moment, a coward drove the Cadillac, unable to say the words, perform the dastardly act Mr. LaBruzzo insisted upon. To do so would end any possibility, any hope of being with Lois ever again. And at the same time, doom her to a life submersed in violent crime.

The words in a cluster wouldn't straighten out. "I...I guess I just wanted to tell you that...I'm—"

She suddenly slid across the bench seat, picked up an arm, and put it around her shoulder. "Harv, if a person waited on you to make a move, we'd both be old and gray. So, I'll say it first, and I hope you don't leave me hanging—I'm quite taken with you. I know it was only one lunch, but I have to say I've never met anyone like you."

She nestled up close. Heat from her body something strange and new and at the same time comfortable beyond earthly description. During high school and college, conversing with women proved impossible, even more so than the most difficult calculus problem. All women baffled and beguiled. And now to touch a girl. To have a beautiful girl sitting close enough to feel her body heat presented as an unrealized fairytale.

She reached up and pinched close to a nipple. The pain brightened the whiteness in the sunlight. "Ouch."

"I just said, don't leave me hanging, and look at you."

The big Cadillac pulled to the side of the road all on its own. She sensed the reason and didn't pull away; she instead lifted her chin as he moved in.

At first touch, her lips, hot and moist, rang a bell deep inside. The desire to kiss her had been a sublime pressure that had continued to build for several days and burst forth all at once. With each passing moment locked in the embrace, his feelings transferred to her, the kiss grew more intense, more heated.

She broke, chuffed, pulled back, and stared. Those green eyes searching for the truth. "Harv, don't think this a prelude to...to something else. I don't know what came over me and...and came over you, but we need to...We *are* going to the lake to ride in a boat and picnic." Her words trailed off as if unsure. Her eyes shifted to confusion. "Talk to me, Harv, say something."

"I ah—" A shaky voice cracked. "I'm quite taken with you as well." Words never said to any other girl or woman. Words a shy introvert could never say without the prompting of a passionate kiss. Words that were grossly inadequate for the moment.

For the first kiss ever.

A fool for waiting so long.

That sublime pressure to do it again now cranked up a notch to an unbearable yearning never before experienced.

"Go." She slapped a leg with adequate force to make the thigh tingle. "Pull out onto the road before someone sees us."

Her feigning of propriety burst the spell. Only a fool would believe going to the lake on a bright sunny day, picnicking, and riding in a boat could go unnoticed. Not by one or two folks, but by hundreds relaxing and frolicking in the sun.

What a day, what a beautiful, glorious day to—

The bright sunlight cutting through the trees as the car sped down the two-lane road suddenly dimmed. An emotional response to fear. Razor sharp fear that snatched the breath away.

The word would get back to Mr. LaBruzzo. Someone would tell him that

Harvey, the "Ledger Man," violated the rule set down while next to a pool under a CinZano umbrella and witnessed by Jackie The Nose.

*　*　*

Current Day

The chair under the doorknob jostled. "Harvey, are you in there? Please move the chair away from the door."

The redheaded temptress had returned from her foraging for new vulnerable victims. Other victims, the same as unattended baby chicks in the nest, unaware the dark shadow of a predator lurked.

The fading sunlight in the tall bedroom windows bespoke of a dying day. What the heck happened to Gurski? Why had he not returned with the "good news," he promised?

The door again bumped against the chair. "Harv, honey, come to dinner. I've made your Friday night favorite: meatloaf, new potatoes, asparagus, and biscuits from scratch. Come on now, baby, let's quit playing these silly games and get back to normal."

The word combination in perfect order describing the meal, clicked into memory. "Ah, hah? Mystery solved. One of them, anyway."

Once out of the chair, Rita's pressure on the door pushed it clear. She entered wearing a stunning red satin cocktail dress with red heels. "Now what are you talking about?"

"The letters. Everything you need to know about me and Sylvia are in these letters. You've read them. Somehow, you gained entry to this house…who knows when or how you read them. That's how you're pulling off this…this scam."

"Fiddlesticks. Harvey, baby, what scam? What are you talking about when you and I have lain around in bed on Sunday mornings, you with the LA Times and me with all of those letters. You said it was okay. You lay there and watched me read them. Now come eat something, you'll feel better."

The mind, once given a task, takes off at high speed. How...? No, when had she come into the house and accessed the letters? Was it before Sylvia or after? The "after" spanned two years back. Many of those grief-laden days nothing but blurs blended into a slippage of time. That's when it happened, when the security breach occurred. Had to be.

In the dining room, Rita pulled out the same chair. At the close end of the long twelve-person table sat a platter of biscuits, fluffy and golden brown, one of asparagus with tabs of real butter melting on top, one of new potatoes, and the pièce de résistance, one beautiful meat loaf. Replete with the baked-in tomato sauce that covered the length. Just like the photo from the red and white checked Betty Crocker cookbook.

One really shouldn't be so enamored of meatloaf, but being raised dirt poor, meatloaf was reserved for special occasions; Easter and Christmas.

The sight of the luscious food could make any mouth water. How could a person sleep through all the noise needed to accomplish such a feat? Had she somehow been slipping a mickey into the food and drink?

Don't give in to her. Walk over to the refrigerator, grab a couple of the corned beef sandwiches made with Wonder bread, and retire to the bedroom. That would show her.

But the food sat there too perfectly, beckoning an old fool to toss out all logic.

Father had said, "*Obstinance will get you nowhere. If you're displeased with a situation, change the narrative.*" Something on that order, the rust on an overused memory clogged the gears.

"I think *I will* have a sit, thank you very much."

She pulled the chair out further, treating an old man like an invalid, then sat in a place directly across. The meatloaf steamed when sliced and doled out.

"Aren't you having any?"

Was the meal poisoned, and that's why she didn't fill her plate?

"Don't be silly, I don't eat anything with a face. You know better than that after all these months at this table." She spooned out the rest of the side dishes, sat back, and watched; a lioness espying a weak and elderly gnu amongst the herd.

The food tasted heavenly. If she hadn't forcibly interjected herself, "by hook and by crook,"—the way Esther would describe it—into this house... well, an invitation might've been forthcoming for her to stay and keep a foolish old man company.

Maybe in another life.

She watched the food moving from plate to mouth, as if the most interesting undertaking ever witnessed. "Do you like it, Harv, my love? Please tell me how much you like it."

"Of course, I do. And I guess I should thank you. I'm not a curmudgeon when it comes to praise, and even though you are an evil, obstinate crook, you are one heck of a cook."

"Watching you enjoy it is thanks enough, though your words are still painful."

"You never let the curtain drop on this act of yours, do you?"

"It's not an act, my dear, and tomorrow or the next day, or the next, you'll wake up and say, "Hello Delores, where have you been all my life? The first words you said to me the day we met out on the Santa Monica Pier. You remember that day, Harv?"

"Not going to happen. Did you really read Sylvia's letters to gather all the information you needed for this...this scam?"

Her green eyes flashed, matching a crooked smile. "Asked and answered, Harv. Do you have another question? I mean, as long as we're sitting here, we might as well have a conversation. Air out *all* the dirty laundry."

"Why did you take off the two bolt locks on the bedroom door?"

"Don't be silly, no one has those types of locks on their bedroom door. It looks like...well, to be honest, it looks like a crazy person lives here."

"Hmm."

"Is that all? No more questions?"

"Why don't you carry around a cellphone?"

The flash of those green eyes again and the smile. "Why don't *you* have a cell phone, Harv?"

"That's an old crook's trick, you know. And I don't carry one because I don't have anyone to call."

"No, I don't know the old crook's trick, enlighten me."

"Using misdirection by asking a question for a question."

"If you must know, I don't like being a slave to an electronic device. Does that answer meet with your approval? And please don't refer to me as a crook."

"As a matter of fact, no."

"Then tell me, Harv, why do you think *I* don't carry around a cellphone?"

"First of all, the really smart criminals have switched to low-tech to avoid prosecution, to avoid leaving evidentiary trails like text messages."

"If that were true, a person just wouldn't use the text messaging app. Or just not text anything incriminating."

"That's a pretty good answer, but it doesn't wash with me. A cell can also historically track a person to every location and route traveled."

"You know what's got to be really scary, Harv?"

"Tell me, I'm all ears."

"This memory loss of yours. How awful it must be to wake up and find yourself old and decrepit when just the day before, when you looked in the mirror, you were young and vibrant. Couple of days ago we lived here as happy as clams. You go to sleep and wake up living in a world that has passed you by. It's so sad. And I am sympathetic, really, I am. But I'm too young, in fact half your age, and I don't have the time, nor the inclination to stay and—"

"Go. Please go. No one is asking you to stay. Believe me, I won't lose any sleep over it. In fact, I'll sleep better."

"Why *does* a person have so many locks on the master bedroom door?" She'd waited to create an ambush with that question.

"I never was bold and fearless when sleeping. I don't want someone sneaking up on me, slit my throat, and I wake up dead."

"Good answer, Harv, my love, but you and I both know the real reason."

"No. No, that's the real reason all right. I think you must've thrown your criminal net over the wrong house, the wrong man. For the life of me, I can't figure your game. Something is afoot, and I can't figure it out."

She slowly stood, wagging a finger. "I don't think so, my love. For one thing, I'm your wife and I'll never admit otherwise." She moved to the counter, picked up a clutch purse. "And your friend Eddie Gurski will discover that I don't have a criminal background. None. I'm clean as a Safeway chicken. I'm not a criminal. You just wasted five hundred dollars. I'm going out tonight, I'll be back late. Don't wait up, my love."

She'd positioned herself in the game as an enigma, first denying culpability and then using a term commonly found on the lips of villains: "Clean as a Safeway Chicken." She liked to toy with her victims, bat around the helpless little yellow tweety bird before swallowing him whole in one gulp.

She did the warm hand to the cheek thing, along with another kiss on the nose.

The thought bubbled up again, no doubt a silly idea to maybe let her stay a little longer, a few days, maybe. The great food, the great Rita Hayworth impression, and the touching. Most of all, the simple touching. Something an old man desires the most is human contact of any sort. But as soon as the idea rises, it's tamped down with self-conceit. No one wanted to be gaslighted, even by a Rita Hayworth. That left only one option: figure her game and then kick that nice butt of hers to the curb.

The front door closed. The silence returned, smoothing out the approaching dusk. With the dimming yellows and oranges came the horrific loneliness. At least with Rita, there was someone else knocking about in the huge, empty house. Criminal or otherwise.

How did she know about the five hundred dollars? Playing back the entire conversation, nothing she said could influence a grand jury to indict. Her words very carefully side-stepped every topic and yet could still be interpreted either way: criminal or wife. A phantom memory gone missing, or what she said, the truth.

Pshaw to the phantom memory.

Chapter Nine

Current Day

E yes eased open, leaving behind a dreamless night. Another morning sun, bright and cheerful, entered through the windows. A glorious day.

Until noise from the kitchen snuffed out all possibility of further glee. Reality set in. The situation with Rita the malefactor, intruding in the home—into a life, remained unchanged.

The chair had again been moved from under the doorknob. How did she keep accomplishing such a feat? Was she part Houdini?

The bed, warm and soft as a nest, begged consideration for him to donate another hour or more to the slumber bank. Why get up just to step back into a nightmare? The contradictory side of the mind remembered all too clearly the great food, the conversation, and most importantly, the warm touch from the night before. If she stayed much longer that side of the mind could win out—say to hell with it and let her stay. Why not? How many years were left?

No. No way could that vixen win at the game of her own design.

Through the open bedroom door, the sound of the front doorbell rang. The click-clack of Rita's high heels on the hardwood floor pinged her path to welcome the guest.

The pressure in the air changed as the door abruptly swung open.

The sound from a frantic woman. She screamed. And continued to scream.

A clue something had gone terribly wrong.

Unintelligible words mixed with the click-clack of high heels as Rita fended-off a kind of whirling disturbance that blew into the house.

Rita yelled to the crazed woman. "Stop it. Stop it right now. Calm yourself."

The covers flung off, the slippers ignored.

In the quick flight across the Asian rug to the open bedroom door, an object underfoot caused great pain to shoot up the right leg.

Hopping around, the obstreperous words muttered all on their own.

The sun through the bedroom window winked off a bit of silver. The yelling in the other room intensified.

"What the—"

Old age wouldn't allow an eighty-two-year-old to bend at the waist far enough to touch the floor, and forced the need to go down on one knee to recover the item. Bones cracked and creaked, muscles threatened revolt.

The object oddly enough, a ring. A lump of silver fashioned after a skull with two red stones for eyes. The skull ring tickled a memory that eluded and fled when trying to bring it forward. When that happened, it was an uncommon symptom of advancing age.

Rita, in close pursuit, followed a harried Esther who hurried into the master bedroom. For the first time ever, her hair, unencumbered by a hairnet, sprang out in every direction, eyes wild like a bull moose falling off a cliff, spooked by a lobo wolf.

She pointed. "What did you do? What did you do to my Eddie? This is your fault. All your fault. You were the last to see him."

Rita held onto the woman's shoulders with both hands. "Get out. Get out right now or I'm calling the police."

Esther whirled on Rita and shoved. A four-decade kindergarten teacher resorting to violence. What had happened to cause the world to go berserk?

Esther turned back and advanced, eyes large behind the thick prescription glasses. Spittle flew escaping into the air mixing with the rant. Her finger pointed the same as a weapon. "You did this. You. You. You."

"Did what? Esther, dear, please sit down and get hold of yourself. Rita, get her some water, make her some hot herbal tea. Calm yourself and tell me what in the world you're talking about?"

"What's that you have in your hand?" She leapt forward more agile than her age should allow and snatched at the ring.

But missed.

"What, oh, this. I found it right here on the floor. I don't know who—"

The brain had continued to search the memory bank, the origins of the ring finally locked in. *Oh, Sweet Baby Jesus.*

Too late. Esther had seen the ring.

The implications now obvious.

"I think that's Eddie's ring. What are you doing with Eddie's ring? You found it, where?" Confusion flourished in her dazed state.

Rita took a step back with an all-knowing expression, smug, and allowed the mystery afoot to play out.

The early bird, the red robin just ate the worm.

"Oh, dear lord." Rita had set the whole play in motion. She had to have dropped the ring on the carpet in a place sure to be discovered. But what did the ring have to do with anything?

Esther suddenly deflated, the same as all the air released from a toy balloon. Her expression and shoulders slumped in equal measure. Tears filled her eyes. She came forward in desperate need of consoling. Her tears wet pajama fabric, her arms gripping tight enough to restrict air in the lungs.

"There, there, it can't be all that bad." What else could a person say?

Tangled up in chest and pajamas, her words came out muffled. "He's dead, Harv. My good friend Eddie...he's dead."

"The hell you say?"

She nodded, not pulling back, and hugged tighter.

If Eddie was dead, what the hell was his ring doing on my bedroom floor? The answer is stark and obvious, and at the same time difficult to believe.

Two men in Sears and Roebuck suits and ties appeared in the wide bedroom doorway. The taller one said, "Police department. We found your front door open. We followed Ms. Esther Goodacre over here from her house."

Rita stepped out of the way with no attempt to intervene. She folded her arms under bountiful breasts, poofing up the cleavage. Not saying word one.

The shorter detective with straw-colored hair and a baby face stepped into the room, aggressive in demeanor. "Are you Harvey Usher?"

Good thing Esther stood close for support. The air turned too thin to breathe and wobbled like a heatwave. "What's that? Why?"

Oh, dear Lord, the ring. An airtight frame job for murder. Why else would the ring be on the floor in plain sight? Placed where an old fool could kick, or step on it.

Rita.

Rita said, "Yes, this is Harvey Usher, I'm his wife. What is it you want from him?"

Off the cuff, easy as you please, Rita rolled over and gave up her husband. No, *not husband.*

Or had this been the plan all along?

"I'm Harvey Usher. What can I do for you?" Back in the day, fear would not rule over all else like it did now causing knees to shake, and voice to quiver.

"We'd like you to come down to the station for an interview."

"I don't think so. I've done nothing wrong."

For the past fifty years, the police station was a place avoided at all costs. A black hole where a person disappeared and never returned. Once inside they didn't have to let a person go. They could…and probably would uncover the name, "Dortmund." Uncover a dirty little secret.

Not so little, really.

Rita, the Red Robin, would win her game of deceit with her black-hearted deception.

Neither detective made a move to get physical. Rita took another step forward. "Unless you have a warrant, my husband's not going anywhere. He has a very nervous heart that, if stressed, will give him fits. You don't want to deal with a witness on the floor having a fit, do you, Detective?"

Nervous fit, the woman was daft. She had no idea who she was dealing with.

The short one hooked his thumbs in his dress belt, a move that pulled back his suit coat far enough to allow a holstered gun to peek out along with a badge clip. The gleam of the badge bellowed out his silent authority. "Who said we'd be interrogating him *as a witness?*"

Dortmund.

Dortmund.

The world started to swirl down a large drain. Along with it came a dizziness that could very well see an old man down on the floor face up, having a "nervous fit." The silver metal ring with the skull, squeezed so tightly in hand that it would be hours before the fiery red indentation disappeared.

"I'm innocent of anything you two buffoons think I've committed. I will go with you on two conditions."

"We don't do conditions."

Rita took a quick step forward. "You will do no such thing, Harvey Usher. You were here all night, and I'll attest to it."

The tall cop with a long, narrow horse face finally spoke. "Who said it happened last night?"

"Hah."

The words of a fool almost followed along with that ignorant reaction. Words that would describe how the woman—Rita—had burrowed into a life and held on like a bloodsucking tick—a rant that she wasn't his wife at all. They would quickly recognize the ramblings of a person who fit *Booby Hatch* criteria. And if mentally ill, all the easier to hang a bum rap.

That pitfall side-stepped and came with a warning: keep your damn mouth shut, you fool.

"Condition number one. I want to change out of these pajamas into regular clothes."

Esther had calmed and stood silently to the side watching, now stepped forward. "What's the second condition, Harv?"

There hadn't been a second. The demand for conditions originated from the need to "take control of the situation leading up to a hostile interrogation." Rule number one in Alfred Manfredi's, "How to corner the Obstinate Spy," the 1942 first edition. Odd how that information just bubbled up all on its own. Dementia, pshaw.

A book studied in great detail after the unfortunate incident with Lois at Tomahawk Lake. While on a sailboat for a month on the way to the Cayman Islands.

"For the second condition, I want Esther, my dear friend, to drive me to the station. I know how you storm troopers operate. You grapple up a truckload of innocents, take them to your lair, and put them under the heat lamp. Maybe pour water down their gullet until they drown. Then you ring them out and kick them out the door to find their own way home."

Horse face said, "Sounds like you've done this before."

Everyone looked at him, mulling over an uncovered kernel of truth. He would be the one to watch—to carefully parcel out answers to his questions. Strictly yeses and noes. Rule number two from Manfredi.

The straw-haired one looked up at horse face who nodded.

"Fine. We'll wait outside and escort you to the station. Don't try to run out the back."

Rita harrumphed. "Does he look anything like an Olympic contender in the forty-yard dash?"

Sometimes she said the most extraordinary things. *A forty-yard dash in the Olympics.*

* * *

Twenty-five minutes later, Esther steered the big Lincoln down the narrow streets, headed for downtown, the plain, pastel blue cop car glued to the back bumper.

No words had been exchanged inside the Lincoln regarding the emotionally charged situation.

She had gone back to her house and slipped into the old Esther garb with the hairnet, and fresh clothes ironed smooth, the support hose, and black orthopedic shoes. Fatigue hung off her like a thick wool blanket.

She kept her chin up, trying to see through the top of the steering wheel. "Harv, I didn't mention to the cops the ring you had in your hand."

What to say? To agree to possessing the ring could later be misinterpreted as an admission of guilt and critical evidence in a crime.

But this was Esther, a good friend.

"Yes, the ring. I found it just after you burst into my house. I got out of bed and stepped on it barefoot. I swear I have no idea how it got there."

Her head turned away from watching the road, a dangerous proposition. Her eyes, too large behind the thick prescription glasses, blinked. "It's that redheaded bitch who did this, isn't it?"

Never in all the years Esther lived next door, not in all the times Sylvia had her over for tea or to play cutthroat Canasta, to share Chinese takeout, did such a word disparaging a person slip past her lips.

A loud bang shook the entire world. The big Lincoln shuddered.

Metal screeched. Crunched.

The car moaned and screamed, side-swiping a car parked at the curb. Then another. And another, until the Lincoln rammed into the back of a vehicle stopped in the middle of the street. The Lincoln came to an abrupt stop, jerking muscles in the neck and back.

The rush of violence brought back a memory buried deep, one involving a convertible filled with teens five decades ago. Lois had screamed that awful day. All the blood. The screaming. The mangled flesh. The end result is too horrific to ponder.

"Harv? Harv, are you okay? I'm so sorry."

"What? Yes, I'm fine. No harm done. Are *you* okay?"

"I ruined my damn car."

"Esther, your language. What's going on with you?"

Tears filled her large eyes. "I loved him, Harv."

"I know you did. I'm sorry." In the hug, her body seemed too fail to maintain a life. She wept, wetting the white on white dress shirt donned in an effort to appear sane in front of the local constabulary.

A loud knock on the window caused her to jump. Outside, Horse Face, bent over, yelled, "You all right? You need medical aid?"

"Egad, man. Just give us a minute, would you please? We're fine."

A long moment passed. "Esther, hon, we need to get out of the car."

With her face still buried in shirt and chest, words came soft and muffled. "Wait. Please, can we just wait a minute? Just a minute, that's all."

"Of course, take your time."

"I need to tell you something important. I should've told you before now."

"I'm right here. Take your time.

Another pause.

"Eddie, he was in prison in Chuckwalla, a nightmare of a place. He was in for something stupid, really. Embezzlement from this job. He took some power tools. He told his boss he was sorry and would pay it back. But the big government machine ate Eddie, Harv. Chewed him up and spit him out. I moved to Blythe those two years I was gone. Lived in a ratty motel at first, then rented a room in a small house cut up into four small apartments. I did it just to be near him. The place always smelled of burnt chemicals. Fellow borders smoked something off crumpled-up tin foil.

I visited every day they allowed me to. He wouldn't have made it through without those visits.

This was right after…right after Sylvia passed on. I shouldn't have left you to deal with that, not by yourself. A true friend wouldn't have left. I was torn, Harv. I'm sorry, I chose to go with Eddie to help him with his ordeal instead of yours. I think…I…I might've been in too much pain over Sylvia leaving us like that. So abruptly without any notice. One minute she was with us the next…"

Only Sylvia's exit wasn't abrupt. There had been plenty of notice, and just enough planning.

"You did the right thing. All of it worked out. I mean until today. I'm so sorry, Es."

Her head moved up and down as she silently wept. "Eddie…Eddie said that if they ever had to give California an enema, they'd stick it up Chuckwalla." A chuckle mixed with tears.

"I only knew him for a short time, but I could tell he was a special person."

She pulled back to look, her eyes large and wet behind glasses now mushed against her face. "You think so, Harv? You really think so?"

"Of course, I do."

Another knock at the driver's window, the rest of the world that disappeared, returned, shifting from diffused grays to bright technicolor.

The long front end of the Lincoln smashed into an accordion of metal and flaked black paint, melded into the back of a Secure Guardian One, armored car parked in front of The Great Bank of the West, GBW.

Guards in gunmetal gray uniforms stood with their guns drawn, held down by their legs, still not sure the ramming of the armored car wasn't a prelude to a robbery. The short detective with the straw-colored hair held his hands up flat, trying for diplomacy and tact.

A crowd gathered.

Horse Face pulled on the passenger door that wouldn't yield. He yelled, "We have the fire department on the way to pry it open. Just stay calm."

"No one's overly excited in here. Go about your business. Go on, leave us be."

"If you start to panic, we can break the window to get you out."

"Nobody's about to panic. Go about your business and leave us be."

A block and a half down, on the left, a Channel 11 TV truck in front of the police station, started up and drove to the crash. Made it before the fire department. The occupants, a Hispanic fellow with a shoulder mount camera, jumped out with an Asian gal and ran over to the Lincoln.

Trapped like a rat, unable to move.

The camera closed in on the window to get a shot of the Lincolns' occupants. How had this happened? Five decades of staying away from the media, and in two bad days, the whole world came tumbling down. All of this mess started with that red-headed witch entering the house where she didn't belong.

"Harv, I like you and all, but please get your face out of my neck. What will people think?"

"Right, sorry." The attempt to hide a notorious face hadn't worked. Based on the flash, the camera caught a good shot, not a profile but a full front view.

Had old age changed enough of the contours, the sagging skin, and tired facial muscles to create a natural disguise?

Besides, after five decades, who held a grudge that long? Right?

Outside the car, the Asian news 11 gal tapped the window. "Are you okay?"

"Oh, dear Lord," Esther said, shifting now to hide. But her motivation came from vanity and the shame, as if two lovers were discovered at a lookout point. "Go away."

The tap again. "Come on, I'm on deadline for the five o'clock segment, gimme something, please?"

Esther lifted a hand and gave News 11 the finger.

The absurdity of it caused unavoidable mirth to rise and burst forth. Esther followed suit, laughing right along.

The fire truck arrived siren blaring and bleated a triple honk before stopping, the noise loud enough to cause a rolling echo that bounced off the business buildings and drew even more attention to the wreck with the armored car.

A blue-uniformed cop appeared and ushered the obstinate and intrusive reporter back. Five minutes later, firemen applied a monster hydraulic device and pried open the driver's door that screeched, unable to resist the laws of nature. Metal tore further, ruining a wonderful vehicle—the source of many pleasant trips with Esther and Lois...no, not Lois. Sylvia. A dangerous mental slip. Outside the car, the bright sun blinded and snatched away eyesight for several long seconds.

Esther held on to a shaky arm while balance returned under protest, the long bench seat of the Lincoln preferred to the crazy world in the street. Out in front sat the metal carnage, the Lincoln melded with the Secure Guardian One armored vehicle. Another SGO vehicle dispatch had already arrived, and money handed in a daisy-chain of burly guards was transferred from the crumpled one.

Behind the Lincoln, Esther had really done a number. Four cars lay in ruin, the same as if a tank had driven down the street, the mechanized track rolling over parked vehicles at the curb. A small blue thing unrecognizable, a bright red convertible BMW, a beige company truck with a trailer filled

82

with lawn mowers and edgers, now thrown to the side, mashed in a ruinous jumble, and the last, a silver Mercedes coupe. The left side of all four, damaged beyond recovery.

Totaled.

A woman in a tight black skirt, white blouse, and heels stood beside the candy apple red Beemer, weeping. A man in a suit stood next to the Mercedes on the phone, yelling at his insurance agent about losing a full day's work.

Horse Face and his sawed-off partner came and escorted their two criminals down the middle of the street, walked the block and a half to the police station. People on both sides stared, gawd, as if the circus had arrived in town and the freaks—two elderly people—had somehow escaped from the back of their caged wagon. Too many held up phone cameras memorializing the walk of shame for their many social media apps.

Now, if only the two cops didn't insist on using the Live-Scan machine to take fingerprints, at least part of the beastly little day could be salvaged. Live-Scan prints meant the instant discovery of the name Dortmund. Live-scan meant incarceration for the remainder of a life, which, of late, had turned outrageously sour.

All due to the arrival of a red robin.

Chapter Ten

1968

Warm wind blew through the open Cadillac windows lifting Lois' beautiful raven hair. The kiss still rattled around in Harvey Dortmund's mind and held his body in a kind of stunned trance, the same as a curare-dipped dart to a buttock.

Ignorant words from a fool could only ruin a now-perfect day. But words needed to be said to dispel the confusion. The biggest question: Why kiss a "Propeller-head?" Mr. LaBruzzo's tag that everyone glommed onto and wouldn't let die. His way to ensure his Ledger Man never rose above the bottom-dwelling station within his organization. The Ledger Man was, "Lower than whale crap." Only he had used the more vulgar definition of excrement.

The association with Mr. LaBruzzo no longer mattered. Only one thing mattered now.

Lois.

Lois nuzzled in closer under a welcoming arm as if she truly enjoyed being in that position. More importantly, though, she acted as if the kiss affected her in a similar manner. That it melted away the rest of the world, narrowing life down to just two people, and at the same time generating a warm glow in the chest. One that, by the second, grew exponentially. An extraordinary feeling. With an emotion like this, one loose in the world, why were there wars?

But how could she feel the same thing? She was nothing short of gorgeous. She could literally have…well, kiss anyone she pleased.

So then, why kiss a Propeller-head?

"Can we talk about this…this…I mean, what just happened?" The trees along both sides of the road blipped by the same as slats in a white picket fence, a mind hyper-focused on the undeniable need to find the answers to important questions while keeping the car in the lane.

"Don't be a silly goose, Harv. You act like this was your first—"

She pulled away to get a look at the confused expression of the fool maneuvering a motor vehicle down the highway at fifty miles per hour, while navigating fresh, wondrous emotions.

A hand came up to touch his cheek, warm and inviting. "Harvey…please tell me that wasn't your first kiss?"

Hot blood flushed his face red, no different than a thumb smacked with a ballpeen hammer.

Say something, you dummy? Use your words or remain buried deep in that "Propeller Head" category for the rest of your natural life.

"Of course not, I've kissed before. But I have to tell you, *that* kiss right there…That kiss was the cat's meow. No kidding. That kiss could make a man feel like William Holden, martinis, and…and white dinner jackets, all at once."

Then the guilt set in. Truth, a pEsthering interloper. "No, I don't ever want to mislead you or lie to you. Yes, that was my first kiss. I didn't mean to lie. Would you like me to turn this land-yacht around and take you home?"

"Don't be silly, it makes me like you all the more. Your honesty is refreshing."

She snuggled back into her place under his arm, one hand resting on the thigh, that connected to the foot that worked the accelerator and the brake. Without careful concentration, the big boat of a car would veer off all on its own and crash into those blurred, picket-fence trees.

After a moment, she said. "Okay. We're being honest here, right?"

"Egad, I knew this was too good to be true."

She slapped his thigh. "Don't be a big wuss."

Another big secret she would eventually discover. He *was,* in fact, a wuss, a very large one. And in the deepest part of his soul, understood how cowardice controlled the majority chunk of Harvey Dortmund III.

"I would like you to know," she said, "That ah…initially, I did come to your house with a picnic basket under false pretenses."

The brightness of the sun dimmed. The internal joy dropped down from his chest and flowed through the wingtip shoes into the floorboard. "Please hurry, say it before I shrink so small I won't be able to reach the pedals. Tell me the rest of it."

She giggled with a wonderful lilt that bespoke of an uninhibited innocence. A laugh that gave strength and, oddly, at the same time, solace.

"Wait. Wait," she said. "But that all changed with one kiss. I think it changed a few things for you as well. I mean, I have never kissed a man like…I mean, you are different in so many ways. Refreshingly different. That's the word, refreshing. You are nowhere near the arrogant, pretentious daddy's boys that haunt the country club, strutting around like stags in rut."

"What was the false pretense?" The ugly question came out in a half-croak.

"It doesn't matter now, does it?"

"Please tell me."

"Okay, but remember, it doesn't matter and has nothing to do with you or me. Not now. After I tell you, we will never speak of it again. It's officially locked in the vault, never to be brought out to the light of day."

She had lost the affect in her language and syntax, the hint of snobbishness gone. The real Lois now sat on the car seat, snuggled up, talking to a propeller head.

"Father heard about our luncheon at the country club. Of course, he would; he has spies everywhere."

One darn lunch had changed the entire world.

"Father is overprotective and sometimes a loud-mouthed lout when it comes to his only daughter, but I do love him dearly. He…well, he forbade me to ever see you again."

"Hence, the picnic basket and the knock at my door?"

"Yes, hence the picnic basket and the knock at your door. I was being

86

an obstinate child showing he could no longer control my life. I'm twenty years old for crying out loud. But Harvey, my love, that all changed. I mean it really all changed with that kiss. I know I sound like a hopeless romantic. I mean…well even a pretentious deb shouldn't talk about a kiss like—"

"Please?" The word croaked out again, the mind having a difficult time digesting her use of the term "My love."

Dear Lord, those two words struck with enough force to snatch the breath from a fool trying to talk to a beautiful woman without saying something ignorant.

"My darling Lois, I'm sorry about your father not wanting you to associate with the likes of me, but first thing after this excursion, I'm buying him a box of Cuban cigars. I'll track him down and we'll have a talk. I'll dispel his worries."

This time she laughed long and hard, a sound that made the top of the head tingle with joy and the world at large brightened by several lumens.

She calmed. "I am sorry, I shouldn't have been so forward, knocking on your door or getting into your car. But Harvey Dortmund, you can kiss me like that any day of the week. I'd just recommend not talking with Daddy, not for a good long time. At least until—"

"Until when?"

"Until snowballs are sold for half-price in a very warm place."

Forget her father; what she just said meant there would be additional kisses. "You said any day of the week?"

The question caused her to hesitate. "Well, no, that wouldn't be prudent. Not *any* day. Shall we just say any day that ends in a "Y"

Laughter rolled out of the car windows dispersing out into the world.

Life could not get any better.

The Cadillac hummed down the road, the warm air blew in the window, a beautiful girl snuggled in close. But most of all, the memory of that glorious kiss lingered like a good Swiss chocolate on the tongue.

"Harvey? Harvey, you better find a filling station. Look."

With the bombardment of romantic distraction, the gauges had taken a backseat. The little red needle bounced on, "Empty."

Just as a Sunoco Station appeared on the right. The caddy dipped down off the crown of the road and into the filling station. A man in his late thirties clad in all white, with a black belt and a white cap outlined in black piping, hurried out. "Fill 'er up, sir? Ethel?"

"Yes, please, and could you check the oil?"

"Will do, and I'll get those windows too."

"Oh, look, Harvey, in the station window. They sell those Styrofoam ice chests. Wouldn't it be grand to drink ice-cold Coca-Cola while sunning on the lake?"

"Yes, it would." Just as the door opened to exit the caddy, a conga line of cars sped by on the elevated highway. High-schoolers in their parents' cars headed to the lake for sun and fun, their glee-filled voices echoing off the tall trees.

Most were convertibles with their tops down. In several of the convertibles, four or five kids sat up on the back edge, their feet in the seat, packed together. They yelled, waved, and horsed around. One of these cars peeled off, zoomed in, and stopped on the other side of the pump. Everyone dismounted the back, and in a covey, ran into the filling station. At the counter, they purchased Coca Colas, candy bars, and bags of peanuts. Their pure innocence lay bare.

Ten minutes later, the newly purchased ice chest filled with cubed ice and Cokes sat comfortably in the backseat. The attendant asked for eleven dollars for the tank of gas. Harvey gave him twelve. He gave a smile and a two-fingered salute to his cap brim. "Thank you, come again."

Off to the right, a scrape and thumping noise drew his attention just as Lois yelled, "Oh God, no. Harvey, look. Oh my God!"

The candy-apple red convertible with the kids remounted on the back edge, took off from the pump and rose up the incline to reenter the highway. The young driver had paused to let traffic go by and then hit the gas at the wrong moment to enter an opening in traffic. The front of the car surged forward and upward on the steep incline. The rear dipped with inertia.

Three teenagers sitting on the back rolled off and landed hard in a writhing pile of skinned arms, legs and knees. Screams rose to a crescendo.

"Those poor kids." Harvey had never seen anything like it. The abrupt violence. The immediate pain and suffering.

Lois jumped out and ran to help. Two girls fought to stand, tears already streaming, chests heaving, the carefree world caving in on them. For the rest of the kids in the car fear froze them for a stunned moment. Then all at once they snapped out of it with screaming and sobbing.

Chaos.

One black-haired girl didn't get up and lay inert face down on the hot asphalt.

The driver aghast, realized his error and jumped out of the car. In his haste he failed to put on the emergency brake. The big car rolled backward.

Everyone saw it happen unable to do anything to stop it.

The car backed over the girl's legs.

The car kept rolling down the incline and crashed into the service station.

One of the girls who stood frozen in place, fainted dead away.

Harvey took off his tweed blazer, covered the injured girl on the ground, and scooped her up. "Come on, Lois, you're driving. We have to get her to a hospital."

Lois didn't hesitate; she set her jaw and ran for the car.

The caddy had a huge backseat with enough room to administer first aid taught in the BSA, the Boy Scouts of America. The black-haired girl bled from a deep laceration above her forehead in the scalp line. Her jaw looked broken. Both shins no longer ran in straight lines, with multiple fractures in each.

"Oh, my God. Oh, my God." One of the girls from the other car, now in the front seat, leaned over to see. She must've gotten in before Lois took off like a bat out of hell, headed back to the city.

"Sit back and be quiet. Lois, slow down, we don't want to crash on the way. Give me your scarf."

With one hand, she unwound the beautiful silk from her neck and tossed it back.

"Robin! No, not Robin. This isn't happening."

Harvey spun on her. "I said be quiet."

"Harvey, don't talk to her like that. Come on, Sweetie, turn around and let him be. Your friend...Robin will be all right. Everything will be all right."

"I'm sorry," low words uttered to Lois. While his hands mottled with blood, fit the scarf over a hanky monogrammed with "HD."

The newly purchased ice, now bound up in the white dress shirt, would help with the swelling.

The injured girl started to come around and rose to the edge of consciousness, emitting pathetic little moans that ripped your heart out.

The ice stemmed the blood flow to a trickle.

"How's she doing, Harv?"

"I think she's as stable as we can get her. How much farther to the hospital?"

Lois looked down at the speedometer, "At eighty, the thirty-mile drive should take us about...oh, no."

Her eyes in the rearview begged for sympathy.

"What?"

"Behind us. It's a policeman. He's pulling us over."

"Pull over, then. What's your name, Hun?"

"Louanne. My name's Louanne Stephens

"Louanne, when we stop, run back to the cop and tell him we need an escort to the hospital."

Lois had already slowed almost to a stop on the road shoulder. Louanne jumped out, with the car still moving, and ran. She spoke rapid-fire to the policeman, hands and arms waving, her panicked voice not quite reaching all the way back to the caddy. Louanne returned as the cop car roared around the caddy, red lights and siren blaring. Louanne jumped back in the car and slammed the door. Her knees and elbows skinned, the blood drying brown on forearms and shins.

Lois pulled in behind the cop car, the big Caddy engine easily keeping up. "Now we're talking. Won't be much longer."

Louanne turned pale and sat back against the door. "I told the policeman to radio in to Robin's father and have him meet us at the hospital. Mr. LaBruzzo isn't gonna be happy about his daughter. He's going to blame us all."

Harvey half-whispered. "Mr. LaBruzzo? Did you say *Mr. LaBruzzo?*"

Louanne didn't answer and slipped into a quiet solitude, the shock of the entire incident had caught up and took its toll.

"Dear Lord, no. Not Mr. LaBruzzo's daughter."

Lois' eyes caught his in the review as she nodded. She understood the ramifications.

More moaning came from Robin LaBruzzo lying across his lap leaking blood. A numerical mind automatically calculated the odds. The variables too many to render a valid sum. How could this happen?

Only one highway led from Hoboken to Tomahawk Lake, that road a choke point—a funnel. If you calculate the best time of day to attend the lake, the one road in…even so, to have one particular girl fall off the back of one particular car in front of the, "Ledger Man, those were some long odds.

A few minutes later, Louanne's eyes defused as her mind mulled all that occurred, she muttered. "Tommy's dead."

Lois asked, "What did you say?"

Louanne came out of her trance for a second and looked over at Lois. "Tommy doesn't know it yet, but he's dead. He was the one driving the car that ran over Robin."

Chapter Eleven

Current Day

Harvey jerked his arm out of Horse Face's grasp on the way to the interview room. "I can walk unescorted if you please. I'm neither criminal nor invalid."

Upon entering the office, a secretary called Horse Face, "Detective Clevenger." Clevenger left Esther sitting in the waiting area out front.

Clevenger ignored the comment. "This won't take long. Would you like some coffee or water?" A common ploy, reassuring your victims as if nothing at all were amiss. All the while, the guillotine hung suspended over an exposed neck.

Two of the four interview rooms on the right side of the hall stood open. "If this isn't going to take long, then no, thank you. And you shouldn't leave Esther alone. She just lost a good friend."

Clevenger didn't care.

At the first open interview room, Rita sat inside dressed in a signature, off-the-shoulder black dress, red open-toed heels, and a faux pearl necklace that dipped down over an improper amount of exposed décolleté.

Legs crossed at the knee, she smoked a cigarette. Her foot with red-painted nails bounced in a nervous but silent rhythm. Deeper in the small room, on the opposite side of the desk, sat the junior G-man, the detective with straw colored hair.

The door, left open on purpose. "Allow the subject of the interrogation to view a government witness giving a statement." The ploy landed number five on the list in Manfredi's book: "Whenever possible, keep the subject off-kilter and reeling with enough stimuli to control the narrative. Utilize witnesses who aren't really witnesses in a gaslight technique. Give the subject a quick glimpse, then slam the door before any interaction occurs."

A pause at the open interview room door didn't solicit a response from Clevenger; he let it happen on purpose.

"Rita," Harvey said, "it's illegal to smoke in a government building."

She took the cigarette from red lipstick lips, blew out a long stream of white smoke. She uncrossed her wonderful gams and, in the first unladylike gesture since entering the House of Usher, kicked the door closed.

Clevenger hesitated at the next open door and held out an arm for a brief moment, indicating a similar seating arrangement as in Rita's room. He then tried to enter but got bumped out of the way.

"That's my chair," he said, "you're supposed to sit—"

"Seriously? You drag me down here on false pretenses that made me a party to a horrific car accident, and you're worried about who sits where? Childish. Where's your supervisor? I want to speak to a supervisor."

"Fine, sit there and shut up."

Graffiti from black felt-tipped markers littered the faded split-pea green walls and depicted various logos and moronic names like: Casper, Lil Insane Duane, Fat Jimmie, Norte, Sueno, and Peckerwood. The brown wooden desk, circa 1950s, displayed similar defacement. You'd think they would search the delinquents before sequestering them. Sharp objects and felt-tip markers shouldn't be difficult to find on a person.

Clevenger didn't have a notebook or recorder. That meant the room was wired. Up in the corner, hardly visible unless a person looked, was a small pinhole camera lens.

Clevenger opened a file folder filled with Xerox copies of documents. He took one out and slid it over. "Do you recognize this item?"

"Am I under arrest?"

Clevenger squirmed. "No."

"Then I'm free to go?"

"If you leave, we will get a warrant, and we'll have to go through all of this again."

"In Arizona vs Miranda and subsequent decisions handed down since, states that I am not obligated to make any statements against my penal interest. If I'm not free to go, then this will be considered a custodial interrogation and you have to admonish me of my rights."

Clevenger's face flushed, unused to victims understanding the law. "You're saying you might have a penal interest in this matter? Is that an admission?"

"Of what matter are we speaking? You came into my house, yanked me out of my bed, and insisted I accompany you to your station to be interviewed about some mystery as yet revealed. How do I know what crime I'm being falsely accused of unless you tell me?"

Clevenger slapped the table with a loud crack. He took out a card from his pocket and read the Miranda Warning verbatim:

"You have the absolute right to remain silent. Anything you say can and will be used against you in a court of law. You have the right to an attorney, to be represented, and have an attorney present before any questions are asked. If you can not afford an attorney, one will be appointed by the court free of charge.

Do you understand these rights I've read to you?"

"Yes, I do."

"With these rights in mind, are you willing to talk to me?"

"No."

Clevenger slapped the desk again, face flushing bright red.

"However, since I have done nothing wrong, I'm happy to answer a few questions."

To further tug the tiger's tail might result in a nasty bite.

"Are you kidding me?" He took a deep breath, steeling himself. "Okay, for the record, state your name and place of residence."

"Harvey Usher. And you know where I live. You were there, remember? Without a warrant?"

He shoved the paper closer, crumpling it in the process under angry fingers. "Do you know what this is?"

Uh oh, notes from Gurski's notebook.

"Hmm. The hand scroll is that of a child in elementary school and difficult to decipher."

"That's your name, your wife's name, your address, phone number, and notes on a conversation with your wife from night before last."

"Okay, and?"

Clevenger grunted as if battling intestinal issues. *"Do you know* Edward T. Gurski?"

"Yes, of course. What's this about? Did something untold happen to Edward? Esther ranted about something earlier, but you really can't take her at her word. She's a bit eccentric, you know."

Clevenger pulled out an 8 x 10 photo that depicted an unfortunate man lying broken face down in a field, legs and arms akimbo. "Edward Gurski was run over last night."

"The poor, poor man. Was it an accident?"

"No, it wasn't an accident?"

"How do you know?"

Clevenger, at the end of his rope, leaned across the small desk. Minute bits of spittle mixed with his words. "Because he was running away when he was run over. Then the person in the vehicle backed over him a few times just to be sure."

He said vehicle like, "Vee-hickle."

"As a homicide investigator, you're not supposed to give away more information than you receive. You probably shouldn't have told me that part if you truly believe me capable of driving a car over a person in a homicidal manner. For the record, I haven't driven in the last five years. Haven't even sat behind the wheel."

Clevenger let that one slide by in an attempt to maintain control of the interrogation.

"Why did Gurski have *your* name with notes on a conversation concerning your wife?"

The need to blurt out that "wife" no longer applied; Rita was not his wife, and Sylvia had passed two years prior. The words made it all the way to the lips before being wrestled down. Instead, Clevenger got the obligatory stare.

He again leaned forward. "You going to answer the question?"

A conflict in the answer with what Rita said in the next room would give Johnny Law a fingerhold in their investigation. "Why don't you ask Rita?"

"Rita?"

"Delores. Rita's…Well, Rita's a pet name of sorts."

"You're saying you don't know why Gurski took notes on a conversation with your wife?"

The stare again as a forlorn stomach growled in a pitiful demand for attention. "Please make an official note that before too long, I will need my medication, or your city will be dealing with yet another in-custody death. And yes, I do read the papers."

Clevenger's jaw muscle bulged as he ground his teeth. "Where were you last night? Account for your hours between eight pm and zero-five thirty this morning."

"Me?"

"*Yes, you!*"

"If you haven't noticed, I'm quite elderly. I go to bed with the chickens and get up mid-morning every day. That's my life in a nutshell. The latter part you can attest to. You and your friend raided my home like a couple of jack-booted thugs when I was still abed."

"So, you were home all night and your wife will back you up on that alibi?"

"I don't know if I'd call it an al—"

"Yes, or no?"

"Detective Clevenger, if this is the way you conduct your interrogations, you might consider seeking psychological counseling to deal with anxiety and overt social inadequacy."

Clevenger sat back and smiled. A sudden shift in demeanor. Not good. Pushed him a little too far.

Toss out something to pacify the beast. "I have no idea what Delores might tell you. You will have to ask her. Can we please move on to the second half of this interrogation? The part where you and your partner switch places to confirm information each of you has gleaned from your respective victims. A method used to catch us in our blatant lies? I do need to get home to my medication. And I'm concerned about leaving Esther alone too long."

Clevenger stood a little too fast, the chair knocked against the wall. He retreated from the room, closing the door.

Now came the wait. According to Manfredi, "Allow the subject to fester in between interrogation sessions." Fester, a rude and improper adjective, but the correct quote just the same. The manual dictated that the wait could last as long as twenty minutes or as long as four hours. But that was 1942; things had changed a bit since. There were laws, after all.

Clevenger left the Xerox copy of Gurski's notes and the 8 x 10 photo of his remains on the desk. Left on purpose to allow the suspect's guilt to enflame, hence encouraging a confession. A cheap ploy.

The camera up in the corner caught every movement, so what did it matter? He picked up the photo and started to fold it in half. But found something written on the back. Words listed Gurski's name and date of birth. The location where he died and the case number. The poor soul was fifty-one years old. He looked early forties.

After a person turned eighty, all ages melded and blended into one solid lump. The photo folded in half slid inside the button-up shirt. If Clevenger checked the digital record, he'd have evidence of a petty theft. What was a petty theft when someone had been run down and then backed over?

Ten minutes later, the door opened. Rita's head appeared, "Come on, slick, let's go home."

"Slick? Isn't that a common term used by the criminal element?"

She grabbed hold of an elbow and tugged too hard, "I'm tired of your abusive banter, let's get the hell outta here before they change their minds."

She'd experienced the same pressure, the same vulnerability sitting in a police station, a vulnerability that jeopardized future freedom.

Out in the waiting room, Esther was conspicuous in her absence. "Where's Esther?"

"Quit lollygagging, I wanna get out of his place."

"I'm not leaving without—"

Another aggressive tug on the elbow. "The cops gave her a ride home. I guess they thought we'd be here longer."

"With that severe car crash, Esther should really be seen by a doctor. Don't you think? She's elderly, you know, and—"

"Harvey, move your ass." A demand that came through gritted teeth.

Outside, the bright sunlight blinded, and a stomach, believing the throat had been cut, cried out for attention. A funny saying Sylvia used to say, repeated from one of the many crime novels she read: Erle Stanley Gardner, Raymond Chandler, and the other more minor dandies who wrote Red Harvest.

Initially, after Sylvia passed on, her image rose up in memory a thousand times a day and gradually diminished to five hundred the first year; two hundred the next. Two hundred times still kept her foremost on the mind.

Until two days ago. As if out of the ether, Rita appeared and ruined everything. Now Sylvia slid further back in memory, popping up a mere one or two times an hour.

All because of Rita. A blight. A plague.

Rita stopped at a convertible red Mercedes 450SL and opened the passenger door. "Get in."

"Do you mind if I first check the car for damage? The kind sustained when driving over a man running for his life?"

Her green eyes narrowed, her red lips turned to a frown. She slowly leaned over, breath hot on the ear. "Harvey, my love, get in the damn car before I forget you're my husband and commit a graphic and bloody display of elder abuse."

"Ha, nice talk. Interesting that you didn't try to deny the damage to your car."

She closed the passenger door, the seat too hot on tired old legs. She came around and got in the driver's side, closed the door, and hesitated. She put her head down on the steering wheel.

Her shoulders shook as she wept. For real this time, not faking or putting on airs. Something had gone terribly wrong with her scam.

"I'm sorry I said that about checking your car for damage. I meant it to sound boorish, but it came out accusatory."

She suddenly twisted, leaned to the side, and grabbed hold in a firm hug, her cleavage pressed in, soft and…and lusty against the arm and chest. Lusty, a word long forgotten in the vocabulary of an octogenarian. Her right arm around the shoulders, her left hand used as support, pressed down upon a most unlikely spot; just below the belt. Yikes.

Ungentlemanly stirrings gone for a decade or better rose to the occasion. The shame. The pure, unmitigated embarrassment.

Rita pulled back to look, to check the eyes for an explanation. "Harv? It's been two years since—"

And just like that, she broke the spell with the vile little lie. She had only been around for two days, not two years.

She held her gaze not inches away, eyes…her eyes this time did not transmit the obvious prevarication like before. She moved in closer and kissed. In another first, her tongue parted lips and explored, hot and wet.

Dear Lord. More stirrings.

The mind gave orders to the arms to push her back, but they would not comply. The kiss went on and on, breaking down the ability to repel the unwanted and lewd advances of a beautiful woman, one with criminal intent.

Then all at once, the memory of Lois' first kiss on the way to the lake popped up for comparison. The warm, wonderfully wild experience. Rita's nothing anywhere close in comparison.

"No." He shoved her away. "I love my wife."

Rita hesitated, lips inches away, eyes still right there searching for the truth. The old Rita would've sat back and mocked the reaction. Not this new Rita, fear appeared in her eyes.

She sat back in her seat, started the car, and drove. After a minute, she asked. "Why in the world would you think I ran over Esther's man, Eddie? What you must think of me, Harv?"

The adrenaline from the kiss made it difficult for a quaking hand to reach in a wrinkled pants pocket to retrieve the skull ring. He held it out for her examination. "Because I found this on my bedroom floor this morning. It's Gurski's. It wasn't there last evening."

Her eyes jumped from the road, not unlike Esther's had moments before the ugly crash. Her mouth turned into a small "o" of disbelief. Genuine surprise. Like the kiss, real, yet all too lurid and lacking the most important ingredient: love. Just as quickly, she looked back to the road, her expression turned to anger. She hit the steering wheel with an open palm. "Dammit to hell."

Chapter Twelve

1968

Harvey Dortmund sat in St. Mary's surgical waiting room holding Lois's hand. Clutched it too tight. Lois didn't seem to mind. Luanne Stephens worked the pay phone before allowing the nurse to clean up and bandage skinned elbows and knees. A boisterous group of teens burst through the double doors and clustered around Luanne, all talking at once, a phenomenon common to the recent teenage set. Ten years ago, they would've been respectful, solemn.

The room's wallpaper, pea soup-green with little white and yellow daisies, did nothing to soothe nerves perched precariously on the razor's edge, all the while waiting for the guillotine to drop.

Mr. Luca LaBruzzo had not yet arrived and only made the wait worse. The idle time allowed an overactive imagination to take up residency, shoving out all logical thought. Brutal, sociopathic images that wouldn't go away. Black and white bullet-riddled gangland figures dead, in a barber's chair, by an open car door, and more often sprawled out on the sidewalk in front of an Italian restaurant.

The large clock on the wall said Robin had been in surgery for a mere twenty minutes. Instead of four or five hours. The minutes continued to crawl by on hands and knees.

The double doors to the room burst open a second time. In rushed Jackie the Nose with the limo driver close behind. Jackie's eyes scanned the room for threats. He backed out. A second later, he reentered with his boss, Mr. LaBruzzo. The world they must live. Believing that his daughter Robin might've been nothing more than a ruse to lure Mr. LaBruzzo out into the open, into a hospital waiting room, targeting him for an ambush.

Luca LaBruzzo didn't look harried or distraught. Instead, he appeared the same as he did in the overactive imagination, angry. Vengeful.

He looked around, spotted his prey, and hurried over. "Dortmund, stand up when I'm talking to you. What happened? Keep in mind, I've already gotten phone reports. The brainless teenager who ran over my daughter is in police custody and being interrogated as we speak. I hope you had nothing to do with this. Wait, is that blood on your clothes? Oh my God, that's a lot of blood." He moved in, eyes fierce, breath garlic-sour, as he spoke through gritted teeth. Is that Robin's blood? Tell me that isn't my daughter's blood. You...you—"

Lois had also stood. Her chin held high, eyes meeting Mr. LaBruzzo's. "Back off, Bucko. The doctor already said Harvey may have saved your daughter's life with his quick-to-action response in getting her here. He also...he also administered the bandage and ice to her head, which reduced the swelling and stopped the bleeding."

"Lois, please don't. I'll handle this." But in reality, fear ruled everything in this new violent world, making even simple speech difficult.

Luca LaBruzzo took a step back, not used to anyone talking to him in a rude and heated manner. His eyes suddenly softened, his tone lowered. "Is that true, Dortmund?"

Words still would not cooperate.

Lois continued. "What happened to Robin was an accident, pure and simple. No one should be jailed...or otherwise penalized for it."

She didn't know about Baby Bertha, or the dirt naps out in Meadowlands that awaited those who went against the family.

Was that reason enough to allow fear to steal words? Wouldn't a man with any modicum of intestinal fortitude step forward and speak for himself? How did Lois find the unmitigated nerve—the backbone to stand up against such a threat to life and limb?

Maybe she truly was Lois Lane.

LaBruzzo held out his hand to shake, the other he extended toward his flunky, "If that's the case, Dortmund, I thank you. Whatever you want, it's yours. Jackie?"

LaBruzzo wore tan kit gloves, soft as a baby's bottom, his grip vice-like in the handshake. Jackie stepped forward and handed his boss a folded sheaf of US currency. LaBruzzo took it and started to peel off several bills. "What the hell am I thinking? Here. I can't put a price on my baby's life." He shoved the money into Harvey's wrinkled white dress shirt, mottled with brown blood.

Robin's blood.

"I can't take this. I didn't do it for money."

LaBruzzo wouldn't touch the money. He nodded to Jackie The Nose, who snatched it back, tore the pocket to the dress shirt, and left the flap hanging. He made the cash disappear with a grunt. Translated, he thought only a fool turned down a wad big enough to "choke a horse," Jackie The Nose's frequently used description. For all of those who populated LaBruzzo's world, money reigned king, and nothing else mattered. Especially not human life.

Harvey's mathematical mind did everything to avoid the situation and instead calculated the amount just surrendered. Based on weight, thickness, and observation of the top bill: Twelve thousand, six hundred and fifty dollars. A close estimate.

Who carried that kind of cash?

LaBruzzo suddenly startled out of his emotionally charged angst. "Hey, ain't this the girl we talked about that afternoon by my pool. Am I right, Dortmund? The girl I wanted her for my son. You promised to take care of it for me, remember?"

Lois stepped forward, her eyes going wide. "Harvey, you talked about *me* with this...this man? Harvey, say something?"

"Please, let's discuss this later."

"Giorgio, come here, son."

With Jackie the Nose and LaBruzzo standing close, blocking the rest of the room, no one noticed Giorgio enter. He wore a light blue dress shirt open at the neck in a deep-vee. The shirt covered with an expensive blue blazer that sported a college emblem with hand-sewn ticking. The perfect example of an Ivy League collegiate student who could blend in anywhere. Except for the fat gold necklace that mingled with thick black chest hair and the gold tiger's eye pinkie ring, a common "Family" identifier.

He was blue-eyed handsome except for his inheritance, his father's long, hawkish nose.

"No," She insisted. "I want to talk about it right now. What did you two have to say about me? At this man's home. At his pool? What were you doing at his home in the first place, Harvey?"

Everything that happened that afternoon, the beautiful drive, the wondrous kiss, her saying those magical words, "My love," swirled down the drain already too far gone to recover. The moment Robin LaBruzzo rolled off the back of that convertible and hit the asphalt, the world shifted on its axis and moved the earth into a permanent darkened state.

A cruel, egotistical way to think about all that happened

"Giorgio," LaBruzzo said, "This is that nice piece of fluff I told you about. What's your name, kid?" LaBruzzo took Giorgio's hand and tried to take Lois's to physically join them in the introduction as if LaBruzzo had the ability to wed on the spot like a ship captain.

Lois jerked her hand out of LaBruzzo's and swung around. "You talked to this man about me as if I were a piece of chattel to be traded?" Tears filled her eyes. Her bottom lip quivered.

"No. Wait. Please? Please, can we talk about this later?"

"Harvey Dortmund, you're...you're a horse's ass." She fled, headed for the double-doors.

LaBruzzo shoved his son. "Giorgio, go after her. Take her ona date. Get her an espresso ana cannoli. Go on, you know how ta handle it."

Jackie The Nose stepped in the way, put a hand on Harvey's dress shirt with Robin LaBruzzo's dried blood on it. "You're not going anywhere, Palie."

"Lois, no. Wait. Please wait." To say any more risked a terminal fate for The Ledger Man, someone in the organization lower than whale crap.

Jackie The Nose chuckled, "Tough shit, huh, Palie?"

The doctor came through the doors on the opposite side of the room dressed in surgical scrubs. The matching mask hung from around his neck. Sweat darkened chest and underarms.

LaBruzzo hurried over.

Jackie The Nose took hold of Harvey's scruff and squeezed with an inhuman strength. He whispered, "Be a good Ledger Man and I'll keep Baby Bertha in my pocket. Heh, heh."

LaBruzzo said, "How is she, Doc?"

"She has a pretty severe skull fracture, which we stabilized for now. She's going to need several surgeries on both legs. I can't emphasize enough how the fast action in getting her here saved her life. She's critical and will be in ICU for at least a couple of days."

"That's good news. Thank you for all you've done. But I want her transferred to New York-Presbyterian as soon as possible. I've already made arrangements."

"Like I said, that won't be for several days at the earliest."

"We'll see about that. Can I see her?"

"Not for two or three hours."

LaBruzzo poked the doctor's chest. "I want to be called as soon as I can see her, you understand?"

The doctor opened his mouth to protest when he caught the fierce glare from Jackie the Nose.

"Yes, when she can have visitors, you will be called immediately."

LaBruzzo suddenly turned and looked around the waiting room as if he didn't understand how he arrived in the surgical wing of the hospital. From his expression, the grief finally penetrated his "Kill-them-all-and-we 'll-sort-it-out-later," mobster veneer. Exposing a wink of humanity before quickly returning to the business at hand. "Come on, Propeller head, I'm gonna buy you the best dinner in Hoboken. You've apparently earned it."

Out in the hospital parking lot, the driver of the black stretch-limo held the door for the boss, who climbed in.

Harvey paused before entering behind the man, forcing down a myriad of hot emotions. The biggest one, Lois's words crushed the life from the chest, his heart, his soul. The memory of her expression, the vile contempt in her eyes, could melt a man of steel into a molten puddle. Where did that leave a man in the wuss category?

Emotions clouded all logical thought. The most important one: Don't get in the car, not with these people. Instead, duck and weave while running for your life.

Get the hell out of there.

The next emotion moved up fast, moved up stronger than the others; anger and hate. The kind of hate that created fuel to power a long dormant engine in a "Propeller Head," calling him to action no matter what the cost.

At the same time, the answer to the question arose, in how there could be war with love so prevalent in the world.

Well, maybe.

Jackie the Nose had veered off to make a couple of phone calls at the phone booth, one just outside the emergency room where the ambulances parked. The place where attendants shuffled in the unfortunates on gurneys who didn't know if they'd ever come out.

Jackie stood under a dim light, talking on the phone and smoking a cigar stub. The butt end mashed and wet, the smoke a gray cloud mixing with the eerie yellow light. His eyes invisible in dark shadow yet casting a sense of malevolence and immorality.

Inside the limo, made darker by the tinted windows, Mr. LaBruzzo was nothing more than a shadow. He sat across, smoking a cigarette. Each time he took a drag, the glow from the red ember lit up his face. The quiet snap and pop of burning tobacco, the only sound except a heartbeat that ran out of control. The yearning. The urge to chase down Lois, hold her tight, whisper in her ear that it was all a mistake, that everything would be okay, was all but impossible to suppress.

Finally, the anger rose enough for Harvey to speak. His voice croaked. "You said in there that I could have anything I wanted. That's what you said."

"Sorry, Dipshit, you can't have the girl. I explained all that once. I don't wanna talk about it again. You understand? That's a done deal. How can you even discuss something like that with my daughter in there fighting for her life?"

The coal-red ember again lit up his face that resembled Lon Chaney's in a cheap horror movie; pale gray skin with half-moon circles under the eyes. This new Mr. LaBruzzo was a lobo wolf emotionally injured over his daughter and not someone to trifle with.

"Hey, Propeller Head, talk to me about this week's receipts, how'd we do? The Eastside crew comes up short again? The monthly shipment to the Cayman is ready to go? I think I might want you to go along on the shipment this week. You talk to Jackie about it."

He wanted the field cleared of all other suitors, leaving room for Giorgio.

Math always came easy, always first up on the tip of the brain. Not now. The heated emotions snuffed out all else. Except what needed to be said to Lois. The apology that would fall short by tens of thousands of miles.

A child-sized penny loafer abruptly appeared out of the darkness and kick-started an addled mind with a sharp pain to Harvey's knee. Oddly, the first thought should've been survival. Instead, the size of Mr. LaBruzzo's feet instantly rose to the surface. Small, too small for a man who ran such a large and complicated criminal organization. Had anyone ever mentioned it to him, chided him about it when he was a kid on the playground?

Jackie the Nose opened the door and slid in. His fat body shoved over, demanding more room. His sour body odor fought a pitched battle for control with the smoke from LaBruzzo's unfiltered Camel.

"Well?" Mr. LaBruzzo said to Jackie.

"I greased a few palms. They know to call or pay the price."

The limo started and cruised through the parking lot. Down the driveway, across the street, and into the parking lot of the public park. The sign at the entrance said, "Park closed at dusk."

The driver stopped, got out, and used bolt cutters to cut the chain draped across the entrance. He got back in and drove into the empty parking lot. He pulled around until the front of the limo faced north. The hospital across the street stood tall and regal. The limo conveniently parked right next to a phone booth in the closed public park.

Time ticked on and on. No one spoke.

Finally, Mr. LaBruzzo said, "Robin's mother, God rest her soul, passed on two years ago." The comment wasn't meant for Jackie the Nose, who would already have that information.

A follow-up reply didn't make it past jumbled thoughts focused on the terrible pain from the loss of Lois. An emptiness never before experienced.

"Robin's been without a mother to set an example. Robin's gone a little wild. I think her mother's death hit her hard. She was supposed to be at school today. Instead, she headed out to the lake with her friends. A bad choice on her part."

A stake-bed truck drove down the street too fast, braked hard, and slid into the park's parking area, driving over the downed chain. Two men jumped out. They set up two tables with chairs replete with soft cushions. Next, out came red and white checked tablecloths.

Two other cars arrived but parked at the red curb in the street. Four men in suits, two in each car, got out, lit cigarettes, crossed their arms, and eyed the passing cars.

Five minutes later, an old Helms Bread truck arrived, repainted on the sides in black and red letters, "Monte's Trattoria." A heavyset man and woman wearing white aprons spattered with red tomato sauce jumped out and arranged food on the table that included two bottles of chianti covered in wicker. Along with two red-jar candles they lit with long matches.

The penny loafer came out of the dark again kicked Harvey's knee. "Come on, Propeller Head, as a reward, I'm gonna feed you the best Italian food in two cities."

The limo door opened almost as if the car read the owner's thoughts. But in reality, the driver had taken some kind of silent cue from his boss.

Mr. LaBruzzo climbed out, straightened his suitcoat, and shot his cuffs. He flicked his cigarette out into the dark. The ember struck the asphalt off in the distance, sparked, and snuffed out.

The man and woman forked out the steaming spaghetti with meatballs from long serving platters, enough food to feed eight to ten people. They poured wine and served garlic cheese bread.

Mr. LaBruzzo sat down and started eating with a voracious appetite, as if his only daughter wasn't across the street in the ICU. He stopped, raised his fork, and pointed with it. "Tony? He can't sit at my table with that..." He waved the fork. "With that shirt. Wouldn't be proper."

Not proper? Two words thick with irony. What did this man know about proper?

Tony, the limo driver, didn't hesitate, he yanked off his jacket exposing a long sleeve white dress shirt, a thin black tie and a brown shoulder holster with the stock of a Colt 1911 .45. Tony took off the gun, laid it on the hood and unbuttoned his shirt leaving him with just a strap tee shirt. He put on the gun rig.

Jackie the Nose took the shirt from Tony. He came over and ripped off the blood-stained shirt. The buttons skittered off into the dark.

Now with Tony's shirt on and sitting at the table with the beast of a man who hadn't slowed his gorging, words needed to be said. Strong words to let LaBruzzo know Lois would not be traded, like 'So much chattel.' "That was an expensive dress shirt he tore off me." Pitiful words, but the best available from a Propeller Head with a weak, almost nonexistent spine.

Mr. LaBruzzo grunted and nodded. Jackie the Nose pulled out the wad of cash that could *choke a horse*, peeled several bills, and threw them. The money fluttered down onto the untouched spaghetti. Money from a person who thought they could buy everything with either currency, threats, or death.

One thing they couldn't buy, love. A startling revelation.

LaBruzzo pointed with his fork, "Happy now?"

"No."

LaBruzzo stared. The candlelight flickered from a disturbance in the mild breeze. "Don't you say it again. Don't you do it."

"You said I could have whatever I wanted?"

"Jackie!"

Jackie the Nose hurried over, his hand going in his back pocket for Baby Bertha, the black jack hungry to crack a fool's skull.

A midnight blue Chevy Corvette roared down the street. Catching

THE OBSESSIONS OF HARVEY USHER

everyone's attention. LaBruzzo held up his hand. The movement stopped Jackie the Nose in mid-swing.

The Corvette braked hard, tires squealing. The car made a sharp turn, slid sideways and bounced over the driveway into the Sundowner parking lot. The men at the curb, the security people didn't raise an eyebrow; they recognized the car.

From down the way, under the streetlights, two cop cars rushed along with overhead red lights flashing in a delayed pursuit. The two cars slowed when they observed the four thugs standing on the red curb, right hands out of view in their suitcoats.

Out of the car stepped Giorgio LaBruzzo. He turned toward the passing cops, smirked, and grabbed his crotch with both hands in a lewd gesture. The cop car's red lights shut off. They cruised on. They too recognized the driver Giorgio LaBruzzo, recognized the red curb violations, the cut chain leading into Sundowner park, the trespassers eating food from "Monte's Trattoria," and decided correctly that tonight, discretion was the better part of valor.

Giorgio walked over and took a seat at the table. Mama Monte served him.

"Evening, Pop, anything on Robin? How's she doing?"

The words came out the same as if underwater. The world a blur. Giorgio's shirt was torn, his partially naked chest raked with fingernail claw marks matching the ones on his face.

Chapter Thirteen

Current Day

After leaving the police station parking lot, Rita drove the red Mercedes convertible, jerking the wheel this way and that, all the while smoking a cigarette. The filter end smeared with red lipstick. Her eyes squinted from the smoke. Her foot worked the pedals, and the beautiful dress crept up to expose a smooth, naked thigh.

Consternation in her expression said she'd given up for the moment, on conning the eighty-year-old man sitting next to her in the passenger seat and now busied that crooked little mind mulling over questions asked by the cops. Questions that pushed her closer to the edge, linking her to a murder indictment.

The spurious comment about checking the undercarriage for damage caused by Eddie Gurski going under the wheels could only have inflamed already heated thoughts. Add in finding Eddie's ring on the bedroom floor, and the inside of the woman's brain had to be spinning like a toy top.

She'd clubbed the wheel when hearing about the ring. But why? The ring wasn't in her room. She acted as if the ring somehow tossed her into an unwanted game. One with criminal exposure to more years in the slam than normally offered for a white-collar grift. She had to know more about what was going on.

Warm wind whipped her red hair into a frenzied aura.

"You know, smoking cigarettes ages your skin something awful."

Her eyes glanced over then back at the road. She turned off the main thoroughfare and took side streets, the tires screeching at every corner. The residential area, her own little auto-cross track.

She tossed the cigarette out overhead. The wind caught and snapped it away. "I'd apologize for dragging you into all of this, but you've said some absolutely nasty things to me."

"Nasty things to *you*? Little lady, you entered *my* home with the intent to gaslight a feeble old man. To con him out of—"

"Out of what? What exactly do you think I'm doing? Have you not once thought that I could be genuine and it's actually your memory creating this little blivit? A blank spot in time."

The hum of the wind made normal talking difficult, worse on an old man's voice. "You finally ready to talk? Come on, let's talk. Tell me what's going on. What are you doing in my house? I don't have any money. What exactly is your intent?"

Her foot covered the brake and slowed while she took a moment to look over. Her eyes searched for something in his. The truth. Or was she just trying to decide which way to jump, deeper into the con or abandon it and run like hell? She had enough of the facts to make that informed decision. Maybe the only person who could.

She put her eyes back on the road, took her foot off the brake, and hit the gas. The moment gone, dispersed into the air as if it never existed. She'd play a little longer in a con game turned murderous, while still trying to ferret out the goal.

Only, what was her goal?

Five minutes later, she pulled up in front of the house. "Get out. I have some important errands to run."

He got out and stood with the door open. "You don't have to do this alone. I can help you."

"Help me with what exactly, Harvey? You don't even have a memory of our loving and endearing marriage. You're living in some kind of delusion where everyone is out to get you. Your silly actions, your hurtful words only make things worse. You're just a tired old fool."

She couldn't leave, not with the car door still open in his hand. "You're talking in contradictions, first you almost tell me what's going on and then you clam up. Then once again, it's all about a loving and endearing marriage, and I'm a tired old fool living a delusion. You can't have it both ways, my dear."

She slammed her foot down on the accelerator. The right rear tire spun, spewing white smoke. The car leaped forward, the door jerked closed, leaving an old fool standing in the street.

Esther appeared on the sidewalk not two feet away. "She have something to do with what happened to Eddie?"

"Geeze, you about scared the water out of me."

"You didn't answer the question."

"No, of course not. How could Rita have anything to do with what happened to Eddie?"

"Coincidence, Harv. I'm not a fool, I read crime novels. That evil woman shows up, Eddie starts looking into her, and the next day he's dead. Run over." Tears filled her eyes. "I can't even imagine what went through his mind when that car chased him down like some kind of rabid dog. Then...then striking him like that. Afterward, he lay there all alone. He died by himself, Harv. He had to endure that by *himself*. That's the worst part of it. The loneliness in death."

Suddenly, the 8 x 10 photo of the dead Eddie Gurski, the one folded up inside his shirt, turned warm. It couldn't happen, but it seemed that way. The power of the mind.

A white Toyota Camry with tinted black windows pulled up and stopped. Esther stepped into the street and opened the back door.

"Wait. Where are you going?"

"The Paradise Lost group home."

"What? No, you can't go there. Not by yourself. That's crazy, Esther."

She climbed in and started to pull the door shut. "You in or out, Harv? I don't have all day."

"Ah, what the hell."

She moved over, and he slid in.

"You know," she said, "Sylvia wouldn't like the way you've started using vulgar language."

The door closed, the Camry took off. "Me? What about—"

"What, Harv, finish what you were going to say."

"Nothing."

The Uber driver followed the tiny blue car in his navigation app, negotiating the streets and intersections, and didn't say anything.

Esther's words about Sylvia caused the last memory of her on that morning two years earlier to bubble up. The gut-wrenching grief, a fresh wound now the same as if no time had passed at all. The emptiness, a hole in the chest that never closed. Could he have done anything differently the night before that morning? Used words to convince her otherwise?

"Esther, why are we going to Gurski's place?"

She stared through thick prescription glasses, her eyes larger than normal. She blinked. And blinked again. "I'm going to find out who killed Eddie."

The craziness of the statement proved the woman wasn't thinking straight. Grief had her by the throat, choking off every last bit of common sense. Masking the real world. What could a woman in her late sixties hope to accomplish trying to discover who had murdered a close friend?

And then what? What if she did happen into a murderer? What else could she do but scream and hope someone could hear?

The Uber driver slowed almost to a stop and dropped off Van Buren into the lower parking lot of the Paradise Lost group home. An old rehabbed motel in the county area far enough away from the NIMBs folks (Not In My Backyard) for them to care. The faded sign on the street had at one time read, "The Blue Ocean Motel," and was now painted over by hand in black paint. A painter with a shaky hand. The single-story structure sported a white rock roof, the rock missing in wide patches, exposing black tar paper to the sun that faded it to an ugly brown. The doors faced outward into the parking lot, an area marred with cracked asphalt and weeds. All the rickety doors had outside hasps for padlocks. The entire building was painted faded blue, at one time mimicking an ocean.

The Uber driver stayed long enough to disgorge his passengers and drove off a little too quickly.

Two motel doors opened in different places down the row. Sketchy folks in ratty clothes and dirty hair stepped out, both of them a Nosy Gus. Or maybe they just recognized two elderly and defenseless victims ripe for the plucking. Curtains in other windows down the line twitched from people who looked out. Paranoid speed freaks, hyper-aware their world could collapse on them at any given second.

"Esther, this was a real bad idea."

She leaned up, took hold of a shoulder, pulled down, and put her mouth close to his ear, her breath warm, humid. "Harv, you need to grow a pair. This is one of those situations, like out on the African Savannah, that if you show any weakness at all, the hyenas will come eat your ass."

Her words again shocked and awed. Where was the Esther of old, the kindred soul who brought over molds of green Jell-O with cottage cheese and pineapple chunks, played Yahtzee and Canasta, and sipped vintage sherry late into Friday nights?

She let go, saw the reaction, and shook her head. "I told you, I spent two years in Blythe, the butthole of California. I had to stay close to Eddie; he was in Chuckwalla. That kind of place, that prison town, will either break you or make you stronger."

"Right. Right, you did what you had to do."

Even so, the stark contrast from the kind, elderly woman, the ex-kindergarten teacher, compared to her crude words…well, it almost seemed like someone else said them, a puppet master of sorts.

"All right then, come on." She led the way and had obviously been at The Blue Ocean before.

Another door opened. A skinny woman with straggly hair and two missing teeth on her uppers smiled. "Hi, Esther." Her tattered T-shirt had a tear down the front, creating a makeshift V-neck. The grossly underweight woman resembled a twig.

"Sorry, Kari, I didn't bring any food today. Maybe tomorrow."

Kari lost her smile. "I heard about Ed. I'm real sorry."

Esther suddenly shifted direction and headed right to her. Esther put a hand on Kari's bony chest and moved her back into the motel room. Esther turned, "Harv, close the door."

The door didn't fit the frame, and when closed, a rectangle of light shone through the edges.

Esther took Kari's arm and guided her over to the sway-back bed and sat her down. "Tell me what you know."

Kari scratched at a scabbed-over arm and twitched. "The cops were here. They talked to everyone."

"Kari?"

Her head jerked to the side, a nervous tick. "What?"

"This is between me and you. No one else will know. You know me."

"What about him?"

Her accusatory finger made the wrinkle skin on his back ripple.

"Forget him. He's so old he can't hear a thing. Deaf as a stump."

That one hurt. As the years ticked by, many aspects of the human body went missing, gave up as if "planned obsolescence" hit the maturity date and simply shut down. Hearing remained the last holdout.

Kari still stared at him.

Esther turned, used an index finger along with the one next to it, and moved them like legs, indicating she wanted her deaf partner to turn around and face the wall.

What the hell, why not?

"There," Esther said, "Now talk to me."

"Eddie, he was upset about something."

"What?"

"He wouldn't tell me."

Facing the front window now, people outside—their shadows walked by the motel room on the other side of the curtains. They stopped as if talking about what went on inside. It caused an uncomfortable sensation, one of being trapped in a zoo enclosure with hungry animals outside the bars looking for a meal.

"You're holding something back. Come on, you can tell me."

Esther, the ace interrogator. Alfred Manfredi, author of, "How to corner the Obstinate Spy," would've been proud. Maybe reading all of those crime novels also helped.

Sylvia had watched all of the old black and white Perry Masons shows on TV, the one with Raymond Burr, and had said, "Hey Harv, I learned enough about the law watching this show I could pass the Bar. What do you think, should I give it a go?" She'd shot him that knowing smile and winked.

The woman was dearly missed.

All at once a mushy memory kicked in bringing up words from Eddie the day he asked for his pay. Still facing away, the words bounced off the wooden door, "Eddie told me that he 'Needed the green.' He also said, 'I got a few people on my ass. The five hundred will go a long way to cool their jets.'"

Movement from behind—by the sound of it—Kari jumped up from the bed. "He can hear. You lied to me. He can hear."

"No, he can't. He just remembered something that's all. Here, I'll prove it. Harv, I'm right behind you. I'm about to kick you in the back of the leg."

"See. If he heard me, he'd move, he'd turn around and protest."

The kick came in hard and abrupt, her orthopedic shoe unforgiving and almost took him to the floor.

"Ouch, son of a—" Hopping around on one leg, there was nothing left but to play along with the sham, "What was that for? What did I do to deserve that?"

Esther used the fingers again, the sign to turn back around.

"I will, but don't you kick me again."

"Okay, he's turned around. Kari please. Tell me what you know about the money?"

A fat pause bubbled up between the two women. All the while, the leg throbbed.

"He owes Aussie Mike."

A long, low sigh escaped from Esther. She loved Eddie and didn't want to believe that he'd slipped back into the criminal world. Not after two years of hell in Chuckwalla.

How could he not backslide, living at the Blue Ocean?

"Who is this Aussie Mike, and where does he live?"

No, it's more important to first ask why the money was owed. The sequence of questions is important in an interrogation.

Kari said, "Aussie Mike is here illegally. He came on a visa to visit on holiday. He never intended on going back. He says the courts and prisons here are a lot nicer. He brags about how border patrol can't catch him."

"Where can we find him?"

Kari must've shrugged.

"Kari, you know I'm going to find out anyway. You might as well be the one to tell me."

"Aussie Mike runs this whole place. He has everyone dealing for him."

"Where does he live?"

"You can't tell anyone I told you."

"Lips are sealed. Tell me."

"You know Casa Blanca?"

"No."

"It's the barrio in Riverside. The cops won't even go in there. His place is on Grace, this side of Lincoln. A yellow house. Solid yellow. A weird yellow. You can't miss it. But you can't go there, that's a real bad place. That entire block is bad."

"Thank you, Kari."

Esther came around, headed for the door, typing in another request for an Uber on her phone.

She wasn't really planning on going to Casa Blanca, was she? In that district of Riverside, the papers reported gang shootings every other week.

"Wait. There's something else."

Esther turned back to Kari, eyes behind thick glasses peering into the gloomy room. "Yes."

Kari squirmed as she sat on the edge of the bed. Her dirty bare feet twitched on dark carpet that looked like it might've once been gold but had been spray-painted green and crunched a little with each step. The whole place radiated a faint reek of sour milk. "I wouldn't ask," Kari said. Tears brimmed and rolled down her cheeks. "If I didn't really need to. I wouldn't ever put the bite on you, Esther, you know that. If I didn't absolutely have to."

Esther came back, sat next to her, and patted Kari's hand. Esther looked up, "Harv?" She made a motion with thumb and forefinger, continuing the deaf ruse, asking for money.

Out of the pocket came the ten-dollar gold piece money clip, a present from Sylvia, thirty-odd years ago. Back when money wasn't so tight.

Before a couple of bills could be peeled away from the meager sheaf, Esther snatched the whole thing. She pulled the money from the clip and handed the clip back. She gave all the cash to Kari.

"Thank you." Kari hugged Esther. She got up, moved to the TV, the old boxy sort with a tube instead of a flat screen. She tinkered with the back until it came away, revealing the inside. She pulled out an 8 x 11 envelope and handed it to Esther. "Eddie gave that to me to hold in case something happened."

Esther let loose with a long, "harrumph," and headed for the door. She didn't slow down once outside and leaned forward, climbing the slope up to Van Buren, where the Uber waited, another Camry, this one dark blue. Was there an army of Uber Camrys out there just waiting to be summoned?

His breath came hard following along the steep slope. "Come on, slow down."

She didn't. Determined. Nothing was going to deter her.

Back in the car and headed for Casa Blanca, Esther sat with the envelope clutched to her chest, staring straight ahead.

"You going to open that?" The need to see the contents, to find some answers, was an urge difficult to suppress.

She looked over. "Don't we already know what's in it?"

The odd question gave pause. "I guess we do. It's probably what Eddie discovered about my problem. The background on Rita and her friend Andy Johnson. The wedding certificate and its bona fides. Maybe something about my background. I asked him to find out what he could about me."

She nodded and again looked forward.

"Don't we want to open it and see what he found? The evidence we need

119

to kick Rita out on her keister." The idea of kicking Rita out caused an emptiness in his chest. For the last two years, living without the love of his life had been lonely beyond belief. To have a woman, a companion to talk to, even if she was on the grift, what harm could it do? To...to just let it happen. Not be lonely anymore. And, man oh man, that woman could cook. Sure, that was it the cooking.

This time, Esther kept looking forward. "You know, I lived next door to you and Sylvia for forty years or more."

"Yes."

She said, "Me and Sylvia talked just about every day. We were like sisters. At least I thought we were." Esther looked over this time. "And right now, when I think back, I really didn't know her at all. Did I, Harv?"

"Huh." Now, after four decades, Esther had finally started asking the right questions. And at this, the most inopportune moment. Or was it? What did it really matter? Who cared anymore about ancient secrets?

"Is that all you're going to say, Harv, is Huh?"

"Huh, and that I'd really like to see what's in the envelope. You did kick me in the leg, you know. I think I'm owed that much."

"Did I hurt you, Harv?"

"Well, yes, you did. It was shocking more than anything else. I didn't think you had it in you."

Esther stared, her eyes blinked. "That morning...I know you don't like to talk about it. I wish you would, though. That morning, did Sylvia leave you a letter? I know she used to leave you letters here and there, and all over the house. Did you find a letter from her that morning, Harv?"

The air in the Camry turned thin and difficult to breathe. How did she know about the letter?

"Harv. I'd really like to see that letter." She blinked those abnormally large eyes, again and again. She gently handed over the envelope held against her chest, placed it on his lap, and patted it once. "Go ahead. I'll show you mine if you show me yours. I want to see the letter Sylvia left you."

Sweet baby Jesus, a deal with the devil.

Chapter Fourteen

1968

Mr. LaBruzzo dropped Harvey off in front of his house, the one paid for with ill-gotten gains. The house next door to Lois'. The place where it all started.

For Harvey Dortmund, the entire world had shifted. His perception of the false myth that The Ledger Man was nothing more than a math guy whose work had nothing to do with what actually happened in the business. A numbers cruncher.

The biggest error that sat heavy on the soul was the notion that participating in a criminal organization didn't hurt others. A soul now all but snuffed out by guilt.

And overwhelming sadness.

The grocery bags filled with currency brought into his office over the donut shop had to originate from somewhere. Hiding his head about that mystery no longer worked. The LaBruzzo organization wasn't a Fortune 500 company that took in cash only. No company dealt exclusively in cash. The IRS didn't like it.

The more obvious answer. The money came from victims of extortion, prostitution, gambling, theft and mayhem. Now the part of the business, the one other than numbers entered into ledgers, had slopped over into his life and ruined it. But worst of all, it hurt Lois. Crushed her.

Standing in the front yard staring, the house changed into something different. No longer comfortable and stable. An invisible shroud of evil hung from the roof peak all the way to the ground. A house purchased with tainted money.

Nowhere in the world did certified public accountants make the kind of money LaBruzzo Threw at him." That's what he'd said in the pitch to employ the "Propeller Head," what he said to get Harvey to come work for him. He'd used benign words that first time, coming nowhere near the truth. An insidious truth that now cornered a hapless fool, leaving him nowhere to turn. The cost for working with a criminal enterprise came due with a price tag beyond reach.

No matter how many feeble explanations were used in trying to solve the equation, the claw marks on Giorgio's face and chest told a story too horrible to contemplate.

Exhaustion set in. With it, warm tears rolled down wretched cheeks.

The dark eastern sky turned pewter as dawn peeked over the earth's curvature to see if all was clear before starting a new day.

Morning dew settled.

Time spun along unencumbered by common emotions. Legs started to shake and threatened to give out leaving one option, move or face-plant.

Behind, on the street, a car pulled up. A door slammed. The meaning, slow in registering.

"Lois?"

The sudden slow-motion spin. The abrupt smile creeping out. Lois had come home with forgiveness in her heart. Of course, that's what it had to be. Love that immense, that important couldn't be snuffed out so easily.

"Lo—"

The fist met a fool's face with a snap and a thunderous clap.

Bright lights. Stars. Pain. The ground, unforgiving in the bounce.

The black wingtips came in again and again, in a long, slow arc. Time slowed even more. The pain from the blows dulled the smothering guilt, and, in a way, acted as a soothing balm.

The yelling finally penetrated the fog, "Where is she? Where's my daughter, you son of a bitch? I'll kick you till you're dead. Tell me where she is?"

Mr. DeFrank stopped out of exhaustion, stumbled over to the porch, and plopped down on the steps. He put his face in his hands and wept.

One kick had landed a glancing blow to the jaw loosening two teeth and swelled the bottom lip that battered the words as they spilled out. "I don't know where she is. I'm sorry. This is all my fault. Please, come kick me some more. I need it. I deserve it."

"You're a smart ass ta boot. Your damn right, it's all your fault. And I think I will." He staggered to his feet, came on fast. Skip-hopped to get the rhythm right, the timing of the next kick.

This time, the long black wingtip came around low and quick. In that instant, something shifted. All that had happened that day, the ungodly highs and equal lows coalesced, allowing an instinct to survive to skulk out.

Harvey Dortmund caught the foot mid-strike and pushed up. DeFrank fell to the perfectly manicured lawn and tried to roll over to gain his feet.

Too slow.

This new person leapt, landed knees on the chest. Fists knotted into hard balls that pummeled DeFrank's arms, covering his face.

Until exhausted.

This new person shifted back to the Ledger Man and fell off to the side next to him. Neither spoke, both breathing hard. Both scared to death over what had happened to the same girl. A different kind of love for each and yet the same.

DeFrank said, "If she's not with you, and you truly don't know where she is, tell me where you saw her last."

"Why did you come here?"

He turned his head to the side to look. "Robin Stephens. She said something ugly happened out on the highway. Said you were involved along with the LaBruzzo girl. That girl just died, and my daughter's missing. Tell me what you know."

"Oh, dear God. She died?"

"The surgeon was found outside the hospital. Around back by the trash bins, with two broken arms and crushed fingers. He refused to make a statement. Where's my daughter?"

"I honestly don't know. We had an argument at the hospital. She left mad. That's the last time I saw her. I was waiting here for her to come home."

Tears of guilt, sadness, and loss wanted to come on again with freight-train fury not easily suppressed. "Before all of this, before that horrible little accident on the highway at the gas station, I told Lois I was going to come find you. Bring you a box of cigars. Convince you that I was good enough for your daughter."

DeFrank said nothing.

"But now, I know for sure. You were absolutely right in telling her to stay away from me."

DeFrank again said nothing.

Everything about the Ledger Man's life, all at once, flashed the same as bitter ptomaine poison. It rose up and out onto the grass in projectile vomit.

The shirt.

The shirt belonged to the limo driver. A part of that life. In a rabid melee of struggling and tearing, the shirt fell to tatters on the grass among the embarrassing results of the emesis.

DeFrank struggled to his feet, dawn in full swing behind him, his mouth agog.

"What?"

"You're back."

The ragged scars. That kind of shame no longer mattered and now became insignificant. "Lessons from a strict father who believed life's edicts took hold better with leather. His favorite catch phrase, 'better with leather.'"

"I'm sorry. Maybe you're not who I thought you were. Maybe I should've had more faith in Lois to find someone who…" His body shook as he wept. "Do you know where to look for her? Can we go now and look for her?"

"Neither one of us should—"

DeFrank leapt forward and shoved him.

"Don't you worry about me. You show me where to look. Then you can just step aside. I'll deal with these bastards."

"I think Lois is somewhere safe, lying low. We just need to figure out where. Do you know any of her friends she might go to when she's upset?"

No way could DeFrank be told about Giorgio and the claw marks on his chest and face. That would only get DeFrank a sweet kiss from Baby Bertha and an all-expenses-paid trip to The Meadowlands. Helping no one.

"I've checked everywhere."

"Then do you have a key to her house? Can we look for an address book, some evidence of where she might be?"

DeFrank scowled. He struggled to his feet, staggered out to his car, got in, and drove away.

Nothing remained but to sit on her porch and wait.

And wait some more. Head against the post, eyes closed, the conjured kiss in the front seat of the car wouldn't come. Only the look. The one in the hospital after the betrayal.

* * *

Time passed in a blur.

The body and mind, out of self-preservation, slipped into neutral, unaware of anything at all.

Then time slammed back into gear.

Dazed. What had happened? Where was he?

Standing in a front yard.

Emotional shock. He'd read about it and thought the syndrome nothing more than egg-head doctors justifying their own existence.

A bone-deep chill rose up past bruised or broken ribs to make sore teeth chatter and shake loose the lingering nightmare. This new mindset: was it a survival instinct recently acquired, or maybe something that came with an abject fear of dying? He kept his eyelids closed while questions ran through his mind, just starting to ramp up. First, the where?

Yes, yes. The porch next door at Lois'.

Why?

The memory returned in a rush. Oh, dear Lord, the "why." Too horrific to contemplate.

Off in the distance, not too far away, a car door slammed.

Lois?

Eyes open wide, adrenaline electric to the heart.

Out at the curb, Jackie The Nose walked around his big silver Buick and came into the yard. "Come to daddy, punk. We're going for a ride."

"I'm not going anywhere with you."

He stopped, held up his hand. "Don't you do it. Don't you look around like you're about to rabbit. You know I can't catch you. But you also know I'll eventually find you when you least expect it, and then you'll pay a dear price. So just be a good little sonny boy, and let's go for that ride. You're gonna like this, trust me."

Was he kidding? Trust *him*?

"Where's Lois? What'd Giorgio do to her?"

Now, halfway across the yard, Jackie the Nose grunted. A warning heard many times in the past. Peons didn't disrespect Capos with insolent demands or questions; they simply obeyed. Did so or incurred the wrath of Baby Bertha.

But maybe Mr. LaBruzzo gave orders not to hurt the merchandise, the all-important Ledger Man.

With each of Jackie's steps, the ability to run, to evade, slipped further away. Until Jackie stopped almost nose to nose, a position he liked best. That way, his victim looked into his eyes, black as pitch, unable to see or even sense what Jackie's hands were doing.

His breath, always sour—worse that morning—could make wallpaper sag. Bitter, acrid. What did the man subject his stomach to that caused that kind of reek? Dead cats?

Jackie's shoulder drooped. His hand whipped out, found Harvey's neck and squeezed, jerked the LaBruzzo's hand-puppet across the front yard and back to the big Buick. He shoved hard. "Get in."

He waddled around to the driver's side. "Hey, Punk," he said over the roof of the car, "I won't tell ya again. Get your sorry ass in the damn car."

Inside, the cloth bench seat looked new. The entire car, only two years old, looked like it had just come off the showroom floor and smelled of fresh pine trees. The scent popular at high-end car washes that used human

126

hands instead of machines.

The Buick listed to the driver's side when Jackie entered. One hand on the outside roof for support and one on the steering wheel to assist pulling in all the bulk that depressed his part of the seat. He eased the door closed, as if the car was a delicate porcelain cup. He started up and turned on the air conditioner focusing the vents on his hog-body. With the seat all the way back, the steering wheel still pushed into his gut.

Not on the road two blocks, he said, "The boss wants me to be sure you understand your position in life. He thinks—"

"I know my—"

"Shut your mouth." His right arm shot out.

The beefy hand connected like a thick block of split wood that chunked into the face.

More pain masked guilt and shame that ruled the day.

Jackie said. "Don't you talk ta me like that, Punk. You want me ta give the boss a bad report card?"

"Would it matter? What's happened to Lois?"

A fat index finger shot over close to the eye and hovered. "You want that I pull this car over and show you how the cow eats the cabbage? Cause I will. You know I got no problem doin' it. That girl is no longer your concern." He looked away to the road to keep the car in the center and not plow into the ones parked on either side.

The finger hovered a moment longer then retracted.

Silence for several miles until he maneuvered onto the turnpike. The big Buick picked up speed.

Finally, Jackie spoke again. "The boss put you on my crew."

"He did what? I can't do that kind of—"

"Not as an earner, you jack-off. It means he made me responsible for you. This thing with Giorgio and the girl is important to the Boss. He doesn't want it screwed up. That's why he made you my responsibility. And Palie, you will not screw it up. You understand? Because now it'll come back on me. And that's not going to happen, you understand?"

More miles slipped under the tires, the humming sound monotonous.

127

Warm summer air whipped in the open windows.

"Since you're on my crew now, you get your pay from me. The way I work, until you've proven yourself, you get half of what you were making. Once I can trust you, you'll start getting the rest."

This wasn't some training method. Jackie was just greedy and simply pounced on the opportunity to cheat an employee out of his due.

"Does Mr. La—"

"You're not gettin' it. You. Work for *Me*. Get that through your little propeller head, or we're gonna have a problem. I won't bring out Baby, because I might hurt that beautiful brain a yours. But I can damn well guarantee I'll hang you upside down in a meat locker 'til your teeth crack from rata-tat-tatting. We got an understanding here?"

Jackie cranked the steering wheel hard to the right, cutting across three lanes to make the offramp. Horns blared. Tires screeched. He kept his eyes on the road. "You didn't answer me."

"I understand."

The grunt, a standard Jackie the Nose reply when he wasn't happy about something.

Twenty minutes later, he pulled into a middle-class neighborhood, turned into the driveway as his hand reached up to a clicker above the visor. The automatic garage door opened. He pulled in and hit the clicker again. The door rattled closed. When the car shut down, everything turned silent except the engine that ticked, cooling down.

"What you're about to see in here is way above your pay grade. You understand?"

The blink and the stare were the only responses available. No words would come from a mind in neutral. Numb. Beyond tired. Forty-eight hours had passed since Lois showed up on the front porch with the picnic basket. Forty-eight hours that had somehow defied physics and now stretched out into years. Decades. An hour for each year sounded about right. An emotionally crushed body no longer possessed regular cravings for food, water, or coffee. The only desire left was to lie down, allow eyelids to close, and sleep for an eternity.

"You gonna answer me, punk?"

"Yes, I understand."

"You better understand. You screw this up, and nothing will keep you out of The Meadowlands. Get your ass out."

Jackie dismounted the car that rose up on his side when he exited. He led the way over to the door into the house. He opened it and walked in as if he owned the place. And probably did.

The door opened to the kitchen. Two rough men sat at a table in a small nook. They wore strap tee-shirts and denim pants, with brown leather shoulder holsters. They played cards, drank cheap beer from cans, and smoked unfiltered Camels. White smoke hung from the ceiling in an even fog bank. The center table was cluttered with toothpicks used as poker chips. Off to the side, close at hand, lay two sawed-off shotguns.

Jackie grunted at the men as he walked past. They grunted back.

Maybe with every miss-out in the chain of human evolution, the beasts, the ones one step closer to Neandertal, used the grunt as their number one form of communication.

The two men looked up and stared, probably burning the image of the new interloper into their brains.

Jackie stopped when he caught their expressions. "This propeller head is now on our crew. This is Tommy Tee and Jimmy. They're filling in while two of the regulars take a short vacation in Bayside. Come on. We're runnin' late."

He waddled down the hall to a steel door that had replaced the common wooden one. He took a ball of keys from his pocket, large enough to be used at the end of a medieval mace. He selected a key and unlocked three padlocks in hasps up and down the door's edge. He hesitated. "You know why you put three locks up and down the side of the door like this?"

A teaching moment in the life of a criminal. Who cares. Lois was the only one that mattered.

"Not talkin'. Probably smart until ya get the lay of the land, huh? Usually, you'll put 'em like this on the inside, not the outside. I jus' did it here outta habit. Locks won't keep those two turds from takin' sledge hammers and breakin' it in if that's what they wanna do. But that's not what keeps this room safe from them. Do you know what does?"

Harvey's words came out in a half-whisper. "The threat of a long, drawn-out, agonizing death."

Jackie the Nose chuckled. "That's right. I might be able to teach you something after all. Now pay attention here. You put three locks—the slide-bolt kind on the inside. One in the middle, one above, and one below because it makes it impossible to kick the door in. And if it's the cops come a knockin' with sledge hammers, it'll give you the time ta arm-up and go ta guns. This is important, make a note." He pushed into the small bedroom.

One empty except for six canvas bags sitting in the middle of the floor.

Heavy wrought iron bars outlined the room on all four walls and the ceiling, effectively turning the place into a makeshift safe.

"Grab dem bags and get 'em loaded into the back of the Buick. Snap to it."

Chapter Fifteen

Current Day

The Uber driver pulled up and stopped at the intersection of Lincoln and Grace. The yellow house, three houses down and on the right, just as Kari described, stood out from all the rest. The Uber zoomed off, not wanting to stick around Casa Blanca. Harvey still held the unopened 8 x 11 manilla envelope from Kari. To open it would consummate the deal with Esther and mean the last unopened letter written by Sylvia would have to be surrendered. And reveal to the world her last words just before she died. Words in Harvey's mind, that if left concealed, in a strange kind of way, kept her alive.

The essence of Sylvia remained in that sealed letter. Along with the lurking fear of what she had to say.

More thought needed to go into that choice before the 8 x 11 manilla envelope was opened. Was it worth the trade? Was finding out about Rita worth dispelling the silly idea that Sylvia resided in her last words?

The world came back into focus. Local inhabitants moved around on foot and in slow-moving cars. Sketchy, furtive kind of people, hygienically incorrect. Shaggy and shabby. What Esther had said about hyenas on the African Savannah was more real than ever.

"Hold it," Esther grabbed onto his arm to stop him while her attention remained in the opposite direction on a car parked at the curb. A gray sun-faded Chevy Tahoe with left front-end damage. She stared at the driver, a young girl with mauve and green stripes in her dark brown hair. The girl got out and walked over with deliberation, and stopped in front of Esther.

Esther didn't take her eyes off her. "Harv, this is Lissette, Eddie's girl."

"Nice to meet you." The girl refused to shake hands and continued to stare at Esther.

He looked around. "We should get another Uber and get the hell out of here. What do you say, girls? Or we can just take your car, Lissette? Yes, why don't we just take your car?"

Lissette broke her gaze and looked over. "This the guy who caused all this?"

Esther said, "He didn't cause—"

"Just wait one darn a minute." He said, "Esther, I can speak for myself. I'm the victim here."

Though not really, not after what happened to Eddie. Throwing the victim card carried little impact and pinged hollow and boorish.

Lissette looked thirtyish, though competent age estimation long ago fell to the wayside. He'd thought Eddie was forty or forty-five, not fifty-one. She wore a black long-sleeved shirt with a black leather vest adorned with silver rivets. Her Levi's frayed and holey showed more skin than they covered. She reached over and snatched the unopened envelope.

"Hey, that's mine."

Lissette held up the envelope. "Don't be a jerk. *I* gave this to Eddie. Forget the envelope. You two were at the cop shop. What'd you find out in there?"

"How do you know that? Have you been following us? Esther, has she been following us?"

Esther said, "They didn't interview me. Though they had *him* on the grill for a while."

"On the grill? Really, Esther?"

Lissette ignored the comment and looked him in the eye. "What'd they ask *you*?"

"They think I'm somehow involved with what happened to Eddie. Me and the woman who's living in my house. I'd like to have that envelope back, please?"

132

Lissette's emotionless and somber expression didn't change. She ripped the envelope into little pieces and let them fall to the sidewalk.

"Hey. Hey, I paid for that, it's mine."

"Then trade me something for it." She poked a finger at her temple. "I got what's in that envelope all up here."

A man twice the size of anyone standing on the sidewalk approached. He wore heavy black army surplus boots, denim pants, and a Rolling Stones tee shirt with a big red tongue on the front.

Lissette stood aside. Her hand disappeared under her vest and into her waistband. "Keep walkin' Bad Luck Charlie or you'll rue the day you stuck your fat nose in my business." The man hesitated, sizing up all three victims, analyzing cost vs gain, and decided to keep moving. Good thing with those thick arms, he could've gone through them like a ten-pound ball in a game of ninepins. Was Lissette bluffing, or did she really have an equalizer hidden away? The same as Jackie the Nose with Baby Bertha.

"Bad Luck Charlie," and "rue the day," where was this girl raised? She'd been reading too much cheesy fiction from the sixties.

Esther didn't appear the least bit concerned. She was on a mission, mind locked on revenge, and no longer cared what happened to herself.

Lissette took off down the sidewalk, headed for the yellow house.

Nothing good would come of it. The three of them sticking their noses where they didn't belong could only end badly.

Esther fell in behind Lissette.

What the hell, why not?

Lissette knocked on the door as if mimicking some church representative there to spread the "Good word."

Ironic.

No one answered. Lissette knocked again.

The front yard matched the neighboring houses, arid-tan and bleached out dirt with scrub weeds having a difficult time gaining a foothold. Several people, criminal types, stopped on both sides of the street to watch what would happen next.

The front door, composed of a solid wood bottom half, sported glass panes on the top half. Hence, vulnerable to incursion. A vulnerable door in that kind of neighborhood meant only one thing. The criminal types watched because they'd been given the word, "Hands off," or suffer severe consequences committed upon their body and soul.

Lissette took a step back, looked at the house's elevation, and then scanned around on the ground until she spotted the target: a fist-sized rock in a planter wall. She retrieved it, walked back to the front door, stutter-stepped to get the right leg out front—much like a bowler in cricket—and threw the rock through the glass pane. The rock continued on into the house and shattered something else before rattling to a stop. The level of force wasn't necessary; a subtle elbow to the pane would've sufficed. Lissette was making a point for the witnesses who would later describe to Aussie Mike the bold and brazen violation of their criminal code.

What the hell was wrong with these two women? But it was obvious they epitomized the always judicious, "Hell hath no fury like a woman scorned." Maybe it was Aussie Mike who had better run for the hills?

When the glass broke, the people on the street scattered, running for cover, in no way wanting to be linked to the ensuing mayhem. The urge to do the same and flee was difficult to overcome.

Lissette reached in and unlocked the door. Her polished black boot crunched broken glass on the floor. She stopped at a tall potted fig, reached in, and pulled out a length of rebar with one end wrapped in gray duct tape. Put there by Aussie Mike to have a weapon close at hand if and when a local got his nerve up and came knocking to challenge the current king.

Inside, the place looked perfect, like right out of a magazine, replete with modern furniture and decor. Tile floors, Crown molding, expensive Asian area rugs, and unique art on the walls. The place smelled of pine trees with an underlying acrid chemical reek.

Lissette swung the rebar and shattered a lamp. Swung again and smashed a turntable for 78 vinyl records. She kicked over a rack close to the floor filled with antique albums, then stomped on them. She stopped and looked back toward the front door. "You two going to help or just stand there with your thumbs up your asses?"

"First, tell me what was in the envelope."

She glared and walked back toward him. "Is that all you care about? Don't you care the least bit about what happened to Eddie?"

"Of course, I do. But if you'd stop and think for one second, you'd realize this Aussie Mike is only one of two leads to what happened to Eddie. And this one is the lesser of the two."

"So now you're a cop?"

"Don't be ridiculous. We need to get out of here before Mike comes home. We're no match for him or his ilk."

"I'm thinking of sitting in that easy chair right over there and waitin' for him. What's the second most important lead you got locked up in that pea brain of yours?"

"Eddie was working for me when it happened. He was looking into the woman who was squatting illegally in my home."

She stopped less than a foot away, purposely violating personal space. "You think that a trespasser, a woman, is more likely to kill someone than a known drug dealer with a violent reputation?"

"How could I know for sure you have all the information on the woman? A variable missing from the equation I'm not privy to." He reached up and tapped her temple.

She knocked his hand away, her eyes fierce.

Esther moved on. "You two keep playing your silly games, I'm going to look for evidence like drugs or guns. Something we can turn over to the police to get them looking for this turd."

Lissette didn't take her eyes off his. "You want to know about your woman?"

"She's not my woman, but, yes, I do. If I didn't, I wouldn't have hired Eddie."

"Okay, but it doesn't mean a damn thing. Her first arrest was ten years ago in Vegas for solicitation. She apparently started late in life. *Arrest, no conviction.* Two years later, Beverly Hills PD, same thing, arrest, no conviction. Then, in the next five years, there were three arrests for criminal trespass in Brentwood, Pacific Palisades, and again in Beverly Hills. Got two years' probation for the third trespass conviction. Then, about a month ago, she was convicted of Grand Theft in Santa Monica. Suspended sentence."

"She's never done any prison time?"

"None."

"What do you think about those kinds of offenses?"

"There's nothing weird about them. It just says the woman likes to take advantage of old, stupid men. Ergo." She held up her hand, pointing at him.

"What about the no jail time?"

"This is California Bud. The Governor let out 2500 criminals doing life and closed down prisons. Anymore, crimes against property isn't even a blip on the radar."

"Hmm."

"Hmm? That's all you gotta say?" Her cell phone rang. She took a step back and grabbed it from her back pocket. "Yeah, baby doll? What? No, honey, mommy will be home soon. Yes, I promise. Yes, I'll bring you some ice cream. Now put Katie on the phone. Please, honey, put Kate on the phone."

A pause. Lissette turned her back and took a couple of steps away, the rebar in one hand, the cell held up to her ear with the other.

"Kate, I told you to keep her off the phone. I'm working. I know. I'm sorry. It's…" Her words tangled in the grief that rose up in her throat. "Tell her I won't be much longer. I'll be home soon. Yes, goodbye."

Esther came out of the room, her expression confused. Shocked.

Lissette hung up and kept her back turned away a beat longer, then turned and faced Esther.

Esther said, "You have a *child*?"

Lissette didn't answer.

Esther took a step closer. "Does the child belong to Eddie?"

"That's none of your damn business, old woman."

"How old is the child?"

"Don't call her 'child', she's my daughter. Her name is Maribelle." More emotions filled Lissette's words as she choked.

"Two years old, two and a half?" Esther asked.

"Leave it be."

"That's why Eddie committed those crimes. He had a daughter on the way. I always wondered why he didn't come to me for money. He was too proud to ask. Eddie was like that. He would want to be the good husband, the good father, and support you on his own. Prideful. He wouldn't take a handout. The poor misguided fool." Now tears filled Esther's eyes. "I'm sorry. I...it must've been difficult for you as well. I'm being selfish. Can I see...will you let me visit with your daughter, Maribelle?"

And just like that, the disclosure of a child snuffed out the bitter, all-encompassing revenge in Esther, shifting her back to the kindergarten teacher shifting her back to the real world where she belonged.

Lissette's back straightened. She took a deep breath. "Fine. When we get done here."

Words bubbled up that had no business coming from him. "If you have a daughter, you shouldn't be involved in this sort of activity. You have a respons—"

She rounded on him, her eyes shifted back to fierce as she again approached and stood in his personal space. "Back off, pal, or I might just cave in your head. You mean nothing to me. You got Eddie killed."

"If I got Eddie killed, then what are we doing here?"

She pulled back the rebar to strike. Esther grabbed her wrist. "That's enough. He can be a real horse's ass, but this time I think he's right. Come on, let's get out of here."

Lissette hesitated, her eyes moving back and forth as her mind processed the new information. "Fine. We'll go, but first..." She whirled and kicked over an end table. Then swung the rebar again and again, shattering anything and everything; the art on the walls, the vase with fresh flowers, delicate knick-knacks on shelves. She reached under her vest, pulled out a gravity knife, flicked it open, and slashed the couch and loveseat. A frenzy of destruction that left the living room decimated and her gasping for breath. Chest heaving.

If Aussie Mike was anything like Mr. LaBruzzo and Jackie the Nose, he wouldn't be happy and just let it lie. Lissette's intent from the onset. Why hunt the lion when you could have the lion hunt for you?

Lissette had driven to the house in her own car with plates registered to her. But, far from the gossip grapevine, the criminals used worked better than law enforcement radios and computers.

Anger, grief, and revenge were communicable diseases that spread as quickly as Ebola and just as devastating. Aussie Mike would be coming after her. After all, three of them.

Esther moved slowly over to Lissette, cooing like a cowboy to a wild mustang. "Come on now. It's over. Everything's okay. Let's go. Let's get out of here while we still can."

Lissette let Esther guide her to the front door. Lissette's eyes defused as her mind tried to rectify all that had happened in the last twenty-four hours. Sweat beaded and ran into bright blue eyes. She didn't blink and returned to the real world.

"Okay," Lissette said, "Let's ride."

On the way out the door, she stopped and with the toe of her boot nudged a black cylindrical object that lay among the detritus she'd created. A blue ring of light circled the top. She bent over, righted the thing, and smiled.

Harvey leaned over to Esther. "What's going on?"

"Just watch."

Lissette said, "Alexa, order dog food, a fifty-pound bag."

The black cylinder responded in a woman's voice, giving several buying options.

"What the hell?"

"Shush," Esther said.

Lissette said, "Alexa, change that to forty of those fifty-pound bags."

Esther giggled. "A ton, that's a whole ton."

Lissette smirked along with her, then went on to order what had to be a full pallet of tampons, toilet paper, Captain Crunch, paper towels, nails, hammers, and finally, a pallet-sized order of Summer Breeze feminine rinse. "There, douche for a douche. *Now* let's ride."

On the way out, Esther said, "All of that stuff is going to be delivered, dropped right in his front yard. The people on the street won't be able to resist."

"Seriously?"

Outside, Lissette said, "Old man, you're still living in the Stone Age."

On the street, Esther opened the passenger door to the gray Chevy Tahoe and indicated she wanted Lissette in the passenger seat. Lissette didn't argue. Esther looked up. "Get in, Harv, I'm driving."

"Oh no." The wreck in front of the bank that totaled her big Lincoln was still too fresh. The violence of the event returned in the form of an acrid taste on the tongue. After a moment's hesitation, and not wanting to be left behind in Casa Blanca, he got in and closed the door. Esther fumbled around looking for the ignition, turned, and asked Lissette, "The keys, dear?"

Lissette handed them over her mind obviously busy running scenarios of what she would do to Mike when she caught up with him. Or in this case, vice versa.

From the backseat, leaning forward, Harvey asked, "Esther, didn't the police take away your license to drive?"

She started the big Tahoe, "Just sit back and buckle up, buttercup."

"Oh, not this Esther again." Shaky hands reached for the shoulder strap seat belt, took the sage advice, and buckled up.

Esther pulled out into the street, her diminutive form far too small to be driving such a large vehicle. The woman had no fear.

After the first turn, a jet-black 69 Chevy Chevelle passed going the other way. The big engine emitting a guttural rumble felt in the chest. Lissette sat up in the seat. "Go back, that was Aussie Mike. Turn around and go back."

Esther drove in the same direction. Thank the Lord for small favors. Something Dad had said, but usually in situations involving sarcasm.

"Turn this thing around right now."

Esther didn't look over, keeping her eyes on the road. She'd learned a valuable lesson from the crash. Keep your eyes on the damn road. She said. "I didn't know you had a daughter. I won't allow you to jeopardize her future."

Lissette said, "I want to know why Eddie owed Aussie Mike money. Eddie might not have taken the screwed-up job looking into that woman if he didn't owe the money. We were doing okay, we had bills, sure, but he didn't have to get in bed with Mike."

Esther shook her head and kept driving.

He stuck his head forward. "What else was in the envelope?"

Lissette scowled, angry that Esther wasn't turning around. "Eddie said you wanted him to look into you."

From the backseat, "That's right, I did."

"You know how suspicious that sounds?"

"Did you find out anything or not?"

"I'm still working on it. But I'll tell you right now if you had anything to do with what happened to my Eddie, you can't run far enough or hide from what you got comin' your way."

"Hmm."

Chapter Sixteen

1968

With the six canvas bags in the trunk, Jackie The Nose drove for an hour, headed east toward the water and then north until the harbor came into view. He smoked a fat black cigar, the blue-gray smoke whiffled out the open window. He didn't talk and periodically looked askance with slit eyes, never acknowledging Harvey seated next to him.

At the harbor entrance, the security man dressed all in gray, leaned out the tall narrow booth until he clocked the driver of the Buick and hurried to open the barrier to let the car pass. Jackie raised his hand and grunted to the man as he went by. He wheeled into the parking lot and over to a striped area with, "No Parking," signs posted big enough a blind person would know not to park there and stopped. He shut the car down, waited, and puff-puff-puffed his cigar.

After a time, he finally spoke. "You know, you and me, we could do big things together. You just need ta pull that square head outta your ass long enough ta see it."

Better not to say a thing, why risk angering the beast?

"You gonna say something or jus' sit there like a bump ona log?"

"I don't know what you are talking about."

"I gotta trunk load a cash-money and you don't know what I'm talking about?"

"I'm fully aware of the situation as it stands. I just don't know in what context you are referring."

He canted to the side while reaching into his back slacks pocket and came out with Baby. He set the beavertail blackjack on the seat, the throng wrapped tight around his chubby fist. "We're gonna have a conversation here, and if it ever comes out, I'll deny it. And then, first chance, I'll cave in your skull. You with me on this?"

"Yes, I can easily comprehend the legitimate threat you just made against my person. But I'm still not sure I follow what you mean."

Jackie picked up Baby and slapped the cloth-covered seat again and again for emphasis. "You might be smart when it comes ta numbers and fancy words, but you're about dumber than a rock when it comes ta life in general."

"I can accept and acknowledge that crude assessment. Because you are correct, if I were smart in the way of the world, I would not be sitting here with a—"

"Watch your smart mouth. We're not friends. Don't make that mistake. We're boss, that's me, and peon, that's you."

"Believe me when I say I would never make that mistake. Go on."

"Okay, so I guess I gotta walk you through it. It's easy, one plus one equals three. You got it now? I control the physical part of the money as you can see with what I got in this here trunk. A million and a half smacks. And you." His fat finger came over and poked an already sore chest from the DeFrank's wingtip kick-job. "You control the pencil that logs in the smacks in that big ledger book. Is it starting to sink in now?"

Harvey struggled up into the seat, the idea foolish and idiotic.

At first, anyway.

"Ya," Jackie smiled. "Now I see you're gettin' the idea. Are you in?"

He wanted to skim the cream off the top. Steal money from Mr. LaBruzzo. The perfect crime. With a perfect alibi. When caught—and he would get caught—all he had to do was point his fat finger at the Ledger Man. An unimpeachable accusation. A capo's word against, "someone lower than whale crap. A peon." The idea was unimaginable before. But now?

After hitting rock bottom. After your life no longer mattered and death seemed the most viable option. An option preferred over living with the smothering guilt and grief.

Of course. What an ideal solution.

Why not use the ledger as a weapon against these…these lowlife, knuckle-dragging scofflaws? Do it with impunity. Hit them where it hurts the most. Make them squeal like little piglets. They hurt Lois. So now let them feel the sharp bite from the *Ledger Man.*

"Okay, count me in."

"Great. We'll get busy with it after this here load. Now get your ass outta the car. Go over there and get that wheeled cart. See it? We gotta get all this dough down to The Lucky Lady, pronto. We're late already. Some shit about wanting to sail with the tide."

Ten minutes later, Harvey wheeled the six heavy canvas bags stacked on the fish dolly. The wooden dock rose and fell ever so gently with the ocean as large boats motored by. The sun reflected and winked off the blue-water surface. The warm breeze made the air almost neutral.

All the while, schemes instead of numbers populated a mathematical brain. What was the best way to skim? How to do it without LaBruzzo spotting the errors in accounting.

But that was the easy part. When it came to numbers, LaBruzzo couldn't "find his ass with both hands," a saying too often used by Jackie the Nose.

Sure. Sure. First, find Lois and get her somewhere safe. Do that part today. Then skim the money. Enough to set up…Yes…yes. That was the answer to the equation, the variable too difficult to overcome; the fact that there would be nowhere to hide from LaBruzzo. Nowhere in the world. But with enough money, you could hide anywhere. Even hire the best security guards. Yes, of course, the answer to the problem…the impossible variable. Perfect.

For the first time in two days, a ray of hope slipped in, illuminating a dark emotional chasm too wide to leap.

Tied perpendicular at the dock's end sat a sailboat. A man in white shorts, white shirt, with a white sweater tied around his shoulders, worked quickly, preparing the sailboat for departure. He hesitated when he noticed Jackie the Nose waddle toward him. Who wouldn't turn and flee for their life?

The man straightened up, the way a condemned man would stand in front of a firing squad. Straighten a backbone in one last attempt to recover a modicum of pride. "You're late, as always."

"Be careful how you talk to me, punk, I'll put you in the hospital again. This time you'll come out drooling and wearing diapers. I get here when I get here, you understand?"

The man didn't say anything more to Jackie. Instead, he said, "Here, hand me down those bags, one at a time."

The bags took two hands, using shoulders and legs to get them over the dock's edge and down into the sailboat. While Jackie looked on, puffing his cigar.

The weight of that much paper—the significance in the conversion to value—it just wasn't fair that a man like LaBruzzo, with a son like Giorgio, could own so much.

The man in the boat struggled to take each canvas bag and lower it to the deck and out of the way. "Hey," he said to Jackie, "I told you, I need a deckhand to sail this thing all the way to the Caymans. You said I couldn't bring my guy because of security reasons. I can't do it alone."

"I tolt ya I'd take care of it and I did." He kicked Harvey in the butt.

Wind whistled. Arms waved wildly for a second until he fell heavily to the boat deck atop the canvas bags."

"Wait. Wait. I can't go, I have to—"

"Shut up and stay down there. You need to get your mind right about this girl. When you get back in a month, you'll have forgotten all about her." He looked over at the boat captain. He stays on the boat the entire trip. There and back. He doesn't, it's your ass. You understand?"

The captain nodded in agreement.

Jackie grunted, going down on one knee to untie the rope that held the boat to the dock.

"A month? Are you kidding? No, I can't go at all. Not for one day, especially not for a month.

Lois? What about Lois?"

The man moved to the tiller and started a small outboard motor. "You don't want to argue with the likes of that bastard. He's a sociopath. Life means nothing to him. An important lesson you learn quickly, or you won't learn anything ever again."

The man guided the boat out into the open harbor. Jackie the Nose stood at the edge of the dock waving like some kind of idiot might if he had family leaving on a big cruise liner with ticker tape and streamers.

Only there was nothing cheerful at all about this trip.

Outside the harbor, the sailboat rose up on the wide swells and dove down the backside. Tom Slade, the boat captain, helped get the mainsail up and then stayed at the helm, yelling and waving with his free arm, directing the fool of a deckhand who had no idea how to sail. Within forty minutes, the boat heaved over, the sails trimmed, the bow cutting through the water like a knife.

While he held onto the wheel, Slade ate a ham and cheese sandwich he took from a cooler along with a beer. "Help yourself, we're gonna run with the wind while it's here. We're making good time."

"Is there any way you could pull in somewhere and let me off?"

"Are you serious? You know what that animal would do to me if he found out I didn't follow his orders to the letter."

"Yeah, I figured as much."

"Go on, eat something. Have a beer."

"I don't drink. And I don't think I'll ever be hungry again." The words just left his mouth as his stomach growled. When had he eaten last? He took out a sandwich, unwrapped the wax paper, and took a bite. His mouth flooded with saliva. Two sandwiches disappeared in a flash.

With a full stomach, fatigue sauntered in and took control. He curled up on the cushioned bench and fell fast asleep.

* * *

Time on the boat had no beginning or ending. Just days of bright blue skies filled with an orange ball of a sun that hovered over a never-ending sea.

Monotony, a cohort to guilt and grief.

Tom Slade liked to talk. Slade probably wasn't his name. In Jackie the Nose's world, remaining anonymous to all wasn't a bad idea. Slade said that two sailors on the high seas only had each other for company, and it was talk or go crazy.

Slade, an ex-assistant state's attorney for New York, was a "degenerate gambler." He'd thrown cases involving Mr. LaBruzzo's crews until Slade's boss caught on and fired him. Now, Slade just made money runs, content to be away from the world and the lure of OTB ponies and blackjack tables in Atlantic City.

Down in the ship's cabin, Slade kept two long shelves of books, one of crime novels and one filled with law books; court procedure, rules of evidence, and laws of arrest. The constant moist salt air had ruined the books, warped them, and turned the edges spotted brown with foxing. Rather than listen to Slade yammer on, the books gave a quiet solace, a place to disappear. The first part of the day was dedicated to the law and its intricate places to duck and weave and avoid justice. At night, crime novels, with their escapism, their fictive dreams that dropped the reader into the weird world of authors who sat around thinking up crimes to throw against the wall to see what stuck. Good and bad people populated the novels. All the books had a rise and fall in the story arc. The protagonist was always motivated by something, causing him to act. That led to a crisis and then a conclusion. Harvey had the motivation; now he needed to act.

In between books, interesting conversations with Slade added anecdotal information to the book learning. He liked to talk about his life, "before," when he was a "shit-hot" prosecutor. He told wild tales of criminal cases and their outcomes. But more interesting was Slade's descriptions of the people he prosecuted. None of them, "had any right to breathe our air."

Did the man realize the irony? That he, too, belonged to that same criminal fraternity, after he purposely threw cases to get LaBruzzo's henchmen off. Allowed those same henchmen to continue loose among the lambs, committing rape, robbery, and murder?

Days, one after another, peeled away. Memories of Lois never gone from mind or soul more than ten or fifteen seconds at a time.

Until three weeks later, when they pulled into The Grand Cayman Island. The charts said New Jersey to the Caymans was about 1400 miles the way the crow flies. But Slade skirted Cuba and took the long way around Puerto Rico, coming up on the gulf side of the Caymans, adding hundreds of extra miles. And days.

Tanned with hair sun-bleached, Harvey stepped off onto land for the first time in twenty-plus days. But old terra firma continued to move as if still out on the vast ocean. Until the sea legs dissipated and balance returned.

Slade timed coming ashore to the bank's hours. First thing, the six canvas bags were shuttled to the Great Grand Cayman Bank, the GGCB. They sat in the private brown leather and chrome lounge, sipping planter's punch while the money was tallied, and a receipt issued.

While out on the open sea, Harvey was able to put aside the anguish and anxiety, the overwhelming need to get back to Lois, and had accepted his indentured servitude. But now that the first half of the journey came to an end, that jittery anxiety returned with a vengeance along with the need to hurry to get back.

Until the second planter's punch.

Slade took a third punch from the offered silver tray while sitting on the plush couch. He held up the delicate crystal glass and toasted. "To safe travels, warm days, and beautiful women."

Harvey held up his glass and only nodded, his mind elsewhere.

"Thought you didn't drink?"

"What are you talking about? This is just fruit punch."

"Sorry, Bucko, the sweet punch masks the ultra-smooth dark rum. And believe me when I say these folks pour with a heavy hand."

Instead of being angry, Harvey giggled. He didn't remember ever giggling. He took a third punch from the offered tray. "This is…is giggle juice."

Slade laughed. "Take it easy, cowboy. If this is your first time, you're not gonna be happy tomorrow morning when you come out the other side."

What did it matter? The hard edge to the world had softened, eased off a weight that had all but smothered and pile-drove a soul deep into the earth.

Outside in the bright sunlight, they walked through the open-air shopping mall. They bought fresh fruit, ordered supplies down to the boat, and donned Panama hats. On the way back to the boat, Slade asked if Harvey wanted to be his permanent first mate on the quarterly trips.

For a brief second, the offer looked like the best thing in the world with no roadblocks at all to keep it from happening. But grief and guilt suddenly swapped places with anger and a need for vengeance, a vehemence so bitter it tasted sour on his tongue.

They stayed another five days. Grand Cayman was not only known for its banking, it also had a reputation for its gambling establishments. After five days, Slade no longer had reason to stay; he lost all the money paid to him by LaBruzzo to make the trip. On the fifth day, he showed up at the dock in bedraggled clothes and a wizen visage. Under his arm, he carried a case of cheap rum he called "Bust-head liquor."

That first night, heading back on the open sea, they each drank from a single bottle. Slade drank until his words slurred. The fat moon lay on the horizon and shone on a silvery carpet of light that ran atop the water leading right to the boat. Slade sat back with the wheel between his toes, steering.

Harvey sidled up on the cushion close enough to hear over the wind. "Tom, if you, as an ex-prosecutor, were going to kill someone and get away with it, how would you do it?"

Slade looked over and smiled. He started to laugh until, in the ambient moonlight, he caught Harvey's no-nonsense expression. "Well, it's going to be like that, is it?"

"Yes, it is."

"Good for you, Harv." He slapped Harvey's leg. "Good for you. Then let's get down to business, huh? First—"

Chapter Seventeen

Current Day

After leaving Casa Blanca, Esther drove the big Chevy Tahoe in and out of streets in Riverside without a navigation app or a city map. She lived in town her entire life and never ventured out except for that two-year stint in Blythe, "The butthole of California." Did it to be near Eddie in Chuckwalla prison. With her diminutive size behind the big steering wheel, she looked more like a twelve-year-old girl who'd stolen daddy's truck.

The distance between Casa Blanca and the Mission district wasn't enough separation from Aussie Mike. The jungle drums of information would reach past those few miles. Aussie Mike would know soon enough who disrespected him and his home and come looking.

Claws out, fangs sharpened.

He couldn't let the slight go unanswered. In the law of that same jungle, if you looked weak, the animals closed in and ate you. Mike's ego would also come into play.

"Hey, Esther," he said. "Why don't you park this thing around back in the alley. It'll be too visible on the street."

Lissette, who hadn't said a word the entire time, shifted in her seat. "No, park it right out front. Let him come." Down by her leg, she still clung to the piece of rebar taken from the yellow house. That primitive weapon would be several kinds of ironic if Mike showed up and took a beating from his own piece of rebar, which, as it happens, was made out of iron.

Esther parked in the street right in front of the house and shut off the engine. She handed the keys to Lissette, who didn't move from her front seat and sat torso turned, staring into the back.

"Hey," he said. "Rita's little red Mercedes isn't here. Maybe she's—"

Lissette craned her head toward the backseat, ignoring the question. "Who's Andrew Johnson? What's he got to do with this whole mess?"

"He's the contractor Rita hired to 'update the kitchen.' She hired him without my consent. Why? Did you find something out about him?"

"No, dipshit. Andrew Johnson's the same as John Smith. There's ten thousand of 'em."

"So, it's an alias then?"

"You know you don't talk like some kinda retired businessman, not with all your street jargon. You want to tell me your story before I find out on my own?"

"I've got nothing to hide. Go ahead."

The false ID had held up for fifty years. If she thought she could punch through it, let her try her damnedest. "What about the license plate, 'Real Man?'"

She leaned back and pulled out her phone. "I don't have direct access to DMV records. I had to farm out that question. I had to burn a big favor to get it done. My contact in the PD said he'd text me the info when he went into work. I'll check on it right now." She thumbed through the text messages. She looked up, glared at him, and spoke through clenched teeth. "The Mercedes was stolen. The owner, a prominent real estate broker, was found floating in his own swimming pool in Redlands. The car's been recovered, burned down to the hubs. Now my contact, the Riverside cop, is in the grease. The plate was flagged by Redlands, and they want to know why he made the inquiry."

Harvey shook his head. "He burnt the car after running down Eddie. He wanted to destroy the evidence."

Esther spun in her seat. "You think so?" She turned to Lissette. "Give me back the keys. We have to go find this Andrew Johnson."

"Esther, what about what you said back at the house that Lissette has a child to think about? And what happens if you do find him? We were just at Aussie Mike's, destroyed his place, and made a huge enemy. Can't you two see running around half-cocked will get you nowhere."

Lissette looked at Esther. "Yeah, but it feels good. I'd rather be doing something than nothing at all."

"That's right." Esther agreed.

"Why don't you just call your friend at Riverside PD, have him call Redlands PD, and give them Andrew Johnson's description. Let them run the guy down. While you're at it have them stake out my house." He wanted the cops close for three reasons: Aussie Mike, Andrew Johnson, and, now, the lesser of three evils, Rita.

Lissette leaned across the front seat again. "We're not gonna let the cops get to this guy Johnson before we do. They'll just put him in the can where we can't get to him. That's if they get him at all."

Harvey said, "He'll be in the wind, killing that car owner and now...Eddie. Let's go inside and talk about this. I'll tell you everything I know. Everything Eddie and I discussed. You can talk with Rita when she comes back. Maybe you can find out from her what's going on? She's involved up to her pretty little button nose."

"Mister, I'm not in the mood to deal with your chickenshit trespassing issue."

"It's not a trespassing issue if two people are dead over it. Can't you see she's at the heart of this entire mess?"

Saying the part about two people being dead caused a dark secret from the past to rise up. One buried so long, the possibility had never pinged as a motive for all the current heartache. Not in a feeble eighty-two-year-old's mind.

Who held a grudge that long? The people involved with that ancient incident were long dead. Weren't they?

But with the violent death of Eddie Gurski, Andrew Johnson *was* the kind of a person who'd bubble up from that violent era. Johnson, the kind of someone the LaBruzzo family *would* hire. Cold. Deliberate. Unflinching.

Serving up "Death on a cracker," as Slade would've said.

Esther held out her hand. Lissette gave her the keys. Esther started the Tahoe. "Harvey, we're gonna find this Johnson fellow and teach him a hard lesson. You in or out?"

"My mama didn't raise no fools." Something else Slade said too often. Each time he said it, the obvious—but withheld rebuttal—was always a comment on his current situation; a degenerate gambler living in a sailboat running back and forth to the Cayman Islands while working for the mob. If that wasn't every kind of a fool, what was?

He opened the door, got out, and stood by the driver's window looking in at Esther. "I'm sorry, I don't want to drive off the cliff with Thelma and Louise."

Esther, with her foot on the brake, pulled the gearshift of the Tahoe into drive. "You know, Sylvia used to say that at times you could be a real horse's ass. I defended you, but now I see what she meant." She took off too fast.

"Huh, that was rude, Esther. Rude and boorish." Said it to no one as the big Tahoe barreled down the street, ran the stop sign, and turned right.

The neighborhood settled into a quiet calm. In the tree above, sat a red robin looking down in a judgmental kind of way. Below sat a tabby cat, its neck craned upward, watching the bird.

He walked up the concrete path to the front of the house. The door was locked. "Crap." He fumbled for the keys, found the right one, and stuck it in the lock. It wouldn't turn. Rita had changed the damn locks. He kicked the door. Kicked it again. The third time, his foot complained with a pain that shot up the leg and into the hip.

The door opened. Rita stood in the sunlight. An angel. One with perfect alabaster skin, beautiful red hair that gleamed, and wearing one of her signature cocktail dresses. This one a black off-the-shoulder number.

No matter how hard he tried not to, a smile crept out. Her presence in the house somehow gave off a weird kind of comfort to a lonely old soul.

But something wasn't right. With the entire package that was Rita, something was amiss. An important component of her persona.

Confidence.

That was it.

Before she exuded a platinum level of confidence, dripped with it. Now she looked harried, a mouse that scurried around under the shadow of a hawk that grew large overhead.

"Well, are you going to stand there all day, or are you going to come in?" She craned her neck out to check the street, making sure no interlopers lurked ready to pounce. Classic paranoia. An insidious affliction he knew all too well. Fifty years of it worked on the body, wore it down to a nub. That constant heavy pressure took a man five foot ten down to five foot eight and hunched over.

"Where's your car? Your little red Mercedes convertible? Did you park it around back? It might get burglarized back there in the alley. The neighborhood has gone to hell in a handbasket."

She grabbed ahold and yanked him inside. "I said get in here." She slammed the door and threw the deadbolt.

"Criminently, take it easy, woman. You just about yanked my arm out of the socket."

She hurried down the two steps into the vast sunken living room. Over the years a place rarely if ever used. Now, almost vacant, many of the antiques carefully chosen by Sylvia were sold off. The highly polished hardwood floor is covered with two large area rugs, both Asian, handwoven, and hand-dyed.

Rita paced the length, turned around, and paced back while wringing her hands. He came in, sat on a restored Toscano Swan 19th-century fainting couch, and watched. Her anxiety tried hard to be contagious.

"My car? You asked me about my car?"

"Come sit, you're starting to make me crazy."

"I can't sit. Can't you see I can't sit?"

"Then tell me about your car."

Her head whipped around. "You. You put the idea in my head. It's all your fault."

"What idea is that, Rita?"

"I'm not Rita, damn you."

"Well, I'd bet this house you're not a Delores either." Her turmoil should

153

have been a welcome balm after the abuse she'd caused over the last couple of days. But seeing her soft vulnerability shift to that of a contrite puppy caught peeing on the floor was heartbreaking.

Suddenly, a scent caught up with her. Not the wonderful soft fragrance that always followed in her wake. But an acrid common reek everyone knows.

Gasoline.

"Rita, what have you done?"

She froze, eyes going wide.

"What do you mean?"

"Come sit. Tell me what's going on? You'll feel better if you unburden your obviously tortured soul."

"Tortured soul, my aching ass."

She stood staring, the consternation plain in her expression as she tried to decide the best path. How much to tell? And the consequences once Pandora's box was opened. She came over and sat on the fainting couch. Too close. Her hip touching his.

She was always working, casting out feminine wiles to confound and confuse the male gender. A disruptor of all common thought patterns.

She reached down and flipped off the backstrap to one high heel, then the other. She leaned back, closed her eyes, and raised her leg over his lap. "Harvey, be a love and rub my feet. I think better if someone's rubbing my feet."

Why not do what she asked? The arthritic pain in fingers and wrist yelped in complaint. "Are you going to tell me why you smell like gas?"

"It's all your fault."

"You've already said as much?"

"You have a gun, Harvey?" Her eyes were still closed, making it impossible to read exactly what she had in mind. But the gun request didn't bode well for a quiet future.

"Why?"

"We won't get anywhere if you keep asking a question for a question instead of answering." The bottom half of her dress was too restrictive. She

154

reached down and shimmied it up past mid-thighs, exposing those...those wonder legs.

Yikes.

When the woman turned her game to full power, mountains shimmied and then moved without complaint.

"Aah, that feels wonderful, Harv. Rub deeper."

He said nothing and tried hard to do as she asked.

"Harv, since we are husband and wife, you can't testify against me, right?"

"Partially true. If we were in fact husband and wife, then the law says I can't be *compelled* to speak against your penal interest."

She opened one eye and stared. "So, you mean that either way, if you wanted to you could testify against me? Is that right?"

"Correct. The car, Rita. Tell me about the car."

"I loved that car."

'Loved,' past tense? "What happened to your car?"

With both eyes closed, tears leaked out and ran down her cheeks. How could anyone not feel sorry for this poor child?

"You missed your calling. You could be a very effective actress."

She jumped up, swinging her legs around. She shoved him. "You're a real bastard."

"What? That was a compliment."

"You really meant it? You weren't being an ass?"

"It's the truth or may God strike me dead."

"Too bad you don't know—"

"Rita, the car?"

She eased her head down and rested it on his lap. She looked up at him with those green eyes. "I burnt it to the ground." The tears again, this time with genuine sentiment.

"Why did you burn it?"

Her body shook as she started to sob. "I found..."

"What did you find?"

"I found some hair and a swatch of a shirt in the bumper. You were right. My car ran that poor man down." She opened her eyes. "Not me, Harv. I didn't do it. You have to believe me. I didn't do it."

"There's no reason in this world I should believe you. You have lied to me for two days now. But I do. I believe you."

"You do?"

"I do. Now tell me, who is Andrew Johnson?"

"He's a bad man. He's bad all the way to the bone. There is nothing good about him. Nothing."

"You ready to tell me what's going on. Why are you here in my house?"

More tears streamed down her cheeks. She nodded.

Chapter Eighteen

1968

The Lucky Lady rode the long, wide swells as a high wind whipped up white caps. Slade dropped down out of the chop and into the calm harbor, the moonless night quiet, lonesome. Harvey jumped off, put out bumpers, tied the boat front and aft to cleats, and took off at a jog down the wooden dock. Slade yelled, "Good luck. You're gonna need it."

The taxi dropped him off forty minutes later in front of his house, the one next door to Lois's that sat dark and foreboding. No one came running to the knocks at her door. An invisible clock ticked louder and louder, both houses a target, a place to look for the errant Ledger Man suddenly let free into the world.

Over the course of eight weeks at sea, house keys had somehow gone missing. Without hesitation, a round rock from the planter broke out the glass pane in the door. The reach in found the door...*unlocked*. When was the last time—

The day Lois knocked came in and offered a lovely picnic at the lake. Only eight weeks ago. Seemed more like years. On that fateful day, had the beautiful woman in the house befuddled a mind to the point of not locking the door when they left?

A shaking hand eased open the door that gave a quiet creak.

Suddenly, an acrid scent froze, body and soul.

Cigar smoke.

Run!

The pivot. He took two long steps before running headlong into a solid mass of thugs. Mr. LaBruzzo's limo driver.

"Going somewhere, dipshit?" The man's vice-like hand on the throat shut down all breathing. Stifled all speech. The man shoved hard.

Harvey stumbled backward and fell into his house. The living room lights came on with a click. The fat slob Jackie the Nose sat in the easy chair puff-puff-puffing his cigar. He looked bigger than eight weeks ago. "You goin' somewhere?"

That bastard Slade. He disembarked, went right to a phone, and called Jackie. Thanks, Slade, for nothing.

"Come on." Jackie struggled to get his fat self up and out of the cushioned chair. "You're way behind on your work. All that cash is backed up and needs to be logged in. Checked and double checked. Heh, heh, by the time you get that done, it's gonna be time for another run down south. See how all this is working out? Perfect because I'm brilliant at calendar work."

He took a handful of Harvey's shirt while walking past and jerked. Buttons tore free and skittered away.

Back outside, Jackie said, "Be a good little propeller head and get in the car. Keep the jibber-jabber ta ya self. I gotta a belly-ache ta be all belly aches."

In the limo, Jackie pushed the button that raised the dark window between the driver and the passenger compartment, cutting off all sound to the driver.

"You remember what we talked about?" Jackie asked, "I figure you can skim what, let's say fifty-sixty k the first time around. Can you cover that much in your ledger book?"

Two weeks to catch up, then another eight weeks sailing to the Caymans. This wasn't fair. Not the least bit fair.

"I can cover a hundred. It's all the same to me. The tricky part of my job is spreading the cash over all the legitimate businesses to keep Uncle Sam in the dark."

"A hundred? Very nice."

"What's my end?"

Jackie's expression scrunched up. "Your end? So now you're getting greedy? Okay, make it a hundert and five. You get the five right off the top. How's that sound?"

"I'm taking all the risk. Five doesn't seem fair at all. Not since you already cut my weekly salary."

Sitting back in the seat, Jackie's weight shifted. His immense stomach put pressure on his lungs and heart. His face turned pale, bloated. Sweat beaded and ran into his eyes. Dark half-moons under his eyes made him cadaverous.

"Okay, as of today, you're back on full salary. But you're not getting' a dime more than five on this other thing. And from now on, from this time forward we never speak of it again. You just do it. When you log in the cash you put that extra hunert K in the bottom draw-down on the right side of your desk. I changed out that drawer. Now it has a false bottom. I'll show you when we get there." More sweat rolled down Jackie's face, and his breath came faster.

Was this somehow an opportunity to take advantage of his ill health?

His cigar had gone out. He patted his pockets for a lighter and couldn't find one. Maybe he left it on the coffee table back at the house. A Zippo with a Marine Corp. emblem.

"Hey, Propeller head, you got a match?"

The idea bubbled up unbidden with no time to ponder the consequences. "Yeah, as a matter of fact, I do. How about *my butt and your face?*"

Jackie the Nose's mouth sagged open. The wet cigar dropped to his chest. No one talked to a capo like that. He brought his leg back and kicked and kicked and kicked. The blows landed hard and hurt like hell.

Jackie wheezed like a steam engine going up a hill and started coughing. But was it enough to vapor-lock his already strained respiratory system?

The limo suddenly pulled to the curb as the separating window came down. "You okay, boss? What's going on back there?"

The plan didn't work, not this time.

Jackie struggled to get out. He walked around and recovered his breath. After a time, he got back in. The limo took off, headed for the office and the piles of rolled up brown grocery bags filled with cash.

Jackie smiled as he puffed his cigar. A cold smile that sent shivers up and down the back the same as if kissed by the Grim Reaper. He took the cigar from his mouth, his eyes squinting from the smoke. "Don't think I don't see you, Propeller Head. You're starting to grow a set of balls. I got eyes on you now, so watch your ass."

"Whatever do you mean?"

"You know exactly what I mean. You think you can outsmart me. Think again."

Ten minutes later, the limo pulled up in front of a donut shop in Hoboken the counting room was upstairs. Jackie the Nose got out and held the car door. When Harvey crawled out and took a couple of steps headed for the stairs next to the Hole in One donut shop, Jackie kicked him in the ass. He stumbled and fell, tearing his pants and skinning his knees.

"Heh, heh." Jackie walked by and flicked his cigar, which bounced off Harvey's face with a wet smack.

Upstairs, the apartment door had a steel frame around it. Jackie took out his wad of keys and unlocked the steel door to get to the regular wooden door. Inside smelled of rancid grease from the years of fried donuts down below. A sickening reek that permeated everything: wood paneling, curtains, and gold shag carpet.

Off to the side of the desk sat eight wicker laundry baskets, one for each week out on the high seas. Each basket filled to the brim with carefully rolled-up brown paper grocery bags secured with red rubber bands. The end result from LaBruzzo's crews, their numbers operations, the extortion from business owners, prostitution and drugs. Each one was marked in black felt tip marker, describing "the who" and "how much."

LaBruzzo always asked for an accounting week by week. Sometimes he even called for an audience every two or three days. The chief crook monitors all of the smaller crooks who populated the lower part of the organization chart. No trust whatsoever. After all, a crook was a crook. LaBruzzo had forestalled the scrutiny while his accountant got his mind right on the high seas. Evidence in how much he wanted the relationship with his son Giorgio and Lois to work.

In the office, Jackie lay down on the couch and immediately fell asleep. The wicker baskets would take at least two days, probably closer to three, to count and log assignments to the legitimate businesses. And that would be working around the clock. The log entries that indicated what money came from what crew interested LaBruzzo the most. If the paper grocery bags came up short, Baby Bertha paid that crew leader a visit.

The limo driver dumped the first basket on the desk. "Get started, I'll go get the ledger."

The ledger wasn't kept in the safe room, not with the money. The cops would love that. LaBruzzo, a control freak, kept it in his hidden safe at his home.

Fourteen hours later, Harvey's fingers and hands were dirty from counting all the small bills; banding them, categorizing, and logging. The mathematical half of the mind was doing the work all on its own, while the creative side stayed busy with the scheme, the multitude of options that continued to unfold. Ones discussed with Slade.

Jackie had slept for eight hours, left, and came back with coffees and donuts from downstairs. He hovered too close, looking over Harvey's shoulder. He ran his finger down the numbers in the ledger. He looked up and checked the closed door, even though no one could enter unless he first unbolted the three slide bolts. He looked down at the ledger and grunted. The grunt, a question.

Being around him all the time, the Neanderthal language started to make sense. Harvey reached down, slid open the bottom drawer, stuck a finger in a slot, and pulled up the false bottom that revealed stacks of stolen cash skimmed off the top and now each banded with a thick, red rubber band.

Another grunt, this one of approval. Jackie patted Harvey's hair. "Good Propeller Head. And because you've been such a good boy, I'm gonna take you on a field trip."

"I really need to stay here and get this done." In fourteen hours, only three wicker baskets lay empty and overturned on their sides. Five to go.

The thick, strong hand took hold of his scruff and lifted him out of the chair. "When I say we're going on a field trip, Palie, what do you think that means?"

"That we're going on a field trip."

"Right-oh," He shoved hard. Harvey stumbled to the door and almost went to his knees. Sitting at the desk all those hours, numb legs needed a little more warning before going back into action.

Outside, the cool night air tasted grand.

The limo wove in and out of traffic, taking side streets to avoid the worst of it, and finally pulled up to the country club. The place he had lunch with Lois that first day. Nice expensive cars packed the parking lot. A team of valets dressed in white shirts, black pants, and red vests stood by at the ready.

Yellow light from the broad windows down one side splashed onto the perfectly manicured grass of the practice putting green. The men inside all wore black tuxedoes, the women elegant cocktail gowns. Diamond necklaces, bracelets, and rings reflected the light. Twinkled.

Jackie shoved again. "Come on, don't drag your ass. We'll miss the dinner. It's prime rib with mashed potatoes and gravy, light biscuits and real butter." The description uttered with an unbridled lust.

"Wait. Look at me. I haven't showered in two days. I'm not dressed for this kind of event. Look at my pants, they're torn, and my skinned knees are showing."

"Get in there. I won't tell you again. I'm not gonna miss a free meal, not one like this."

The hand again at the scruff of his neck. The vise-like squeeze. Jackie's mouth came up close enough to sense the humid reek. "We're going to sit and have a nice meal. Then we're going back to work. You're not going to say one damn word once we're in there. You understand?"

The double doors were opened automatically by a doorman to allow them in. The vast country club dining area had been commandeered for the event. Guests disbanded from small groups and moved around with cocktails, looking for their seats. Green salads were placed on chargers in front of each guest. Other servers filled wine glasses.

Jackie, his hand still on the back of Harvey's neck, guided them in and around tables to one empty with ten chairs and a "Reserved" card. "Right here, Propeller Head." He pulled out a chair and shoved Harvey down. The sight of the fat Jackie the Nose dressed in his gangster garb, a striped polo shirt and black slacks, abusing his charge caught everyone's attention. For just a moment, before everyone turned back to being self-centered snobs.

Jackie sat down and scooted his chair sideways—close, in case the Propeller Head lost his mind and made a break for the door. Jackie picked up the basket with fresh dinner rolls, dropped three on his plate, and slathered them with pads of real butter.

A live band over in the corner played soft music and suddenly stopped. They shifted quickly to the wedding march. All the guests froze and then struggled to their feet.

Not until that moment had it sunk in, the true purpose of being there. It wasn't for a free meal.

This was another one of those horrid little teaching moments.

"No. No. No. This can't be happening." Harvey tried to rise and flee to the door and out into the safety of darkness. Anything to get away and not see, not have the coming image emblazoned in memory for an eternity.

Jackie took hold and jerked him back down. The only two in the entire place are still sitting. He stuffed an entire dinner roll in his mouth. Some real butter slid off, smearing the corner of his lips. He wiped his mouth with the back of his hand. His words came out muffled. "Sit there like a good little tot and don't you dare say one word. You embarrass me, I'll whip you with my belt when we get back to the shop."

The crowd clapped. A multitude of gowns and tuxedos were the only things visible from the sitting position.

How God awful horrible.

The bride in all white satin and lace, the groom in a black tux, broke through the crowd. They moved to steps that led to the elevated table at the front of the room.

A table not ten feet away.

Lois turned. Not even a veil could mask her beauty. Her long black hair a stunning contrast to all the white.

Only the lack of a smile turned her into nothing more than a toy doll. The lack of enthusiasm obvious to everyone in the room. And yet no one made a move to do anything about it, their tacit fear palpable.

Abigail, her best friend, dressed in a gawd-awful purple thing, stood at a table filled with other bride's maids. Tears flowed down her cheeks. Not tears of joy, but tears of despair.

Giorgio's smile displayed perfect white teeth. He waved like some kind of fool as if the master of ceremonies sitting in the back of a convertible in a parade.

Mr. LaBruzzo sitting at the table closest to the married couple stood and raised his glass for a toast. The room turned quiet.

Just as Lois' eyes fell upon Harvey. The lack of her reaction hurt more than anything else. Mr. LaBruzzo's toast a blur of words incomprehensible while Lois' stare drilled into him. With each passing second Harvey shrunk smaller and smaller until he could hardly breathe.

Jackie the Nose leaned over and chuckled. "Some party huh? Thought you might enjoy it."

And still he stared at the woman he loved.

Jackie the Nose not getting the desired reaction continued. "You know the other day out by the pool at the boss' house, I saw Giorgio give that girl a kiss that…well, I gotta tell ya, that kiss gave me a little wood if you know what I mean." He elbowed Harvey. "Did you hear what I just said?"

Not looking away from Lois, Harvey said, "Half the room just heard what you said you buffoon."

A server placed a plate with a slab of prime rib in front of Jackie. The fresh meat a distraction that kept a fat fist from punching his lights out.

Everyone else still worked on their salads. Jackie grabbed the sleeve of the server. "Hey, pal, bring me two more just like this one, warm but still mooing."

He dumped the creamed horseradish on the meat, took up the knife and fork, and started in while talking around the beef. "I'll counsel you on that remark when we get outside. You understand? Don't make me get up from this meal. I won't be happy."

Someone in the audience tapped a knife to a glass. Giorgio continued the smile and raised his hand to pacify all the others who tapped in unison. He raised his new bride's veil. He put one hand on each cheek, pulled her in close, and kissed her.

She didn't close her eyes, and her expression didn't change. Once the kiss ended she went back to staring at Harvey. Those eyes ruining him, melting him down into a slab of meat the same as Jackie's prime rib.

Never in his life did he think the world could be so cruel.

Jackie chewed and spoke with his mouth full. "That's one nice piece of grade A tail, don't you think?"

"I can say without reservation that you will live to regret this."

Jackie dropped his knife that clattered on the plate. His face flushed red. Flecks of horseradish flew when he spoke. "No one talks to me like that. No one." He started to rise out of his chair.

Until Mr. LaBruzzo, at the other table, beaming up at his son, turned and glared at Jackie for disturbing the perfect country club evening. Jackie eased back into his seat. "I'll deal with you later."

"I can't wait."

"You little son of—" He caught himself in time and glared for a moment. Then, viciously cut a chunk of prime rib and shoved it into his gaping maw.

Mr. LaBruzzo turned his stare onto Harvey. Harvey sensed it but would not look away from Lois. If there had been any doubt about the plan hatched on the high seas, none remained.

He mouthed the words to Lois, "I love you."

Lois' expression remained stoic, unmoved by the silent words of devotion. The obvious finally became clear. That bastard Giorgio drugged her.

Chapter Nineteen

R
ita's head lay on Harvey Usher's lap while they both sat on the fainting couch in the sunken living room.

He said, "Don't stop now, tell me why you're here. What's you're ultimate goal?"

Her eyes remained on his. Her hand slowly came up, fingers toying with his shirt buttons. "I...ah—"

"I know it goes against the code of the con man, well, in this case, the con woman. Your edict is never, under any circumstances, *reveal* the con. But you have to admit what's happened does not come under normal circumstances."

Her chin quivered. More tears rolled down her cheeks. "I'm in trouble, Harv, deep trouble."

How could a person not feel obligated to do anything and everything to help this wounded little bird?

"I figured as much. Quit stalling."

"Be nice."

"You're here to rip me off. I just can't figure out how. I don't have any money. And now I'm running out of patience."

She turned her head and looked away, lips shifting to a pout.

"It might be easier if you just start from the beginning."

She turned back, eyes angry. "First, promise me...swear you won't testify against me and I'll tell you. You really need to know what I have to say. So, swear."

"Okay, I swear I will not testify against you. Now talk."

She sat up and nodded. "You don't have to sound so coarse about it."

"Rita?"

"Okay. I was arrested a while back for...for grand theft. This time I sat in jail pending trial. It was over a lot of money. A lot. And the mark...he had influence. A pillar in the community, French cuffs, tie pins, on the board of the country club. I was going away for a long stretch.

Harvey, that jail was absolutely horrid. The toilets are right out in the open where everyone can see your business. And...and at night these big ugly women roam the dorm looking for 'Fresh Fish.' Ugh. Awful, absolutely awful."

"What happened?"

"Just like that, you want to gloss over my ordeal? You don't want to first comfort me? At least a little?"

He gave her the evil eye.

"One day, I was sitting in Sybil Brand, that's the county jail. And the matron came to the dorm and said, "Roll it up, you've been bailed." I didn't care how it happened. I couldn't get out of that place fast enough. It smelled sour. Reeked of body odor and despair."

"Keep going."

"I didn't know anyone with that kind of money. The bail matched the amount of the theft—well attempted theft. I never saw a penny of the money I was accused of stealing."

"How much?"

"Two hundred and fifty thousand. But I found out later he didn't post the two-fifty. Instead, he got a high-powered mouthpiece to go into court on a bail reduction hearing. This guy who bailed me really has the juice."

"Who? Who are we talking about?" He knew but wanted to hear it from the horse's mouth.

"Andrew Johnson."

"That's not his real name, is it?"

She shook her head. "I don't know his real name."

"Why Rita? Why me?"

"Johnson somehow found out about the scams I ran on old folks. He came looking for me. He said he wanted to sponsor me, help me. He wanted to pull one or two small cons, see how I handled myself. Then go for a big one. One where I'd never have to work again. A ten or twenty-million-dollar job. We'd split fifty-fifty. I could change my name and live in Spain. Live in, 'the lap of luxury for the rest of my life.' That sounded so good when compared to prison for five to ten. Because I still had to answer for the case he bailed me out on. With that kind of money, I could run."

"What's the scam?"

"You really don't know?"

"Rita?"

"You know how much this house is worth?"

"What? Ah, we paid a hundred and fifty thousand for it."

"When?"

"About fifty years ago."

"A hundred and fifty was a lot of money that long ago. The online apps have this place appraised at five million."

"It's worth wha...Are you kidding me? This old heap of wood. Five million?"

She said nothing and stared.

"But how can that value get transferred to you?"

"It's simple, you own the house free and clear and—"

"The post-dated marriage certificate? Oh, dear Lord. And...and the police coming out when I called them that was all part of the scam. You *wanted* me to call the police, so it was documented that I was mentally diminished. That I didn't even know my own wife."

She reached over and put a hand on his leg. "I'm sorry, Harvey. You are a nice man, and I've grown to like you. A lot."

"But you were going to sell the house right out from underneath me? Put me on the street. I'd be living under a bridge in a cardboard box like some kind of troll."

"No, silly. We just applied for a mortgage. We planned on walking away with a cool two million dollars in a cashier's check negotiable anywhere."

"I'd have a house payment of two million dollars. I couldn't handle a nut that large."

"There would still be three million in equity. You could sell it, pay off the mortgage, and still have about…what two million to start over. It was a win-win on this for everyone."

"Not for me it wouldn't be. I'd take it in the shorts on this game of yours."

She shrugged, gave a coy, half-smile. "Such is life."

"How far have you gone. I mean with the bank?"

"The appraisal was the last thing we needed. Andy was here that day. You saw him in the kitchen. He did the appraisal, forged the name of an appraiser. But he still needed measurements to make it look legit. A floor plan drawn up with the square footage, doors, windows, that kind of thing. We are just days away from closing escrow and getting that check."

"What happened? What screwed the deal?"

She stared. She didn't want to say the next part. Not and incriminate herself. Even if I did swear not to testify against her.

He said, "I hired Gurski, that was it, wasn't it? And he got too close to what was going on, right?"

"Andy was afraid of what Gurski would do. When Andy found out, he didn't even blink. The man's a cold fish, a sociopath. He…he used my car to kill Gurski to frame me. He wanted the entire two million without having to split it. He set me up. I wouldn't have even suspected it had you not said something when I was driving us home from the police station. What am I going to do, Harv? He scares me to death."

"You know that car he's driving with the personalized real estate license plate?"

"Yeah, he said he needed it when he drove up to the bank to take out the loan. It was a prop for the con. Took the banker out to lunch. Andy said he had the woman eating out of his hand."

"He killed the realtor, drowned him in his own pool, and stole the car."

Tears again, not from angst and emotional trauma but from fear of Andrew Johnson. A fear she had every right to own. She was a living, breathing

THE OBSESSIONS OF HARVEY USHER

witness against him.

Something still wasn't right. "Why…I mean, how did you pick me as a target? Was it you or Andy?"

"Andy had the deal all set up when I walked out of Sibyl Brand. He said we do a couple of small jobs and then the big one. This would be the first small one. He drove me right over, briefed me on your history and on the entire setup."

"And the letters? Did you read the letters?"

She nodded. "We came in that first night after you fell asleep. We changed out the picture on the credenza. Took your wife out and put me in. Then I sat at the dining room table reading those lovely letters from your wife. You know, and I'm not just saying this, that if you put them all together in sequence, those letters would make a beautiful romance novel. I cried. I actually cried when she—"

"Did you read that top one, the unopened one?"

"I did not. I don't know why, but I didn't. To open it…I guess I'd feel like…well, a peeping tom of sorts. I'm not a dirty voyeur. The other letters, the ones you'd already read, you already knew about those. The unopened one, that was where I drew the line."

"Ah, crap."

"What, Harv, tell me."

"Can't you see you were played just like me."

"What are you talking about?"

"You need to leave right now. Run."

"Why? What are you talking about?"

"They're not after you. This wasn't about some two-bit real estate scam. It's deadlier than you think. If you run right now, maybe they'll forget about you, let you walk away from this thing."

Chapter Twenty

1968

Two hours later, the limo drove them back to the donut shop. The traffic had calmed, making the ride smoother. Less stop and go. Jackie sat back in the seat his eyes tented about to fall asleep. His belly rounder now filled with three of everything: three servings of prime rib, three glasses of red wine, three gin and tonics, three brandies, and three slices of wedding cake. Harvey, sitting across from him, could only sit back and stare blankly at the walrus-like beast while his mind locked on Lois and her total lack of expression. How her eyes stared at him the entire time.

Pure unadulterated torture.

Never had an all-encompassing darkness descended so quickly as when he saw her at that table.

Jackie raised his fat leg and shoved his foot into Harvey's knee. "Hey, some hoe-down huh, Propeller Head? The boss really knows how to do it right. Heard he dropped a bundle on that little soiree."

"Hmm."

"Talk to me. Maybe some of that intelligence will rub off on me."

Jackie was too sated to physically punish him for the smart-ass remark from earlier. He'd do it now with what he obviously believed was witty banter.

"You know what?" Jackie said, "That same day at the pool. You know what we were talkin' about earlier? When I saw that...that lascivious kiss?"

"That's a rather loquacious word for someone so provincial."

The ugly smile crept across Jackie's face. "I won't pound you into a pile of meat. Not tonight. I won't let you ruin this great buzz I got goin'. But you better check yourself when talkin' to me. I'm a boss. You remember that or pay the consequences."

"Hmm."

"Don't gimme that 'Hmm,' crap again."

"Yes, sir."

He gave me the eye. "Damn straight, giving me that hmm crap. I won't have it." He paused, letting the warning have time to seep in. "Anyway, right after he got done kissing her, you know, out there by the pool. She smiles and says, 'Hey Giorgio, my love, I got your gum.' You know because they were bangin' tongues and all. You know what Giorgio says? He says, 'No ya don't babe I gotta sinus infection.' Get it? Ya get it?" He kicked out with his leg and laughed until his face bloated red and he started coughing.

Harvey's stomach rolled and threatened to disrupt the limo's clean interior. Jackie knew how to be vicious with the black jack, but he could also cut right down to the bone with his words.

Harvey forced out a smile. "My friend, you had better be careful in your overly sated state. Someone might mistake your body, as it were, for an aberrant tumescence that—"

He stopped laughing and tried to sit up, but couldn't; the load of wedding cake in his belly worked against him. "My what? What did you just call me?"

"Nothing bad, I assure you. I'm just referring to your out-of-control vascular congestion that's taken over your entire…well, self."

"My tum-science what?"

The limo pulled up in front of Harvey's house. "I guess this is my stop." Harvey shot him a fake smile and got out before Jackie could decipher the last few sentences. He'd need a dictionary first. And then know how to use it. In all likelihood, by morning, he wouldn't remember anything of the conversation.

Harvey no sooner closed the door when the limo driver gunned it away from the curb.

He stood watching as the long, sleek car drove to the first intersection and made a left. The red brake lights disappeared into the night.

The sudden realization hit. Jackie the Nose left him standing on the sidewalk. Free for the first time in eight weeks and two days. He would never again take his freedom for granted.

The reason became painfully obvious. He was no longer a threat to Lois' relationship. An hour into the meal—an hour into Jackie's three-hour gorge-fest, Lois left with her new husband, Giorgio the despoiler, en route to their two-week honeymoon on a rented yacht in the Greek Isles. The mere thought of Lois' situation made a lump rise in his throat and choke off precious air.

He paced in the grassy front yard as his anxiety continued to rise. He would have to act or die.

He paced back and forth.

In the moon-bright evening, his eyes caught a glimpse of white up by the front door.

What was that?

He hurried up the steps to the porch and found a sealed envelope stuck in the outer screen door.

Lois.

How had she gotten a letter to his house? Only one way, really. Through her maid of honor, Abigail.

On the front of the envelope, written in a delicate feminine hand, it simply read, "*Harvey.*"

Shaky hands gently tore open the envelope as an overactive imagination tried and failed to predict the contents. Eyes blurred with tears that in turn blurred the world and the words in the one-page missive:

My dearest Harv.

I don't fault you for not coming for me. I know you would've if events and circumstances had allowed for it. You have a valiant heart, my love. The heart of a lion that would've done neither of us any good. You are no match for the likes of these...I dare not say it.

Those same events and circumstances have sealed my fate. I am not one to dwell on bad luck or the unfairness in the way of the world. Truly. I have now accepted this foregone destiny and can only hope you will take this note as a final good-bye and escape this life. Run Harv.

Please, just run.

Always yours,
Your most intimate confidant,
Lois

The idea that Giorgio The Despoiler now had Lois under his thumb, able to do with her whatever he pleased, hurt something fierce. Fat tears dropped on the inked letters, smearing words. He looked up suddenly to check and see if anyone was watching. She cared for him. She wanted him to run to safety.

Emotions shifted to a blue-white anger needing a release. If anyone had been around, they would've fallen prey to an unleashed violence like no one in the world ever experienced.

Instead, the shrubs in front of the house, the tall and beautiful gardenias and Jasmine, took the brunt. Thrashed, torn out by the root, and tossed willy-nilly about the yard.

Out of breath, chest heaving, he looked around at the end result. It looked as if a misdirected mortar shell fell from the sky and destroyed the picture-perfect front yard.

After a time, he carefully folded the envelope and tucked it into his shirt pocket.

Inside the dark house, one that now seemed alien, he left the lights off and still found the car keys on the kitchen counter. From the safe in the master bedroom, he took five thousand dollars in fives, tens, and twenties. He walked out to the car parked at the curb, started up, and drove off into the night.

The same car in which he'd kissed Lois for the first time. That wondrous kiss that carried so much meaning. The kiss that would withstand the ages of time.

He wouldn't run.

No way.

He wouldn't leave her to a "Foregone destiny." He'd kick destiny right in the ass.

Bold talk for a propeller head.

Twenty minutes later, he found the safe-house and parked three doors down. The sleeping neighborhood sat quietly except for the normal sounds: the mild breeze that rustled tree leaves, a barking dog, and someone watching late-night TV. The tire iron came out of the trunk in the hope that no one would be in the house. Why would there be if all the money still remained in the counting room above the donut shop, not yet transferred?

He'd start a small fire in a corner, then get out. Sit in the car and watch a house that belonged to Jackie the Nose burn to the ground. Strike a blow against tyranny, no matter how insignificant.

Not a peep came from the dark house. All the inside windows were covered. First with paper. Then on top of that tinfoil. To thwart the curious. Not one ray of light escaped.

If two thugs were in fact standing watch, then visitors were expected to enter through the garage. Only approved guests had garage door openers: the owner/employer, Jackie the Nose, and employees—the thug guards. If the guards were present, knocking on the front door would put them on high alert and risk life and limb.

But life and limb no longer carried the same value.

No one responded to the knock. Not even a peep of sound came from inside. The second knock instigated footsteps that thumped on the hardwood floors, a wooden foundation supported by pilings underneath. The porchlight remained off. The door opened a crack. "Who are you? Whatta ya want?"

Harvey surreptitiously tossed the tire iron into the shrubs and fanned the five thousand dollars. The only way to communicate with the baser species was with money. Especially money they didn't have to earn. Slade's words about guns on that moonlit night struck hard and fast. Time for plan B. "Open the damn door."

Whispering came from inside.

The door opened. Back in shadowed relief, a thug in tan khaki pants and a white sling tee shirt wielded a 12-gauge pump shotgun. The large black hole at the barrel's end threatened mayhem and death. The man said, "You're the propeller head. The ledger man, right?"

Harvey's insides shook with fear. He said nothing. Entered. Pushed on past like he owned the place. "I'm bored. I came to play some poker. You boys up to it?"

The thug closed the door and bolted all three slide bolts. "Hell yeah. We're up for takin' your money. Come on in, dough-boy."

Inside smelled of sour body odor, fried grease, and cigarette smoke.

These were the same two men from eight weeks ago. But if all the money was in the counting room over the donut shop, what were they guarding?

Harvey sat down first and fanned the money out on the kitchen table. "We're not really going to use toothpicks as poker chips, are we?" He gingerly picked up the shotgun on the table, set it on the floor, and slid it closer to the wall. The steel, warm in hand, the weight inordinately heavy.

The thug who answered the door said. "Hell no." He tossed his shotgun on the couch before coming into the kitchen.

"So, if memory serves, you're Tommy Lee and you're Jimmy?"

Jimmy turned the chair around and sat in it backward, forearms resting across the top. Tommy said, "Tommy Tee, not Lee."

"Oh, right. Sorry."

Tee said, "Jackie know you're here?"

"What do you think?"

"Huh. Yeah. You wouldn't risk your scalp comin' here without telling him."

Jimmy leaned in. "We gonna jaw-jack all night or we gonna play some cards?"

"My money's on the table, proof I'm serious. Where's yours?"

Tee looked at Jimmy.

No money was allowed while playing cards in the safe-house. If one of them lost, he might convince the other to make a foolish decision and take down the backroom filled with Mr. LaBruzzo's cash. A fatal mistake. But greed ruined the world in the past and would in the future.

Had LaBruzzo been smart, instead of two thug guards he should've had three. The odds were far better that two might get together and decide to steal the million and a half. But with three thugs the odds greatly favored less cohesion and stronger security. All Mr. LaBruzzo had to do was ask, and Harvey would've told him. Numbers never lie.

Jimmy and Tee both signed IOU's on paper napkins from the local pizza joint. Each for fifteen hundred. A huge amount of money, especially when considering an average house sold for fifteen to twenty thousand dollars.

The game started off in a bad way with Harvey losing the first six hands. With each loss, the piles of cash in front of the other two grew. They laughed and joked. They asked several times if he wanted to come back sometime soon.

"Why are you boys here in the first place? I've been gone. All the money is over—" He stopped short of giving away the donut shop counting room, the name, and or the location. Maybe those two didn't have a need to know.

Tommy Tee let out a gleeful snicker as he pulled in another fat pot. "That's cause while you were gone, Cadillac Frank, him and his crew from up on the northside—that crew gets all the best jo—"

"Don't," Jimmy said. "Jackie said mum's the word on that job. That means don't say a damn thing about it."

Tommy Tee said, "Stop it. This guy's our friend. He's one of us. Aren't you Propeller Head?"

"I am. And you've whetted my curiosity. Please continue."

"Don't."

Tommy shook his head, smug about possessing information wanted by someone else, something that rarely occurred. "Listen ta the way this guy talks, it cracks me up. I'll tell ya why, Junior, if you promise to come back once a week ta play cards." He stuck out his hand to shake.

"You have a deal." The man had a grip that could crush walnuts. Slippery with a disgusting dampness.

"Fine. Cadillac Frank hit a transport plane at JFK, a plane from Suisse Bank or some shit. I know I got the name wrong. I don't speak German."

"It's Swiss, not German, you idiot."

The robbery of that transport company had been all over the news. The police were still scrambling, jacking up every crook, grifter, and hooker looking for a lead and had found nothing. The amount of the theft had been kept from the news.

Tommy shuffled the cards and started to deal. "There's two million in that back room, LaBruzzo's taste for the job. If two mil was only his percentage from one job, can you imagine what the take was?"

Harvey picked up his cards. "Yes, I can. Twenty million."

"How the hell you know that? Were you there or something?"

Jimmy grunted. "You are an idiot. You forget he's the Ledger Man?"

"No, I wasn't there, but it's simple math. Mr. LaBruzzo gets ten percent."

"Ten percent of twenty million is two million?"

"Oh my God, Tee, play your cards. Your skirt jus' slipped up and showed your dunce cap. It's Jacks or better to open, play. Bet. Shit or get off the pot."

Tommy Tee tossed in two fifties. "There, whatta you think about them apples?" He turned back to Harvey. "Guess what else?"

"Tommy! Quit."

Tommy smirked and waved off his best friend, his partner in crime.

Harvey looked into Tommy's eyes that were black as obsidian. Ignorance could be more dangerous than a hair trigger on a loaded sawed-off shotgun.

Harvey said, "If I had to guess, I'd say that since the plane was a Suisse transport, that means there are two million in gold bullion back in that room and not cash."

"Got-damn, you gotta brain on ya. But you missed this one. You were close, though. It's gold bars."

Harvey couldn't help himself and chuckled.

Jimmy glared. "Don't you dare laugh at my friend."

"Sorry. You're right, that was boorish of me. Tommy, please accept my apology."

Apparently, Jimmy thought he had a modicum of pride even though he'd also planted men in the Meadowlands, marrying any and all integrity imagined or otherwise. Harvey recently heard about one of Jimmy's heinous acts. The story came out one night on the high seas on the way back to the States. Another night when Slade drank too much, "Busthead," liquor. He talked about school. A girlfriend of LaBruzzo that LaBruzzo had grown tired of was handed over to Jimmy. Jimmy wasn't kind in the method used on the poor woman before, "Planting her." And Slade wasn't miserly with the details. And should've been. After that drunken evening, nightmares followed for several nights. In the end, Slade warned about staying away from Jimmy and Tommy Tee, said they cared not for human life.

But who did in that mob world?

Alcohol was strictly forbidden in the safe-house, but in their gleeful greed, one chrome flask wrapped in thin, tight leather came out. Then another. Tommy Tee offered it to Harvey, who took it and stuck his tongue on the opening, not allowing any to pass. The side effects of alcohol fogged the mind and eased inhibitions. In the wrong direction.

Two hours later, down to three hundred dollars, Harvey decided to unleash his "Propeller Head—brain," and started counting cards with due diligence toward playing the favorable percentages of chance. Tommy Tee and Jimmy turned quiet and morose as the piles in front of them diminished a little more with each hand. The glee-filled boyishness disappeared. Left in its wake were brutish thugs, angry and having a difficult time holding back a vengeful wrath.

Tommy Tee lost a huge pot. He jumped up. His chair flew back and hit the wall. "You're a cheatin' card sharp." He swayed as he tilted back the flask, finishing off the last gulp.

"Really? If I'm cheating, what's my method? How am I doing it? I can guarantee you this is nothing more than a long stretch of luck."

He took a deep drag off the Camel and flicked the butt into the living room. It landed on the green high-low carpet close to all the previous ones. Ash embers that smoldered and burnt black holes, extinguishing all on their own. A flammable proposition with potential to rain down hellfire on all of them. The burnt chemical reek permeated the entire area; kitchen, living room, and dining room.

"I...I don't know for sure. But no one's that lucky. No one, damnit."

Jimmy said, "There's no luck involved. It's all about numbers and percentages."

Not necessarily true. A pro could read the "tells" of each player at the table and have a better than average chance of overcoming the numbers and percentages. This, according to Hoyle's first edition of "A Gentleman's Book of Poker Hands." Something read on the trip down to the Caymans. Slade had a number of intriguing gambling books. Black Jack held the most promise in making a great deal of money at a gambling establishment.

"Sit down, Tee. He's not cheatin'. We're the *fools* for playing cards with a brainiac." Jimmy threw in his cards. "I don't think it's right for you to hold us to those IOUs. You played us."

Harvey reached out and raked in all the money except what remained in front of each man: a hundred and fifty in front of Tommy Tee and two hundred for Jimmy. "As you know, I'm not intimately familiar with your world, but I don't think the...ah, rumor that you two are welshers will not serve you well."

"Why you little chickenshit piece of—"

Jimmy again grabbed ahold of Tommy Tee and restrained him. Jimmy leaned up and whispered in Tommy's ear.

The liquor worked on both of them, sanding off the rough edges to their combined cache of common sense, one already in serious shortage. Jackie the Nose once said about his two safe-house thugs, "For them two, when God was handin' out the brains, someone jiggled his elbow." An odd affirmation for such great responsibility.

Tommy's words seeped out. "You dumbass he tells Jackie we're playing cards and gambling in here, it'll be our asses. Adiós muchachos. A one-way ticket to the Meadowlands with a stove-in head."

Jimmy let an ugly little sneer creep out, similar to the one Jackie the Nose used a moment before Bertha goes to work. He wagged his finger. "Wait,

I don't think Jackie knows about Propeller Head's little visit. Why would Jackie allow it? For what reason? To play poker? I don't think so. You know what, Tommy? We got this little pecker head by the short-and-curlies."

"I think you're right, partner. We can tear him a new asshole and he can't say a damn thing to Jackie about it."

"Now just hold it." The threat had a strong bite to it. "Let's make a deal, okay?"

"What kind of deal?" Jimmy asked.

"Forget the deal, let's have some fun with his asshole. It'll make the time go by faster."

"Wait. I'll give you three hundred dollars plus tear up these IOUs"

Tommy took a step, coming around his chair. "Hah. We'll tear 'em up our ownselves and keep all the money. You won't be able to do a damn thing about it."

Jimmy chuckled. "That's right, partner. Leave his face alone, just hit him below the neck."

"Wait. A thousand each. I just want two things from you."

"Tommy, wait, let him talk. We got nothin' ta lose."

"Nah, he's got nothin' I wanna hear."

He moved toward Harvey, who backed into the living room.

"I just want two .357 magnums. But they have to have long barrels. Six-inch barrels if you can get them."

Tommy paused mid-step, his expression turned to confusion as his mind tried in vain to process this complex conundrum. "Why do you need guns? You're the Ledger Man."

Harvey stopped backing away and straightened up. "That's right. *That's right.* I *am* the Ledger Man. And you know what that means. That means I have Mr. LaBruzzo's ear. You two forgot that part. I have the absolute ability to call him on the phone. Or even stop in at his house. He'll talk to me anytime, day or night. Do you two have that kind of juice? All I have to do is whisper a couple of well-placed sentences like there *might be* some money missing from the house on Daisy Street."

Tommy lost the color in his face. "You wouldn't do that, would you?"

"Shut up, partner. Let me think." He looked down at his feet while his mind worked a problem too complex for his brain-housing-group to decipher. He looked up. "Okay. Two guns."

"Magnums with six-inch barrels."

"We get the grand apiece now?"

"That's right. No problem."

"And…and we drop the guns off at your house. We don't see you here again. Ever."

"Wrap them in oil cloth and stash them in the barbecue on the back porch."

"And we don't talk about this ever. If someone like Jackie asks us about this, we clam up. We know nothing. You understand?"

"Absolutely."

Tommy said. "What's he gonna do with the guns, Jimmy? He might think he can bump us off and take all that gold."

"Smarten up. You think a guy like this rube can go up against two hardened operators like us?"

Harvey counted out the bills giving them each a thousand dollars. "And you have shotguns against two pistols, a real mismatch. But in truth, if you must know, in the count house, I feel vulnerable. I'm there by myself. Anyone from a rival…er, group could come and take down all that money. If that happened, even if I lived through it, I would be suspect."

"That's true," Tommy said.

The prospect of money put a smile on their faces. But only for a second. Jimmy said, "Now get the hell out. Don't ever come back. I mean it, too. Don't ever come back here."

The front door closed, cutting off the last vestige of light.

Standing in the yard, a devastating feeling of doom descended on his nervous system, one that made muscles in all four limbs shake. He muttered to no one. "No way will I walk away from this alive.

No way."

Chapter Twenty-One

1968

T he next day, after too little sleep, the limo driver knocked at the front door and drove Harvey to the donut shop. A different driver. "What happened to the other guy?"

The driver said nothing and hit the button to roll up the window separating the driver's compartment. The organizational hierarchy of the mob didn't require the driver to talk. The Ledger Man was important and, at the same time, not. A true paradox.

Hole-in-One-Donut shop coffee and a bear claw for breakfast held off the hunger until dinner. The dirty money, the ones, fives, tens, twenties, and the rare fifty, left his hands almost black from grime. Mob money always came from the lower socio-economic strata, the working man. Overused money from blue-collar hands.

Concentration flagged. With the monotony of the job, the green money eventually disappeared, turning into mere paper. Minor numbers that floated by without end. A full-grown man counting paper was no different than a kid who played Monopoly.

An uneventful week passed.

The day-after-day dreariness, counting money, working the ledger, eating and sleeping, was interspersed only with thoughts of Lois. Her lovely countenance. Her eyes. That wonderful kiss. And the amount of time left before she returned home. Was it normal to be so besotted with such limited contact and only one kiss?

To think about the two million dollars in gold sitting in the backroom on Daisy Street made his hands shake. Did he have the nerve to pull it off? Did he have the nerve to strike a blow against those who raped, robbed, and murdered innocent people with impunity? Do something that would cause a domino effect of pain and suffering meted out to those in the criminal organization? A little Quid Pro Quo. No guilt there. It would be to those who deserved it most.

A different kind of guilt, more than anything other argument, made up his mind. If he pulled it off without a hitch, he'd have something to show Lois when she returned. A big *something* that would have to put a smile on her morose expression. And if he fumbled the ball and was killed, would it matter? At least he'd have tried.

Five more days passed with his numerical mind constantly working the variables in the plan. The first and foremost being the weight. Gold sold for forty dollars an ounce. Two million in gold came to 3100 pounds. That's a one and a half tons, give or take a few ounces. Greed had no place in the plan. Money and wealth no longer mattered. Just revenge. Even if the gold did nothing more than disappear.

My God, a ton and a half, though.

A '68 Chevy Nomad weighed 3300 pounds. The weight of the gold is the same as a car.

He was only one man.

How in the world could he move that much weight by himself and get away with it?

Impossible.

The morning of that fifth day, he sat up in bed. The absurdly simple answer came to him in a dream. He chuckled.

Laughed until the move onto the next question: how to overcome the two gargoyles assigned to guard Mr. LaBruzzo's little nest of gold. Jimmy and Tee lived in a world of violence, one where Harvey had never ventured. Slade had said that when the time came, "The person that wins is the first one to pull the trigger." Which equated to zero hesitation. "Don't even think about it. Step in and go to guns. Bam. Bam. Bam."

He hadn't thought to check the barbecue on the back porch for the two .357 magnums. Why? If he couldn't figure out the weight problem. After work on the fifth day since the decision to go through with it—two days until Lois returned—he waited until dark to step out onto the back porch. Held his breath when he opened the lid to the barbecue.

Wrapped in multiple red grimy garage rags, he found two guns, both .357s. One with a six-inch barrel, the other a snub nose. The one with the short barrel wouldn't work nearly as well. Jimmy and Tommy Tee not only kept their word about the guns, but they also left a box of .357 magnum ammunition.

Perfect.

In his house with all the windows closed and the doors locked, he went to work at the kitchen table. First, he opened a box of *Orange Minis*. Tiny jaw-breakers. Candy for kids. Popped one in his mouth and started sucking. Not a real candy person, but the sweetness did taste nice. Next, he dumped out all the bullets from the box of fifty. Long, ugly, lethal little things. He used pliers to pull off the lead noses and wrapped the noses up in one of the red garage rags to discard later. Some place far from home.

The gunpowder from each shell was dumped into a cereal bowl, one used to eat oatmeal on the mornings the limo driver came late.

He wasn't paying close enough attention. The impending threat of the robbery clouded a normally analytical mind. He had sucked the Orange Mini down to nothing. Didn't really notice until it completely dissolved.

Damn.

He tried again. This time, popping five into his mouth. He got up and paced, going over everything Slade had said that first night they headed back to the States from the Grand Caymans.

* * *

On the sailboat, daylight handed off to a moonless sky. The millions of stars supplied plenty of ambient light. The vast, sparkly dome dwarfed all humankind and made life insignificant.

Several hours into the journey, the wind died altogether, and the endless sea turned to a motionless lake. What sailors called the "Doldrums."

When they had first left the harbor, Slade had started to explain how to kill someone. He abruptly clammed up after only a few words. Probably thinking about what Jackie would do to him if he found out. And one way or another, Jackie somehow found out about everything. But Slade kept drinking and up rose his alcohol courage in a countenance flushed red and rheumy eyes. Soon, without prompting, he again started talking.

"The biggest mistake assholes make when setting out to commit a crime is their lack of planning. They gloss over the details. Details that every time without exception rise up and bite them in the ass.

Each decision, each choice they make, should be given careful consideration in how it will play out in court. How the prosecutor will come at you. Then side-step resolve each of those pitfalls. The biggest being evidence. Guns have sealed many a fate of a numskull gunsel. You see, we never catch the smart ones. That's a huge secret the district attorney keeps from the public."

"Okay, then tell me how to do it? How do you kill someone with a gun and get away with it?"

A knife or blunt object was unacceptable. Too personal. Too up close. Too yuck. With a gun, it was just a matter of pointing and pulling the trigger. Do it from an impersonal distance.

"The rifling in the barrel called, 'lands and grooves,' are unique to each weapon. When a bullet is fired it spirals down the barrel and the lead is scarred by those lands and grooves. You shoot someone, the bullet is left behind forever linked to that gun. It can and will be linked. They are now even linking the shell casings to the individual guns based on the striker, the firing pin. Which is also unique to each gun."

"You're not helping. I asked how *you* would do it."

"With candy. Specifically, hard candy. I've been thinking about this for a long time. As far as I know, no one has ever tried it."

"Explain. Candy? Really?" Too much rum caused Slade to spew forth a fantastical theory that, once viewed sober in the light of day, would never hold up. When questioned the next morning, he would inevitably scratch his head, "Did I really say that?"

"Look. You can't leave any shell casings at the scene. You can't leave any expended bullets in the body, in the wall or the grandfather clock. That's all damning evidence to a jury if any of it is recovered and linked to a gun. That's why when a mob guy shoots someone, they drop the gun and walk away. They put rubber bands around the stock to thwart any fingerprints."

"Okay, that sounds good."

"Until we pull fingerprints off that gun cylinder and from those shell casings inside the cylinders. We can also track where the gun comes from. If you're going to do this, one of your biggest hurdles will be finding a cold gun. And...And distancing yourself from that gun once you use it. The guy that gave you the gun is now a witness against you linking you to the gun."

"You still haven't explained the candy idea."

"If it were me, I'd use two cold guns. Magnums with six-inch barrels. One for each hand."

The specific detail in his explanation lent credence to the theory he started to explain. He now sounded like he did actually know the topic and wasn't talking, "out the left side of his ass." A vulgar colloquialism, Jackie the Nose liked to use regarding his numbskull employees.

"How do magnums and candy work together?"

"Look. There was this case back when I was a rookie DA. This is what gave me the idea. This detective believed he had a murder and arrested the ex-wife of the victim. When it was actually a suicide. Once they looked into the guy's background they found he had tried to kill himself a couple of times before. Did it just to get attention in some kind of misguided way. But in this particular instance he pulled the head—the bullet—out of the shell and put the shell back in the rifle. He did this outside the presence of his ex-wife. Now with his ex-wife as a witness he put the rifle barrel in his mouth. The man didn't think the gun would hurt him if there wasn't a bullet in the shell casing. He begged his ex to come back to him. When she refused, he pulled the trigger and blew half his head away."

"Huh. From the pressure generated in the barrel. It had to go somewhere."

"Exactly."

"So, if I understand what you're saying. I'm to pull the bullets off the shell casings and replace them with hard candy."

"Right. The candy has to be seated as firmly as you can get with enough room to allow the revolver's cylinder to rotate unobstructed."

"But that would mean—" The physics ran slipshod through a confused mind. The weight of the candy, the velocity, the drag from the coefficient of friction. Numbers, formulas. "That would mean I would have to…I mean the gun would have to be put right up against the guy's head."

"Yes, it would. The candy is just there to hold the gunpowder in the shell, so it doesn't fall out until you're ready. You'll have to get in real close to Jackie. Which won't be a problem. He doesn't see you as any kind of threat. To him you're a house mouse. I've seen you around him. You're actually perfect for this job."

"Jackie? Who said anything about Jackie?" How had he figured out the target? Was it that obvious? Would other people also see him as a suspect?

"Don't play me for a chump."

"If that's the case, aren't you now just like the would-be guy who sold me the gun?"

"No."

"Why?"

"Because you could claim I'm a co-conspirator *and* make it stick in court. I want that pig-faced asshole dead more than anyone on this planet. I can't do it because one, I don't have the balls for it, and two, he'd never let me get close enough to him."

"I understand the reason for the magnums and behind the longer barrel to burn all the gunpowder and generate more pressure, but why two guns?"

"It's a safety bumper in case you screw up. If for some reason Jackie tumbles to you as you move in. At five, ten feet that candy will come screaming out of that gun barrel. It won't kill him from a distance, but if you aim for the face it'll stun the crap outta him. May even disable him and give you enough time to walk right up and finish the job point blank.

Contact wound." Slade put two fingers to his temple, his thump acting like the gun hammer.

"But there's six shots in a revolver. You still haven't explained the, "why," in having two guns."

Slade leaned over close and spoke. In the still night air his breath was humid and heavy with the sugary scent of rum. "If you use all six and that fat bastard isn't dead then that second gun—"

"*Is for me.*"

Slade smiled and nodded.

Chapter Twenty-Two

Current Day

Harvey sat on the fainting couch with Rita's head resting on his lap, her eyes closed. She'd just confessed to the scam, the purpose of her presence in the house. Her cheeks still wet from tears. Genuine this time.

With her eyes closed, he could stare at those wonderful lips with impunity.

Until she suddenly moved. "Harv. What are you talking about?" One eye opened and peeped him. "What did you mean when you said I need to run? You sound like you know something more than I do about what's going on. What is it?"

"No, I don't. It's just this Andrew Johnson fellow has already killed two people...that we know about. He has nothing to lose."

She closed that eye. "You're probably right, but right now, right this minute, I'm so darn tired I just want to curl up in a corner somewhere and sleep forever."

"That's a definite symptom of depression."

"Can I just rest here a moment? Just a moment without Dr. Harv with his Sears and Roebuck diploma, giving me a psychological diagnosis? All I need is just twenty minutes, Baby, then we can deal with the rest of the world. Go on the run like you said. You'll go with me when we run, won't you, Harv? I'd like that. I just don't know what we'd do for money."

Money. There it was again, the root of all evil.

The last image of Sylvia rose up vivid and all too real. Her eyes milky in death, skin waxy, lips purple. Nothing like Sylvia of old. Nothing like Lois that warm day on the highway, the day of that kiss.

Poor Sylvia.

That last image for the last two years he tried like hell to stuff back into a corner of memory never again be brought out into the light of day. A lump grew in his throat as emotions took over. A vacant hole opened up that begged to be filled. He was nothing more than a doddering old fool who stood on a precipice looking down into a dark abyss. A darkness that wanted him for the violent indiscretions back on Daisy Street in Hoboken, an abyss that smiled and beckoned. Indiscretions, too soft a word.

Rita's eyes remained closed. His hand all on its own rose up and stroked her soft hair. Oh, how he missed Sylvia…missed Lois.

"Hmm, thank you, Harv. That's very nice. And you have no reason at all to be nice to me. I was going to rob you blind."

"None of us are without our faults."

Now the memory of the night on Daisy Street in Hoboken flashed in freeze frame slow-motion. The two magnums filled with candy bullets. The struggle. The gunshots.

"It's strange, but I feel really safe with you." She reached up and put her hand on his arm. The weight from the move lowered his hand until it naturally took a position on an ample breast. A place where any red-blooded American man would yearn to be. Not him. Not in that moment.

Had she made the move on purpose while continuing to play a longer game?

Did he care?

Her breathing slowed. Two minutes later a cute little snore emitted from those red painted lips.

He missed Sylvia something fierce, but after two grief-filled years with all the lingering anguish, the woman on his lap taught a new kind of lesson. How, no matter what happens, human life is insignificant. Time always marches on, never slowing for anyone.

Once, when his father tried to describe The Big Bang, the origins of the universe, the age of the universe, he said, "In comparison, the sixty—eighty years each of us roam this planet is nothing more than a popcorn-fart."

Harvey lifted the hand from her breast. She turned from her back to her side, that button nose inches from the button on his shirt. "Harv, you are always the consummate gentleman. Give me twenty minutes, just a short little nap, and then I'll be right as rain." Her hand came up, took hold of his, brought it down to stroke her own hair. Twice.

Her hand let go and fell away. She emitted a feline-like utterance, a purr, and snuggled in.

No doubt about it, she was on the make. She wanted to secure the foundation needed for an escape from a danger that lurked on the other side of the metaphorical front door. Why choose an elderly man who had difficulty walking, let alone running? A rude and unfair assumption popped into his head: she must think money is hidden somewhere in the house, money needed to aid in their flight.

But he didn't care. Not in that moment.

Time slowed. The ticking grandfather clock grew louder than normal.

The conundrum as to whether Andrew Johnson worked on his own or as a puppet for the LaBruzzo family swirled around and around, ticking off the pros and cons. The biggest part of that question, though: if it was the LaBruzzo's, then why now? Why, after fifty years, would they decide to come looking for him to exact revenge now? What had changed? Had the last five decades of constant fear, the perpetual looking-over-the-shoulder, been their long game of torture?

Mission accomplished. He had not slept through an entire night without getting up at least once to check all the windows and doors. Didn't go anywhere without first peeping the street to see if it contained a throng of beady-eyed broken-nosed thugs who bristled with weapons of violence.

What kind of life was that?

No way. Couldn't be. The LaBruzzos liked their revenge served up hot and messy and most of all immediate. No. Something had definitely changed. The LaBruzzos still had the Lois and Harvey of old on their books and had somehow figured out their hiding place.

CHAPTER TWENTY-TWO

Now Rita wanted to go on the lam and continue that same five-decades-long fear.

Was she really sleeping at a time like this? He continued to gently stroke the soft red hair.

Forty minutes later, a sound came from the front door. The pressure in the room shifted. Back out of view in the hall, the front door had opened.

Harvey held his breath.

A second later in padded the big tabby cat, who'd been out in the front yard looking up into the big elm. The cat came in as if he owned the place. He carried a red robin firmly ensconced in his mouth. The large domestic feline stopped, turned its head, and looked into the living room. Those weird eyes could give anyone the willies.

One tiny bit of blood dripped from the wretched bird. That same cat had often come into the house when Sylvia was alive. But not in the last two years. How odd for it to enter now.

Right behind him, the noise of loud feet woke Rita, who sat bolt upright. "What? What's going on?"

The cat bolted, disappearing down the hall with its feast. Sure-to make a mess of feathers and blood.

Esther and Lissette appeared haggard and worn out. The death of Eddie the day before—the horrible grief, coupled with the trip to the Blue Ocean Motel, the trip over to Casa Blanca, then the hour or so trolling the streets looking for Andrew Johnson and Aussie Mike, took its toll.

Lissette espied Rita and tromped right over. "This her? This is her, isn't it?"

Rita said, "Harv, who is this unruly woman and what's she doing in our home?"

Harv ignored the question one sure to cause conflict and asked. "Esther, why did you let that cat into the house with a dead bird to boot?"

Esther shrugged. "You know that Barney's my cat. He just followed us. I didn't think he'd come into the house. He bolted in when I opened the door."

Lissette kept eyes on Rita. "I won't ask again, is this Delores Templeton?"

Rita stood. "That's me. Who's asking?" The spiked heels made her two inches taller than Lissette.

Then it all happened too fast for Harvey to react.

Lissette quick-stepped over and shoved Rita, who back-peddled and plopped down onto the divan. Before Rita could respond, Lissette straddled Rita's lap and wrapped fingers around that delicate, alabaster neck. "Eddie was my—"

Over by the entry hall, two men stepped down into the living room. The one in the expensive black leather jacket and buzzcut hair said, "The door was open, so we invited ourselves in. Hope you don't mind." He pointed back the way he came. "Does that Chevy Tahoe belong to anyone here?"

The Australian accent was unmistakable. Aussie Mike had entered without any force and now controlled the room and everyone in it. Controlled the entire house.

Chapter Twenty-Three

1968

H arvey leaned forward, resting his head on the steering wheel, his car now parked on Daisy, two houses down from the safe-house. The moonless night sickening in its blackness. An evil blackness. No wonder people feared the dark. Back at the house, he'd loaded the car with the two guns, a wood chisel, and the largest sledgehammer he could wield. Did it just before throwing up. Then threw up two more times. Nothing remained in his stomach. But that didn't stop the nervous tremors or the dry heaves.

That night on the boat, Slade described and in great detail the method that would take out Jackie once and for all. And if that worked, even Giorgio. To rescue Lois.

But two battle-proven thugs in the house on Daisy? Would the same plan work? Logic dictated the odds of success were seriously diminished, taking out two at once with candy guns.

Slade had said. "In that limo with Jackie, don't hesitate. You hesitate, you're dead. Remember. Always. Always. Act. Act. Act."

Tomorrow, Lois came home from...from her honeymoon. And worse—if it could be any worse—the day before yesterday, Jackie the Nose came to the apartment above the counting room. He watched the count and the entries going into the ledger for four hours, twenty-one minutes, and fifteen seconds. Watched his skim money going in the drawer with the false bottom.

He had never been that attentive. He'd come to watch before but always fell asleep on the couch after eating his fill of Little Debbie chocolate cupcakes and six half-pint cartons of chocolate milk. But the day before yesterday, instead, he sat across the desk with his pig-eyes taking in every move until he finally spoke. The words came out cloudy, in distinct. Harvey was too wrapped up playing out a lethal scenario right here in the office. The one where he suddenly stands and shoves the .357 magnum with the six-inch barrel across the short distance over the desktop. Shove it right into his face. And without hesitation, pull the trigger. Jerk it six times. The loud bangs. The blinding flashes filled the room. Jackie the Nose disappearing in the white fog created by the gun smoke.

But every time in that hellish scenario Jackie reappears, his face mangled. Baby Bertha in his hand ready to mete out mayhem.

Slade having played a terrible joke on an ignorant propeller head who bought into a crazy theory about candy bullets. Once it was all put together in a long string, it even sounded insane to Harvey.

To successfully shoot Jackie with a candy bullet in the counting room would point a big ugly finger at you know who. Mr. LaBruzzo would have every degenerate street thug from two states gunning for the poor Propeller Head who had nowhere to hide. And to kill Jackie outright truly wasn't fair to all the other poor victims with caved-in heads and buried out in the Meadowlands.

No. Jackie needed to suffer.

Jackie was entrusted with the gold. No matter what happened he couldn't dodge the blame if the gold went missing. Mr. LaBruzzo couldn't let the error go unpunished or he'd seem weak.

Yes. Yes. Stick to the plan. Stealing the gold killed, wounded or hurt everyone up the line.

Later on, that same day after Jackie got up and left, the pressure off, the urge to go through with the cold-blooded murder, words Jackie had said on the mental rewind returned.

Jackie wanted the loot at the safe-house transported to the Caymans. When though? Two days. He'd said two days, right? That forced Harvey's hand. Do the crime or forget about it altogether.

From the box of fifty bullets, he made twelve candy-tipped bullets and six extras to test fire. In his closed-up bathroom with balled-up toilet paper in his ears, he yanked back on the trigger.

The gun hardly kicked. The horrific noise overcame the make-shift ear protection and made them ring. Billowing white smoke filled the room and coalesced into a smooth cloud bank. The *Orange Mini* hit the tile and disintegrated, leaving a white skid mark. The method would work, but the gun had to be in direct contact with the head. The mere thought of getting that close made his hands shake.

* * *

Out in the car in front of the Daisy Street address, Harvey took a deep breath, let it out and exited. He eased the door closed, reached in, and grabbed the long-handled sledgehammer. Under his shirt, the two guns in the front waistband sweated as if living entities. But that wasn't really the case. His hot skin oozed sweat that turned the blue steel slick with dampness.

He tried to put all else from his mind and focused on those three words. "Act. Act. Act."

But that didn't work. Instead, in Slade's other words, the reason for the second gun nagged and worried him.

Of course, that had to be the way this whole thing would end. The second gun put to his own head. Bam. End of story.

On the porch, he set the hammer down beside the door and knocked. The hammer there in case no one opened the door.

Footsteps on the wooden floor approached.

Dizziness ensued as an already rapid heart rate took off at a gallop.

Lightheaded.

The door opened a crack. Tommy Tee said over his shoulder. "Hey Jimmy, tonight's entertainment just arrived." Tommy swung the door open, reached out, grabbed him by the shirt, and jerked him into the house. Tommy slammed the door with one hand while his other held a fist full of shirt.

But the shirt had pulled up, exposing both guns.

Tommy Tee was too close to see the hidden threat.

Jimmy had been walking over, the shotgun left back on the table. His eyes grew large. He took a step back to get the shotgun. Thought better of it and changed direction. "Gun! He's got a gun!"

Time hung like a fat bubble on a bright blue day. Harvey wanted to act but stood frozen inside that bubble.

Time grabbed hold and took off at full speed. He yanked the .357 from his waistband. The wrong one. The one with the short barrel. The one meant for himself if he failed.

Tommy Tee heard the warning from Jimmy, and instead of reacting the correct way by knocking out all of Harvey's teeth, he turned to look at Jimmy coming his way.

No time to think.

Harvey stuck the gun under Tommy Tee's chin and pulled the trigger. The gun bellowed but was muffled by the barrel surrounded by skin. The powerful, super-heated gases slammed the orange bit of candy upward. Skin parted. Teeth blew out with bits of tongue.

Tommy grunted and started to wilt. Harvey shifted positions, stuck the gun against Tommy's forehead, and jerked the trigger two more times.

A mist of bright red blood mixed with white smoke in an eerie collage.

Tommy fell to the floor, just as Jimmy tackled Harvey, knocking all the wind out of him. Jimmy rolled on top with his legs straddling high up on Harvey's chest, almost at his neck. He pulled back a meaty fist to strike a brutal blow.

Panicked instinct took over. Harvey reached round stuck the gun against Jimmy's lower back and pulled the trigger.

A shudder rolled through Jimmy's entire body. His primal howl drove deep into Harvey's soul with the unforgettable sound.

Jimmy tried to stand, but his legs no longer supported his body. The hard candy and that same super-heated blast of pressure from the double-load of gun powder blew out a chunk of spine. Jimmy flopped on the floor, screeching his face a rictus of pain.

Neither leg moved.

His arms and head thrashed about willy-nilly.

Harvey struggled to his feet shaking all over fighting a darkness threatening to takeover—a fainting spell. Shock.

Jimmy's body spasmed, then stiffened. He stared at Harvey while purple lips moved in a silent merciful entreaty.

No way could Jimmy be left to testify in court. Worse, though, was to leave someone alive to tell Mr. LaBruzzo who hijacked his gold.

Harvey bent over, hands on knees, and dry-heaved at this new deadly prospect. The awful necessity to "snuff out a witness." It was one thing to kill someone while defending yourself. But to take the life of an incapacitated person...well, that would take an entirely different level of wicked deviant. An attribute Harvey didn't possess and never would.

Tears streamed down his cheeks. How had a simple Ledger Man's life come to this?

Only one option remained.

Jimmy's eyes blinked. And then blinked again.

No way. Damn the consequences. He couldn't do it.

Words finally slipped from Jimmy in a mumble. "Take me to the hospital. Come on, man, help me up. Take me to the hospital. I can't walk. I can't move my legs."

Harvey nodded. His feet moved all on their own without orders from the brain. "Yes, of course. I am so terribly sorry. I didn't mean to—"

Harvey took two steps closer. Jimmy rolled onto his side and grabbed onto Harvey's legs. Wrapped both arms around. Pulled him down to the floor. Punched him in the stomach again and again. Jimmy's eyes aflame, gritting his teeth. He said, "I'm gonna rip your damn head off."

Harvey raised the pistol.

Jimmy glommed onto it. Harvey wouldn't let go. They fought over the gun. The primal instinct again kicked in. Harvey let go of the gun with one hand and reached for the second gun in his waistband. He stuck it into Jimmy's abdomen just as Jimmy wrenched the other one away and turned it to fire into Harvey's face.

Harvey fired six times into Jimmy's abdomen. The noise muffled. The smoke followed the super-heated gases into Jimmy's abdomen, doing serious damage to internal organs. Doing lethal damage.

Jimmy's mouth opened. Turned into a small "o." His eyes went wide.

Harvey kicked him off and grabbed the gun from Jimmy's hand. He put it to Jimmy's forehead and pulled the trigger two more times. He stood back, gasping.

Stunned.

How had he survived what just happened? All the odds favored a far different outcome.

Thank God Slade recommended two guns. All twelve rounds were expended.

He shook off the encroaching shock. Too much work still remained for him to curl up on the floor and let depression take over.

The gold had to be dealt with.

Chapter Twenty-Four

Current Day

I n Harvey's living room, Aussie Mike sauntered over and took a seat in Sylvia's favorite Louis XVI chair. He put his feet up on the antique ottoman, pulled a box of Winfields from his pocket, bumped one out, and lit up. Everyone in the room silently watched, mesmerized, unable to take a single breath. To sit among enemies wasn't smart, but he didn't perceive a threat from two women and two old folks ready for the glue factory.

Lissette finally took her hand from around Rita's throat. She swung a leg from around Rita's lap, stood, and stared. She sported the funniest grin, like that of the tabby cat who had, not moments before, walked past with the red robin in its mouth. The fragile bird with that little drop of blood.

Esther recovered her nerve first. "Take your feet off the Victorian ottoman. It's very expensive. And there's no smoking in this house. How rude of you to just light up without first asking permission."

Aussie Mike's man, a burly thug with a square head and a bulbous nose, stood off to the side with his hands crossed at his waist, giving each in turn the evil eye as if willing someone to try something stupid.

Aussie Mike flicked cigarette ash onto the floor. "That's kinda ironic. You wanting to maintain your house in an immaculate condition. You were just at my house. You *saw* my house. Don't you think that ironic? I mean, after what you destructive little shitheels did? Those albums took me years to collect. Some are irreplaceable. The art—" He rose a little out of the chair recovered his demeanor—took a deep breath and eased back down.

Rita straightened her rumpled cocktail dress, leaned over, and whispered in Harvey's ear. "What the hell's going on? Who is this twat with his meat puppet?"

Harvey craned his head backward, shocked at the vulgar words coming from such a lovely mouth. Marveled how a single utterance held the absolute ability to change an opinion of a person.

"Shush." Under such tense circumstances, he didn't know what else to say.

"Don't you dare shush me. I have every right to know who has the unmitigated gall to walk into my house uninvited and mad-dog us." Lissette stood in front of them, partially blocking their view. Rita lifted a black spiked heel and kicked Lissette in the back of the knee.

Lissette floundered for a moment and regained her balance, her gaze never leaving Aussie Mike. One class A predator watching another.

No scenario allowed this gathering to end amicably.

Esther said, "Excuse me I have to use the lady's room." Esther wanted to go in the dining room to use the phone and call the police, her thoughts plain to everyone in the room.

"Oh no, you don't, sister, sit your fat ass down right over there."

Esther paused a moment, then did as instructed.

He pointed to Rita. "I don't know you, babe. You weren't at my house today. But these three over here, they were. You stand up right now, move over to the corner, and stay quiet. If you're quiet, I'll leave you out of this. Leave you outta the punishment these dodgy asswipes got comin'."

Harvey said a little too loudly. "Go on, Rita, do as he says. You don't want any part of this."

Rita stood, walked over to the fireplace where Aussie Mike pointed, and crossed her arms under her ample bosom. A key attribute Aussie Mike noticed and ogled before coming back to stare at Lissette with an expression that shifted to seething anger.

The entire situation was about to get ugly. The bloody and broken kind of ugly.

Aussie Mike stood up from the chair. "Let's start with the old dude. We'll make the women watch. Let 'em sweat what's about to come their way."

The goon took one step before Rita held up her hand. "Wait."

Aussie Mike's grin returned when he looked back at Rita. "Babe, the deal was for you to be quiet. Unless you wanna buy a piece of what they got comin'?"

"Harv, just give them what they want."

"What are you talking about?"

"Yeah," Aussie Mike said, "What *are* you talking about? What do we want?"

Rita smirked. "What everyone wants. Harv, give 'em the gold."

"The what?"

How did she know about the gold? Earlier, when she had said Andrew Johnson briefed her on the con, she'd only mentioned the theft of equity in the house. Nothing about any gold. Was she lying before, or had she just made something up on the fly, and it happened to be a huge coincidence involving a yellow metal? Slade had said, "Always beware of coincidences, they don't exist in our world."

From the moment Rita stepped into the house, she never once let down the façade to display her true self.

"Heh, heh. Like I'm gonna believe this old crow's got any gold. Don't yank on my dick, woman. You won't like me when I'm mad. Right, Pablo?"

Pablo, who looked Caucasian, grunted and nodded, taking another long step toward the fainting couch where Harvey sat. He lifted his leg to take another—

"Harv, it's only money. Give it to him. He'll leave us alone if you give him *that* kind of money."

"Rita…"

How do you politely tell a person, one you've come to like, to kindly butt the hell out?

Rita put her hands behind her back and leaned forward a little for a fuller display of entrancing décolletage. "If Harvey won't tell you, I will."

"Rita, don't. I told you to stay out of this. This guy isn't messing around. He's serious."

"No. No. Let's see what she has to say." Aussie Mike moved toward her, the grin returned, showing a wedge of perfect teeth.

Rita, standing in place, cocked her hip to one side, then the other while flashing sensuous eyes. She had turned on every famine weapon in her arsenal. Activated the tractor beam that drew in all the poor souls who fell helpless to the primal urge to procreate.

Mixed emotions flooded Harvey. The most important one, the need to help and protect her, and the larger, more encompassing one, green-eyed envy.

When Aussie Mike was two feet away, Rita leaned forward a little more and shook her bosom ever so slightly. A shimmy that caused her breasts to quake. Mike's eyes glazed over, his tongue snaked out, and licked dry lips.

Harvey spotted the con, the distraction, a moment before Aussie Mike did. Her hands behind her back whipped around to the front, swinging the fireplace poker in a two-handed grip.

He raised his arm.

Too late.

The poker glanced off his head but still struck hard enough to make a resounding thunk.

Pablo roared, changed direction, and ran to defend his boss.

Lissette stuck out a foot and tripped him. The rebar slid out of her sleeve into a waiting hand. With both hands, the rebar did a brutal tap-dance on the man's back, arm, and ribs. He rolled and brought his hands up in defense. She broke both hands and then both arms. The thuds and cracks mixed with grunts and screams in a horrific display of brutality. The anger over Eddie's death finally finding a vent.

At the same time, over by the fireplace Rita, with her legs spread wide to give balance, raised the poker over her head and brought it down as it whistled again and again.

The men took the beatings until Rita and Lissette ran out of steam. The men rolled to their sides and moaned, curling into fetal positions.

Esther stood frozen in place, her mouth agape. She, too, had never witnessed such brutal violence. Seeing it on TV was nothing like up close and personal. The anguish, the pain, the thumps, cracks, and shattering bones.

Harvey struggled to his feet, lightheaded and woozy, walked over to Rita gently placing a hand on her back. Her chest heaved, breathing hard, face glistening and still flushed with rage. He peeled the poker from her hands. Based on the rap sheet Lissette had recited from memory, Rita was a confirmed white-collar criminal and had never been arrested for violence. For all he knew, this was her first venture into the world of mayhem.

She turned and glommed onto him. Held on tight enough to restrict breathing. "Oh Harv. I didn't mean to. Really, I didn't. He…they were going to hurt all of us. I could see it in his eyes."

Her tears wet his shoulder. Real or staged, he didn't mind at all.

For all her gruff talk, Lissette looked just as emotionally torn up as Rita. Harvey raised his voice at her. "They are not completely neutralized. They will have guns. Search them. Then get some duct tape from the kitchen drawer by the refrigerator and tape their hands and feet."

She looked up with a thousand-yard stare and suddenly returned to earth. "Right. You're absolutely right. Esther, get the tape." Lissette went to work searching Pablo first and immediately came up with a gun from under his shirt at the small of the back.

"Don't stop, he'll have another gun and a knife and maybe some brass knuckles."

Lissette nodded and went to the moaning man again, tossing the weapons aside in a semi-pile: a knife, another gun, smaller, and a roll of quarters.

Rita moved her mouth close to Harvey's ear. "Harv darling, how do you know so much about what happens on the street? What would this thug be carrying?"

He peeled her away to look into her eyes. "What makes you think I have any gold?"

"Don't be a fool. I was 'telling him the tale.' Giving him the bait."

The ease with which the woman flashed in and out of lamb versus wolf costumes shocked and awed. "You got room to talk about me. 'Telling the tale,' and giving him, 'the bait,' are con artist terms."

She again shifted emotionally. "...That's right. That's right. But I've never...I mean, I've never hurt anyone before."

"It's okay. It's all over now." He let the question about the gold hold for later. It was foolish to discuss it further in front of witnesses.

Lissette finished with Pablo, came over, and worked on Aussie Mike. First patting him down taking weapons and then taping him up. Afterward she stepped back and began kicking him.

Esther paced the living room, stopping now and again to look at the tools of violence that had been used on the men, the poker and rebar lying on the floor. Both common and innocuous, and at the same time foreboding. "Now what are we going to do with them? We can't just leave them on the living room floor to...to molder."

Lissette stopped kicking. "I'll start digging a big hole in the backyard."

Aussie Mike struggled and squirmed, but couldn't object to the gray tape across his mouth.

Esther half-yelled. "We can't do that. We can't kill them. This...all this here was bad enough."

"Esther?" Lissette said, "They were about to do the same to us."

Harvey raised his hand. "Don't be ridiculous. Mike is wanted by immigration, and I'm sure for other narcotic-related crimes. Pablo will have the same problem, which turns out to be our solution. Load them up in the back of the Tahoe, drive them to the hospital, and kick them out. Problem solved."

Rita poked him in the back. "I'll say it again. You know far too much about violence and the street to be some kind of retired furniture store owner."

Aussie Mike struggled against the pain and bindings, his face bloating red. He didn't want to go to jail, do time, then get extradited back to Australia. He probably had a lot of pain and suffering waiting for him there.

Lissette went down on one knee and stripped the tape from across his mouth.

"Please don't drop me off at the hospital."

Lissette said, "You know what I find really odd?" She didn't wait for an answer. "That you never once asked what the hell we were doing at your house in the first place."

His swollen and bloodied lips sputtered as if his mind disengaged and slipped into neutral while scrambling for an acceptable answer.

"Tell me what you had on my Eddie? Are you the one who ran him down like a dog?"

Rita reached down, took Harvey's hand, and squeezed. Rita had burnt the cute little red Mercedes down to the hubs because of the front end—the car vs pedestrian damage. To step forward and tell the truth would incur Lissette's wrath, which at the moment Lissette had a difficult time containing.

She picked up the piece of rebar. Held it over Mike's one good knee.

"Eddie?" Mike said.

"Eddie Gurski, the father of *my child!*"

"Oh, Fast Ed. He ah…"

Lissette whacked him, but this time at half strength.

Harvey couldn't stomach torture on any person or animal. "He didn't do it. Please, just leave him alone." She stood up from bent knee and rushed over with an upturned face. "So, you think you know who did?"

"I do. I told you it was Andrew Johnson. And if you think these two are bad to deal with, wait until Andrew Johnson comes for us. And he will come for us. I mean me—he'll be coming for me. It's best if all of you get the hell out of here now before it's too late."

Chapter Twenty-Five

1968

D awn peeked over the curvature of the earth as Harvey pulled up in front of his home. Physical fatigue had never punished a Ledger Man as it did now. Every muscle threw up its hands and said that's enough, no more. Even bad metaphors plagued a tired mind. Lugging gold bars, what a workout.

The walk from the curb to the front door was a bridge too far, yet had to be done. The only thing that kept forward motion in play was the improbable idea that Abigail might've left another letter from Lois. Idiotic. But in difficult times fools grasp at straws.

He traversed the front yard, up the tall, tall porch steps and unlocked the door. It took twenty minutes and every last bit of energy. He fell into bed the same as a Sequoia crashing down in a forest. No one was there to hear the loud harrumph of exhaustion. Nothing moved but lungs and the air needed to survive before sleep took hold with an impenetrable darkness. In that darkness resided a profound fear that two people would forever lurk waiting in ambush with sawed-off shotguns. Both asking why?

Two minutes later or was it eight hours, panic lifted the soul from a bone smothering slumber.

Rising. Rising to the surface. He opened one eye. Sunlight radiated through the bedroom window dappling the floor and undisturbed bedspread next to his swollen hand.

In a chair from the kitchen, not two feet away, sat a slob of monumental proportions. A crass, conscious less killer; Jackie the Nose.

Blubber covered in yards of slacks and poly-cotton of the dress shirt slopped over the edges of the chair.

All of their own, numbers jumped into the Ledger Man's head, weight differentials, structure tolerances resulting in an obvious solution. That poor chair. The man tortured everything he touched.

Adrenaline suddenly shot through heart and soul. The eye winked shut and he froze. The memory from the night before returned ugly and dark. But more important the question: had every iota of evidence been dealt with? What was it, Slade had said, "Pitfalls sealed many a fate of numskull gunsels."

With the thought came a moment of revelation.

Harvey Dortmund had crossed over. Transitioned. He was no longer merely a Ledger Man: he had taken one giant step deep into *Gunsel* territory. A purebred gun thug. Never in all his dreams had he—

Jackie raised a foot and shoved the top mattress almost knocking it off the box spring. "I saw that guilt-riddled eye. Get your sorry ass up. Now."

"Huh? What's going on?" Acting innocent and unaware became difficult with such a huge threat in close proximity. A cold trickle of fear caused every muscle to shiver. He sat up and scooted to the edge of the bed. "What's going on? What are you doing in my bedroom?"

"Has your happy-ass been here all night? Don't lie to me."

Muck from sleep clogged the eyes. He wiped them clear as Baby Bertha suddenly appeared in Jackie's pudgy fist, the blackjack thirsty for blood and bone.

"What's going on? Of course, I've been here all night. Where else would I be? I don't have any kind of life. I worked late at the shop and came right home. I was so tired I didn't even take my clothes off. Look?" The blood-spattered clothes from the night before had been discarded in the dumpster behind the *A&P* on Harrison on the way home. Every little detail dealt with. But Slade said one little bugger of a detail always slips through. Always. That left only the hope no one of importance would, "Tumble to it."

The "little bugger," theory now amplified the terror becoming more difficult to suppress.

If Jackie had found the bloody abattoir over on Daisy Street, the mutilation of his two men—but more importantly the safe room found empty, the gold missing—then why so calm? Why wasn't he jumping up and down about to blow out a major blood vessel?

Cunning, that's the reason. He came over suppressing an internal rage that had to be bursting his insides. All an act to test a Ledger Man's intestinal fortitude. To see if he'd crack in a deadly game of bluff poker.

"What time is it anyway?"

"Doesn't matter." Jackie held out a hand. The new limo driver handed him a *Hoboken Pictorial* newspaper. The headline took a moment to focus and digest.

"Two Dead in a bloody scene on Daisy Street. The Candyman still at large."

"The Candyman? What's going on? Why are you showing me—" He feigned surprise, "Daisy Street? Are you kidding? Someone hit us? Hit our safe house."

Jackie stared into his eyes searching for the truth. This was the big moment why Jackie had suppressed his rage while searching for the person who deigned to go against the family in such a blatant manner.

The moment stretched out fat and treacherous.

Urine pulsed inside a weak bladder and wanted out in the worst way. Hold your water or die.

Finally, Jackie struggled to get his bulk out of the chair. He waddled to the dresser and kicked it. Kicked it several more times then went at the wall denting or creating ruinous holes. Grunts of rage emitted with each effort.

He teetered on unbalanced feet, his right hand clutched to his chest. His bloated rage-filled expression turned ashen. He wobbled back over to the chair and flopped down. The poor chair creaked and settled a couple of inches compressing under the load. It couldn't take much more abuse. The feeling mutual.

Jackie wheezed and coughed.

Die, you fat putrid pig. Die.

But wishes like that never came true. Fate always the prankster. Color returned to his face as breathing returned to normal. One day though...

Now, what would be the normal reaction to what happened in the paper? "Who's this Candyman? Do the police know who did it?"

Jackie took out a white monogrammed hankie and mopped sweat from his face and all the chins, his eyes on high beams glaring. He sat in the bedroom because very few knew the location of the safe house on Daisy. Oh, damn. Karl, the old limo driver. He knew, and someone took his place. Karl, the most recent inhabitant of The Meadowlands.

The new driver had a look about him, dusky and dangerous. Tall with wide shoulders and a thin Ronald Coleman mustache. Dark circles under his eyes added to a tacit threatening demeanor. He wore black livery with gold cuff links visible on French cuffs that peeked out the suit coat sleeves.

Jackie caught him eyeing the new limo driver. "Ha, this is Eugene Lujan. We call him Genie because he works miracles with a knife. Thought I'd up my game a little. Karl, he...well let's just say he took an early retirement."

All the thugs had to have ignorant nicknames as if their personal identity depended upon it.

"Wait," Harvey pointed to the newspaper. "You're here because you think *I* had something to do with this?"

"Those were two of my best boys. They wouldn't let just anyone get the jump on them. They didn't get a shot off. The door was undamaged. No. No. Whoever did this, those two boys knew 'em and let 'em in. No doubt about it."

"And you think I might've done it?" Harvey looked over at the new limo driver, Eugene Lujan, who smirked and shook his head as if saying, "Never in two million years."

Jackie caught the driver's reaction and looked back at Harvey, "Don't be smug with me, you little twat. I'm covering all the bases here. That's all."

"Why would anyone just want to kill those two guys. The house was empty, right? I still have all this month's take in the office over the donut shop? We haven't moved any of it yet."

Jackie stopped wiping his face and again stared, his eyes delving deep, probing Harvey's mind for an answer not forthcoming.

"Yeah, I guess that's right. You're right about that. I hadn't thought of it like that."

"So then maybe it wasn't an inside job. Someone on the inside would know there wasn't any money there. That would make this a hit pure and simple, right?"

"Yeah. You're a smart kid. Go back to sleep. You're back on the sailboat tomorrow heading south."

"Why? It's early. We have another week before the regular trip's scheduled."

"You don't get to ask questions."

"It's the money. You want to keep it safe in case this *was* the first salvo in a gang war."

For just a millisecond, Jackie's angry expression shifted to surprise. He caught himself and shifted back. "Mind your mouth, you spineless, good-for-nothing little weasel. One day that brain of yours 'ill get you a free plot over to the Meadowlands. You mark my words. You heard it here first."

He turned and waddled out; the floor creaked under each step.

Through the window, Jackie stood by the car and spoke with the limo driver, Eugene Lujan, The Genie. Lujan pointed back at the house and laughed. Jackie nodded and got in. The car started up and zoomed off.

A large exhale left his lungs. He didn't know he'd been holding it in.

Harvey picked up the discarded *Hoboken Pictorial,* read the article, and then read it slowly two more times. "The Candyman." Huh. The journalist didn't say why the police tagged the killer that way. The paper withheld the information about the candy residue found in the fatal wounds. From the law books and the cases Slade had talked about, the "Homicide bulls" always withheld a couple of pieces of information in case a whacko, who didn't do it, tried to confess.

Outside the window in front, a car pulled up and stopped. A pretty young woman got out and stared at the house for a moment before walking up. When she stepped out of the shade into the sunlight, he recognized her. Abigail, Lois's best friend and maid of honor.

Chapter Twenty-Six

B ewildered, Harvey watched the women in the living room. Why didn't anyone listen? Did they not believe in the impending danger? The severity of it?

An hour after the mayhem that involved Aussie Mike and his thug-monkey Pablo, all three women casually sat around discussing what to do next. Rita brought up the plan first. "We need to mousetrap him. We have the advantage. We know when he will be here."

'Mousetrap,' a word Slade liked to use.

"Not him, *Them*," Harvey said too loudly. "There will be more than one. Andrew Johnson will bring friends to this insane party."

They all stared at him for a moment. Lissette broke first, looked at Rita, "I like that term. Yes, we'll mousetrap him." She turned to look at Harvey, "*And* anyone else who comes along with Andrew the asshole."

Harvey put his head in his hands. "Oh, dear Lord, help us all."

The women, an odd bunch with Rita in her signature cocktail dress with a wide black belt and heels, Esther in a bland neck-to-the-floor dress, and Lissette's holey denim pants, boots, and an eggshell white long-sleeved blouse now speckled with blood. Blood from the earlier violent confrontation.

All three should be scared out of their skin. Anyone who peeked in the window as an unaware observer would never guess what had transpired in

214

the room. They would simply see best friends quietly organizing a dinner party or baby shower. Cool and casual.

Unnatural under the recent circumstances.

The women should be nervous, frantic about what to do next.

That was easy, run like hell. No ifs and buts or buts. Get the hell out of there.

But the three had never encountered anyone even close to resembling the man the mob sent, Andrew Johnson. Brutal, ruthless to the nth degree. Not in the same league as the two light-weights now rolled up like a couple of gyros and dumped at the ER.

Earlier, Harvey sat and watched, fascinated, while the three women used the expensive antique living room rugs to drag the two thugs out to the Tahoe, backed into the breezeway adjacent to the garage, just off the alley. Loaded them up and drove away, headed to the hospital.

Craziness.

Pure unadulterated craziness.

Now they made plans to do something similar to Andrew Johnson, and nothing Harvey said could convince them otherwise. "He's not here alone doing this job. Believe me, he's going to have help. All the help he could possibly need."

This time, all three stopped the jibber-jabber and looked over.

Lissette said, "He killed my Eddie."

Rita said, "He tried to frame me for Eddie's murder."

"Esther, what about you? Please, go home and let this be. Just walk away before it's too late."

Esther's stare hurt the most. She finally said, "Have you read Sylvia's letter yet? The one you never opened? Her last letter to you?" Esther wasn't even sure that particular letter existed. Yet somehow, she did know.

"Stop it. One has nothing to do with the other. Quit trying to change the subject. Please, I implore you all to go home and be done with all of this. Someone is going to get hurt...or worse."

"That's right, someone is," Lissette said, "Andrew Johnson."

"Oh, dear Lord."

Rita said, "Andrew won't leave until he has the money from the equity in the house. The escrow officer is dropping the check by tomorrow at nine a.m. That's when we have to be ready. Seven o'clock in the a.m. would be best."

"Be ready? What don't you understand? This guy is an animal. He won't hesitate like the other two did. This guy will, 'act, act, act.'"

Rita shot him a patronizing smirk. "You okay? Sounds like you just had a seizure or something?"

"You're not catching on to any of this. None of you are. You're letting your need for revenge cloud logical thought. Listen to me carefully. He is not here for the money. That's just a sideline, a way to torture me a little more before he puts the screws to me. For—"

"For what? Rita asked. She stood, walked over, and sat on the easy chair arm. An intense body heat radiated off her. The woman could power a steam locomotive.

"Never mind. What you need to know is that he will not hesitate when it comes to violence. We have to get out of here, all of us."

Rita put her hand on his arm. "Harv, I'm concerned. I've never seen this side of you. This ego thing you have going on. This is not all about you."

"Stop it, Rita. It has nothing to do with my ego. I'm telling you the truth. I really hate to say this, but we should call the police. Let them handle it."

"The police?" Rita stood and sauntered back to the couch where the women sat. Her hips are doing the side-to-side, 'bang, da bang,' thing. No other way to describe it. "Harv love, I'll ask you again, are you holding something back that we should know?" The mention of police made her nervous and prompted the need to change the subject. She'd had a taste of jail and wasn't ready for any more.

He needed to move her away from any thought of gold.

Slade had said the number one rule, that under no circumstances could be violated. Ever. Was: "Tell no one." The last item he covered that night out on the water coming back from the Caymans, *"Once the deed occurs, it never happened. You understand? No matter what, and I mean under threat of death or physical torture, you never admit to anything. In your mind, as far as you're concerned, it never happened."*

Now the dilemma: break the unbreakable code of conduct set down by Slade and tell the women the whole story, or remain mum and risk someone getting seriously injured or killed? Stepping back and looking at what happened with Aussie Mike and his cohort, any normal, uninvolved person would say a great deal of luck played a part in overpowering those thugs. Too big a part. Rita and Lissette both possessed a twinge of ruthlessness. But not near enough. Not when compared to any one close to approaching Jackie the Nose's level of brutality, which Andrew Johnson possessed as evidenced by the way he ran down Eddie. And the fact that the 'Family,' from back east wouldn't send a slouch. They would pick the most ruthless.

Harvey struggled to his feet, his age kicking in making it difficult. A reminder of many serious limitations. He raised a hand and gave a backward wave leaving the living room. He needed time to think.

But as soon as he entered the hallway the real reason bubbled to the surface. It was finally time. Esther was right. For the last two years he'd been a child refusing to confront the pain in Sylvia's last letter. The guilt. The regret. The sorrow. And even a bit of anger at her for leaving him alone. Okay, maybe more than a little bit.

Tomorrow, after fate took a heavy-hand there might not be time left to read it.

In the master bedroom, the shoebox filled with so many memories sat on the dresser.

The unopened letter right on top.

Hard to believe Rita, the con woman, resisted the urge to open it. When she preserved that little bit of privacy, she revealed a modicum of humanity. A smidgeon of redemption. Both of which a con woman on the make could ill afford.

He took the letter, sat on the edge of the bed, stared at the envelope already yellowing around the edges, and tried to conjure what Sylvia must have thought in those last moments while putting pen to paper.

In a smooth, even hand she simply wrote, *"Harv, My Love."*

He stuck a finger under the flap and tore it open. The sharp edge cut a paper-thin slice across the index finger. A crimson drop wet the flap. With a shaking hand, the folded missive slid out.

He took a deep breath and unfolded it.

My dearest Harvey

Before I start in on my explanation, first and foremost, you must know something terribly important to me. I will love you forevermore.

Now for the difficult part. Please, please don't take my selfish actions the wrong way. After our fight last night, I ground up some prescription drugs (drugs you didn't know about) and dissolved them in the 'Night water,' glass I keep on the nightstand next to the bed. I know I shouldn't have done this awful, selfish thing right on the heels of our fight. But the decision had already been made and had nothing to do with our angry words. This decision was made based on something else entirely.

We have always been honest with each other, (Until a couple of months ago). I feel guilty as hell keeping it from you, (I know, I don't usually use words like, "hell," I apologize).

You're the strongest man I know. Have ever known. I mean that Harv. You saved my life at great risk to your own. You're truly my knight who came to my rescue. I wish I had your intestinal fortitude, but the onslaught of age grinds a person down to a nub. After I tell you my thoughts in the ensuing words I know you'll automatically assume my recent decisions weren't made of sound mind. That I was impaired with pain and medications. You'll think that if I had come to you we could've worked it out. Not so Harv, please don't believe in that wistful whim.

We had fifty good years together. Wonderful storybook years. Fall back on those memories, use them to help get through this. In the past two months I have found great solace in them as well.

A wife shouldn't keep secrets from her husband especially from you Harv. I have three things to tell you. Three very difficult things.

First, I have cancer Harv. The very bad kind. A plague that befalls nearly everyone who lives too long. No regrets my love, truly.

Esther has been driving me to the doctor when we told you we were walking at the mall to get out of the heat. Don't be angry with her. She's a good friend and I have leaned on her far too much over the years. I'll get to that part later. But if you have the chance, take her to a nice dinner and thank her.

That's the first thing, Harv, that awful insidious beast that has invaded my bones and has tried too hard to snatch away my soul.

The second thing is, I recently read a news article online. Brace yourself, Harv.

Oliver Buckingham was taken from The Coconut Tree Assisted Living Home in St. Augustine Beach, Florida. The FBI found him five days later in a defunct, broken-down warehouse. He died strapped to a chair after being tortured. The FBI, in their statement to the press, linked Buckingham to the Jersey mob. The LaBruzzo family. I find it difficult to even write that awful name. According to the article, a family attorney said, "Buckingham, after being disgraced and disbarred as a prosecutor, worked for the LaBruzzos, advising them on 'Delicate legal entanglements.'"

That's the way they described it, too: "Delicate legal entanglements." My aching butt. Right Harv?

Anyway, I hired a PI firm back east to look into this mess, and they found the feds had reopened the gold heist from Suisse Air Transport. The gold was never recovered, and they believe it is still out there somewhere. The feds used the forensic DNA test on some of the old evidence. The results have now somehow linked back to a house on Daisy Street in Hoboken. You know the house, Harv. A double murder. But murder is too strong a word, now when what happened was closer to euthanasia of rabid animals. Harsh words, Harv, but true.

In their search for all that gold, the FBI kicked over a hornet's nest. If you haven't put it together, Oliver Buckingham is the person you traveled with down to the Grand Caymans. Buckingham is Slade, Harv.

Slade was the one who created our new identities. If he talked after being tortured, the LaBruzzo clan will come for us. They'll want the *gold. They'll know our new names. Track us to where we've been hiding for the last five decades. One last thing on this, and it's important. When we stole that gold, it was worth $40.00 an ounce. (What's left, only about a quarter of the whole), is now worth $2000.00 an ounce. That alone would reinvigorate these animals to come looking.*

You have to run, Harv. After you read this, drop everything and run. With this cancer, all this horrible pain, I can't do it. I would be a huge weight hanging from your neck.

Know this, I was angry with myself for making the decision to leave you in such a lurch. That's what sparked the terrible little tiff we had last night before I drank the "Night water." The guilt for leaving you holding the bag. To deal with it all alone. For that, I am truly sorry.

The pain has come on again with insidious intensity, like it tends to do once the sun sets. So, now with great regret, I have to end this missive that I'm sure you will bemoan opening forevermore...I hope you did open it, Harv, and that you weren't so angry with me that you tossed it in the ashcan.

PS. The third thing...well, I'm in too much physical pain now to deal with something so emotional. These two particular emotional companions carried for half a millennium, Mr. Shame and Mrs. Guilt. Go to Esther and ask about it, tell her I said to tell you. She'll know what I'm talking about. Show her this letter. I told her I was going to write it.

So, goodnight, my dear Harv, we had a hell'va run, didn't we?

I'll love you forevermore, my foolhardy knight.

Sincerely, your wife, your friend, your lover.

Lois

The letter fell to the floor. Warm tears streamed down his cheeks. Unbidden, the memory of that horrible event flooded back. The one two years ago.

* * *

He'd awakened the morning after the argument with Sylvia, rueful and determined to make amends. He slinked out of bed without disturbing the covers or jostling the mattress. Hurried to the kitchen and made her favorite breakfast, a three-minute egg, a slice of rye toast, no-butter, two slices of bacon, and plain yogurt with blueberries. Barely enough to keep a bird alive.

Out in the garden where Sylvia spent hours on end tinkering, he clipped one yellow rose with a perfect dew-speckled bloom. The marvelous scent a celebration of life. A musky fragrance, sweet and spicy resembling meadow honey with fruity undertones.

Overhead in a jacaranda, a red robin stared down and then hopped from branch to branch. She spoke, "Yeep. Yeep." Odd, that species of bird had never before graced the garden. A good omen for a glorious day.

He entered the bedroom swinging the breakfast-filled tray, whistling the theme song from Rogers and Hammerstein's *Oklahoma*. Sylvia's favorite.

He froze mid-note. Mid-step. A long golden ray of sunlight came through the window, illuminating Sylvia's lovely countenance.

But something was wrong. Horribly wrong.

Sylvia—prompted up with a pillow the way she always slept due to "a bad tummy"—acid reflux, didn't move. One side of his brain registered something ominous and kept it hidden from conscious thought until he looked closer.

Her chest didn't move. That was it. She wasn't breathing.

The tray tumbled to the hardwood floor. A far-off clatter was dulled by the rushing sound in his ears.

He ran through the scattered detritus, turned an ankle almost going down, and limped the last five feet. He took her in his arms, her body stiff. Cold. Nothing at all like *Lois*. This was nothing more than a chunk of cold firewood.

What happened to his Lois?

The world closed in.

Outside the window, the wind rustled the jacaranda branches, and a red robin heralded in Lois' passing with a "Yeep, yeep."

Chapter Twenty-Seven

1968

Harvey peeked out the window to be sure Abigail was alone, a recent precaution instituted since Jackie the Nose started his spot visits. She stood out on the front stoop. Maybe she had word from Lois.

Harvey ran fingers through tousled hair, smoothing down bed-head, straightened clothes rumpled from falling straight into bed, and hurried to the door. The newspaper Jackie the Nose showed him clinging to his fingers with an invisible adhesive. A newspaper that confirmed the nightmare plaguing sleep and upsetting an already delicate stomach. A nightmare making him out to be a brutal murderer. And undeniable.

He swung the door open and caught the unsmiling Abigail's hand raised, ready to knock.

No smile. Not good. Not good at all. But who in the entire city had reason to smile. Hyperbole most often the product of despair.

"Good morning, please come in." He stepped aside to let her pass. She wore a white collared blue gingham dress with faux pearl buttons down the front, white heels, and white gloves. The sunlight made her oval face glow, and the red lipstick bright.

She hesitated, turned her head to look back out into the neighborhood for anyone who might have witnessed the improper offer to a refined young woman.

"I'm sorry, let me take you to breakfast."

Still no smile. "Sir, it's eleven thirty, almost noon."

"Lunch then? Please wait right here; I'll get my keys."

"No, I don't have much to say. We can talk here on the porch."

He'd held his tongue long enough and couldn't wait a second more. "Is Lois okay? Have you heard from her? Have you seen her? How does she look?"

She shook a head of red hair and muttered, "God's holy trousers. Yes, let's go down to the diner and get a coffee."

"Fine. That's fine. I'll drive."

"No, I'll drive." She turned andmoved down the walk, heels clacking and without waiting got into a canary yellow Ford Mustang, the paint too bright for so early in the morning. He climbed in. Once inside, the car seemed smaller. He sat like a lump, the newspaper inert in his lap.

She drove more like a banshee than a young woman, yanking on the steering wheel to take corners, tires screeching. The heavy tension in the car, a presence, a third person. Of course, she would believe he had something to do with Lois' predicament. That he was the link to the criminal element. Before all the problems started, an accountant for *a family business* was nothing more than a job with numbers put down in a book. Why wouldn't a simple Ledger Man want to take out a lovely woman like Lois?

But the accountant job—the association had been the problem. The LaBruzzo family acted as a swirling vortex of violence. Lois stepped too close to the edge and was sucked in. If Abigail assigned fault to a foolish man who took Lois too close to that edge, then guilty as charged.

She pulled off the street and nosed the car up to the side of *The Last Hope Diner*, a converted railroad car. The sun winked off the brightly polished exterior that lacked any greenery. Just asphalt that ran right up to all the shiny aluminum and glass windows.

Inside, the lunch rush just started leaving only two seats at the counter. Not the best of circumstances. The empty seats left a straggly truck driver on either side who could eavesdrop.

They sat on the red vinyl stools. The harried waitress rattled saucers and cups, setting them down in front of them, and poured coffee without asking. She yanked menus out of the hands of the men on either side and handed them over. The men in unison opened their mouths to complain. She raised a finger. "Don't. You two know that menu better than I do. Get over it." And she was gone, servicing the noisy, hungry crush.

The sudden integration with other people, normal people not involved in the criminal world, brought back the guilt, the reminder almost too heavy to bear that he was now a murderer. The event from the night before again rolled back like a gut-punch. The look in Jimmy's eyes when the gun went off in his abdomen. The way the anger drained away, the eyes shifting to the question everyone asks when the Grim Reaper taps you on the shoulder, "Why me?"

The God-awful waste of life, and for what? Money? No amount of money was worth taking someone's life. And he'd done it twice. The simple multiplication of doubling two numbers also doubled the guilt.

Abigail leaned forward and around in front of his face, inches away. She whispered, "Hey, are you okay? You just turned pale as a ghost. Did some evil spirit just tromp across your soul?"

Without realizing it, a whisper came out, uttered all on its own. "Lois is worth it."

Abigail jerked as if slapped. "Of course, she's worth it, you damn fool." She dumped cream, then sugar in the coffee cup and stirred the light tan concoction. "You're the cause of all this. I don't know how you live with yourself." The contempt oozed off her. "She's the best person...She's the—" The stirring in the cup increased. The liquid overlapped the brim, spattered the worn vinyl countertop. Tears filled her eyes. If he didn't know better, Abigail was also in love with Lois.

"I fired a metaphorical shot last night that—" But caught the slip of the tongue as Slade's words echoed in the empty chamber of the mind. *"Tell no one. Once the deed occurs. It never happened. You understand? No matter what, and I mean under threat of death or physical torture you never admit to anything. In your mind, as far as you're concerned, it never happened."*

But the utterance to Abigail was also wrong. There was no "metaphorical" about it. A meager attempt to veil the truth. The trigger had been pulled, and two men died. The gold was stolen, and maybe…just maybe, what happened lit the match to ignite an upheaval. Now, a ripple of deceit starting with Jackie the Nose would move up and down the chain. The end result from that ripple would leave fresh overturned dirt in the Meadowlands. But most important, an opening to whisk Lois out of the hyena's jaws.

"What do you mean? What kind of metaphorical shot?" She'd caught a whiff of promise in a situation that until that moment lacked all hope.

"Nothing. Please tell me why you came to my house."

"No. You started to say something, and I want to hear it."

He glanced to the side and caught the gruff truck driver paying too much attention to his oatmeal bowl, staring straight down, working hard not to look askance, his regular-sized ears now looking more like Dumbo's.

Harvey leaned over and whispered to her. "This isn't the time nor the place."

She whispered back. "I'll tell you mine, if you tell me yours."

"This isn't high school, this is serious business."

Abigail's violet eyes turned fierce. She gritted her teeth. "Don't you dare talk to me like that. This is not some sort of game. Not with what my best friend is going through. Not after what happened to the surgeon and…and to Johnny, the poor kid who was driving that day on the road to the lake. The day—"

He eased forward on the stool and rested his elbows on the counter, cutting her off, not wanting to hear more of that litany of terror, by saying. "I have to leave tomorrow. I won't be back for a couple of months. Please tell me. I'll go crazy if I have to wait until I get back."

She again stuck her face right up against his with breath Double-Mint fresh. "Do you know what Giorgio *did to her* that first night?" Said the last words loud enough the entire diner heard. Silence rolled through the small confines, the clacking of flatware against plates, the loud talking ceased.

Harvey took her arm, yanked her off the stool, and headed for the door. The yank elicited a small yelp. Three months ago, a certified propeller head performing that aggressive behavior would never have happened. Especially not to a young woman.

Outside in the parking lot, she jerked her arm back and straightened a ruffled dress. "You're nothing like what you seem. You're just like all those animals. You're just like Giorgio."

Anger flushed his face hot. He stuck a finger close to her nose. "Don't you ever say something like that again. I've done something to help Lois, and I'm not proud of it, but at least I've done something."

The frustrated anger left her expression. "What? What have you done?"

As if the words had a mind of their own, the urge to violate Slade's number one edict rose up and almost blurted out. He broke eye contact, or the utterance would've entered the world, on the loose like a deadly virus. "Please just tell me what you came to say."

"I was hoping you would have enough guts to bring a gun to the funeral. I'm going to. If you do, maybe between the both of us we can take out enough of them to make a difference. Shoot that bastard Giorgio."

"Wait, what funeral? What are you talking about? Take guns to a funeral?"

She reached down and snatched the newspaper from his hand, the one Jackie the Nose showed him not half an hour ago. The paper he couldn't put down and was stuck to his hand as if glued. The front page described the previous night's heinous activity and tagged the perpetrator as The Candyman. Tagged Harvey Dortmund a criminal. A murderer.

Did Abigail know something? Was she talking about a funeral for one of the dead men, Tommy Tee or Jimmy? No, that would be too soon.

She opened the paper, thumbing through it. "Here. Right here on page seven."

He took the paper back and first looked up at the windows in the diner. Almost everyone stared down, wondering what the hell was going on between the nerd and a beautiful woman way beyond his social status.

He took a step back and glared down at the newsprint.

Alfred Alister DeFrank III died yesterday in an unfortunate swimming pool accident. At 3:45 p.m., house staff found him floating in the pool wearing all of his clothes. Interviews revealed DeFrank had been despondent over the marriage of his only daughter. In the past couple of months, he had retreated to his home, rarely going out and drinking in excess every night. Authorities believe DeFrank tripped while intoxicated, fell into the pool, and was unable to make it back to safety.

The memory of the encounter with Lois' father—the fight in the front yard—returned in technicolor. His words. His passion for protecting Lois.

Air left his lungs in a long, sad sigh. "It wasn't a swimming pool accident. He was murdered."

"Of course, he was murdered. Those bastards wanted Mr. DeFrank out of the way. He was pounding the drums, trying to get anyone and everyone to listen to him about his daughter. Kidnapped and in captivity. He hired a heavy-handed PI to try to pry Lois away from the LaBruzzos. The man disappeared. Poof."

"He'll be out in the Meadowlands now."

"What?"

"Never mind. You can't go to the funeral, you'll only get yourself hurt or worse."

"Not if we both go. I can distract them by shooting first, then you can—"

"Listen, Abigail, that's a fool's errand. I have something else in the works and—"

"What? Tell me."

The newspaper in his hand turned damp with sweat. It would be too easy to show her the front page and own up to the horrific event. But in turn it would also ease, at least a modicum of guilt that with each breath smothered and snatched at his breath. "I set in motion a catalyst that hopefully will erode away confidence and…and neutralize some of the organization's strength."

"Tell me."

"I can't."

"Tell me or I'm taking a gun to the funeral, with or without you."

"All I can say is that I planted a seed and the end result will be—"

She turned, walked away, and said over her shoulder, "No. You tell me something of substance that will convince me what you're doing will save my friend, or I'm going to the funeral with a gun. I'll teach those bastards not to—"

"Wait."

Abigail turned back and waited, her eyes alive, anxious.

Harvey walked up to her, the newspaper opened to the front page.

Chapter Twenty-Eight

1968

T he shining carpet of light glowed on a dancing ocean and ran up to
a full moon that sat fat and sassy on the horizon. The Lucky Lady
came down off a swell and rolled into the harbor. Slade no longer
gave orders on how to handle the boat. He didn't have to. Harvey did the
mindless chores while his mind worked the coming plan step by step. First
came the phone call from the dock to Abigail.

This trip took nine weeks.

Five months had passed since that first kiss with Lois in the car on the
highway. For her five months of captivity with Giorgio was no different
than a POW, in terms of the emotional and physical torture. In order for
Harvey to extricate his true love and take it on the lam, money was needed.
He had the gold...sort of had it.

Almost.

But in a few hours, he'd take another giant step toward being free with
the love of his life.

The only problem being the plan moved far too slowly. One day, one hour,
one minute was too long to leave Lois with that abusive pig. But to move
fast and make a costly mistake meant an end to all things. A violent, blood
and bone-filled end.

The trip to the Caymans should've let things cool down and allowed the
image of the Ledger Man to fade into the ether. Put Jackie the Nose on

another trail as far as suspecting someone else.

* * *

During that first week of the recent trip heading down to the Caymans, Slade didn't say a word about what happened on Daisy. Harvey began to believe the man lived on his boat like an ostrich with his head in the sand, allowing the world to just wash over him.

On the eighth night, when the Island rum stole Slade's common sense, he sat in the navigation well, back propped against a pillow. One foot on the tall chrome wheel clutched in his toes. He gave a Cheshire Cat smile. "You going to tell me how it all went down?"

"What? How what went down?"

The boat was far enough south that the wind had turned warm and whistled in the ear. Slade's words came out clear enough, but the shock of the abruptness caught Harvey looking.

Slade used his other foot and gave Harvey's knee a shove. "You can't bullshit a bullshitter. Come on, we're friends. You can tell me."

"I have no idea what you're talking about."

In the trips down to the Caymans, living in cramped quarters, a person couldn't help but get to know the other. With no middle ground to retreat to, you either became fast friends or dire enemies. Harvey now understood Slade's every tick and tell. Even with Slade's superior card skills, he long since gave up playing poker with him.

Slade's abrupt question sent Harvey's heart galloping and mind spinning.

"You know exactly what I'm talking about. Spill it."

"Huh. In Manfredi's, 'How to Corner the Obstinate Spy,' the 1942 first edition—right down there on your shelf—Manfredi says that during an interrogation, you should keep the questions general without specifics and allow the subject to make his own conjecture as to the answer."

Slade used his foot again, this time shoving harder. "My God, man, that was almost word for word. I should never have allowed you to read all those books. Okay, that was a general question fashioned to catch an unwary opponent. So, here is the—"

"Are we opponents now?"

Slade laughed again. "Quit it. Stop using Manfredi against me."

"What are you talking about?"

"Diverting questions with a question. My God, you are an apt pupil. Just tell me."

"Okay, wait a minute. If I did happen to know what you are talking about. And I'm not saying that I do. And this…this topic happened to be somewhat of an incriminating nature—this I can assume by your tone and delivery of the question in question—*and* I told you the answer you want to hear— wouldn't I be violating your number one rule about telling no one even under threat or torture?"

"Look around. We're all alone out here. We're friends. No one within a hundred square miles of water. It's just me and you."

When the first trip down to the Caymans ended, Slade had disembarked and used the payphone on the dock to notify Jackie the Nose of The Lady Luck's arrival. Jackie had been at Harvey's home waiting in ambush.

The relationship with Slade didn't fit perfectly in any one category and was more a paradox. Harvey never had such a good friend like Slade, and yet Slade couldn't be trusted. His addiction to gambling ran his entire persona, controlled his entire world. Sad.

The problem, though, was that Slade had schooled him on how to fashion the bullets out of hard candy.

Even though the journalists never mentioned the hard candy's utility, the cops had labeled the perpetrator, The Candyman. Did Slade know about what happened on Daisy or was he just fishing?

"Okay, I'll answer one of your questions but—"

"You'll answer it honestly?"

"Yes, that's what friends do. They don't lie to one another. I'll answer one question if you answer one."

The ocean swished along the underside of the boat as the keel cut through the water. With the smooth swell, the boat gently rose and fell not unlike a baby's cradle.

CHAPTER TWENTY-EIGHT

Slade asked. "What's your question?"

"What's your real name?"

Slade smiled. "Yeah, thought as much. Well, that's not gonna happen." He handed the rum bottle over.

Harvey took the bottle and tilted it back. The alcohol burned all the way down and warmed the stomach.

Slade said, "Hey, down in the cabin, right-hand side cubby, get my small blue bag, would ya please? It looks like a dopp kit."

After some rummaging, he found the dopp bag and brought it out. Slade sat up, moving closer to the wheel, using one hand to steer, the other to grope around in the small bag. "Here we go." He pulled out a clear plastic container. "Saltwater taffy? You want some?"

"No thanks."

Slade unwrapped a piece and popped it in his mouth. "Hey, guess what?"

Harvey saw it coming, smiled, and shook his head. "Don't."

Slade laughed. "Since you brought this to me, doesn't that make you the Candyman?"

* * *

Harvey leaped off the boat with the rope, tied up to the cleat, turned and ran for a pay phone to call Abigail, elated that Jackie the Nose wasn't waiting on the dock slapping an empty hand with Baby Bertha.

The second call was for a yellow cab that arrived and drove far too slowly, the short distance to Washington and Fifth. The cab dropped him in front of The Thomas Soda Fountain closed till the next day. The distance was easy enough to walk, but Abigail was already on the way to the meet.

Nine weeks out of touch left the imagination to run wild. What had happened with Jackie the Nose? Had Mr. LaBruzzo taken him out for losing all the gold? Why wouldn't he? With that kind of money gone, along with two of his best men, CEO's of Forbes 500 companies had been fired for far less.

But those CEOs didn't literally know where the bodies were buried like

Jackie.

The taxi left, drove down Washington, and made a right. The red taillights disappeared, and a quiet calm settled in. After midnight, no one roamed the dark streets. He turned and hurried to the alley behind the store.

Abigail waited in an all-white with a blue stripe *U-Haul It*, rental truck, the kind with an automatic lift gate. The kind that could carry over fifteen hundred pounds of dead weight.

This time, Abigail wore a smile, one that changed her entire persona from the constant solemn and sad to vivacious and beautiful. A stark reminder that she should be out having the time of her life with friends and or socially interacting with men. Instead of "aiding and abetting a murderer after the fact." Another term found in Slade's books back on the boat. In those same books no defense of what happened on Daisy could be found. Justifiable homicide did not apply to the killing of two murderous thugs. If caught death row awaited like a blinking neon light.

Abigail started the big truck, "Hey."

"Hey to you. Do you want me to drive?"

"I got it." She shoved forward the long black gear shift to the four-on-the-floor, smoothly let out the clutch, and headed down the alley without headlights. The incongruence of the petite woman behind the big steering wheel was another reminder not to involve such an innocent.

Abigail wore a blue chambray shirt, tan canvas trousers, and brown brogans. A red bandana pulled her hair back. A cord around the waist cinched up the trousers three sizes too big. If larger in stature, she might have been mistaken for a long-haul truck driver.

With the first turn onto a street from the alley, she switched on the lights.

He wrung his hands. "This is a bad idea. It's the middle of the night. People are going to hear us doing our business and call the police."

"Stop it. *We have* to do it right now. During the day, people would also see us and call the police. We'll be more visible in broad daylight. It's one of those six of one, half dozen of another."

"That doesn't even make sense. I never did understand it. They are both the same."

She maneuvered the truck over to the curb, put the stick in neutral, and both small feet on the big brake pedal. "Did you lie to me about being The Candyman? Because you're as nervous as a longtail cat in a room full of rocking chairs."

"I'm okay. I'm just worried I'm about to drag you into this mess."

"I was going to shoot up a funeral, remember? In comparison, this is a cake walk." She put a foot on the clutch, depressed the pedal, shoved the stick into gear, and took off without jerking.

"You drive this thing like you own one."

"I rented it four times while you were out on your vacation cruise."

"I wasn't on a vac—You rented it four times?"

"To practice. I don't want anything to go wrong. I worked on the plan. Practiced everything. Speaking of going wrong, I've had a lot of time to think about this project of ours."

"Is that right?"

"That's right. What do you think about…I mean, instead of holding the gold in storage, we offer it up in exchange for Lois?"

"No."

"Just like that, no. You don't even want to think about it? Talk about it first?"

"You don't know what these people are like. They are pros at this kind of thing. At mayhem. They are not restricted by any laws and do exactly whatever they want whenever they want. Human life means nothing to them. We even try to make a trade; they'll start killing everyone near and dear to us. They will hunt both of us down and torture us until we tell them the location of the gold. And worse, Giorgio will start beating Lois, just because."

"Oh, you're probably right. I guess I didn't think it through. I just want to…I just want to get her back, that's all."

The unfamiliar urge to reach over and place a consoling hand on her shoulder passed as the *U-Haul-It* truck made a wide sweeping turn onto Daisy. Just the sight of the street made his stomach churn.

Two minutes later, she slowed to a stop in front of the safe house. The death house.

He said, "Hey, what are you doing? We agreed to park around back in the alley."

She shifted into reverse and backed up into the driveway of the house next door. "After the double murder, and with the Candyman still on the loose, these folks put their house up for sale and moved to "the crime-free," Midwest. I called the realtor and rented it while the owner tries to sell it."

"That was some smart thinking."

"In back of the truck I got a long board, two ladders, and a big tarp. I figured we'd hang the tarp across the two ladders between the two houses to cover our movement."

"I guess you're right, I have been loafing on vacation. You have really thought this through. Great plan."

She smiled, beaming.

The safe house stood on a foundation elevated a foot and a half off the ground. After the shooting, he moved the carpet in the safe room with all the gold, pried up a couple of boards, tossed the heavy ingots under the house, replaced the boards and the carpets. Effectively hiding the gold in plain sight. Who would steal that much gold and just leave it three or four feet away? Sure, some smart guy might think to look under the house, but the shock of all that gleaming yellow metal gone would baffle and confuse the most conscientious criminal. But most of all raise an ire never seen before. After those emotions passed, a stark fear would take over, clouding all else. Jackie on the hook for the loss.

Now the difficult part: crawling under the house next door, dragging out the individual ingots, carrying them through the next-door house, and loading them on the truck. Dirty, heavy scut work.

They still sat in the dark truck. She said, "I calculated this job should take us ten hours. We do five hours tonight and finish the last three or four hours tomorrow."

Two days of exposure. Harvey's mind flitted off as light as a bird to something Slade had said:

"The biggest mistake assholes make when setting out to commit a crime is their

lack of planning. They gloss over the details. Details that every time, without exception, rise up and bite them in the ass.

Each decision, each choice they make should be given careful consideration in how it will play out in court. How the prosecutor will come at you. Then side-step and resolve each of those pitfalls. The biggest being evidence."

Evidence left for the police was still a problem but leaving a trail Jackie the Nose could follow was lethal and in the most brutal way possible.

"Hello?" Abigail snapped fingers in front of his face. "Earth to Harvey. Where did you go?"

"What? Oh. I'm here. Sorry. I was just going over in my head this whole…this whole caper." Never in all the world did the word "caper" ever fit into the day and the life of a certified public accountant.

"Forget all this gold. I'm more concerned about my friend. When do we go for her? Get her away from that bastard Giorgio? I could shoot him right in the dick for hurting my friend."

Violence and mayhem changed everyone who touched it. For Abigail, the vengeful attitude overcame etiquette and decorum in the form of vulgarity and the need to pull a trigger.

He couldn't tell Abigail the part the gold played, that the money would be used for new identities and to support a life on the other side of the world. That once gone, Lois could never again contact Abigail. Every time that thought arose, the deception caused an ache in Harvey's chest.

"How is she doing? Have you seen her, talked to her? How does she look?"

Abigail's shadow turned to look out the truck window. "She's doing just fine."

Something about Abigail's tone wasn't right. Maybe a lie lurked in the sparse words.

"Can you look over here, please?"

Abigail turned, half her face in dark shadow, the other half gray from ambient streetlight. "The only thing keeping her going…well, the only thing she has to look forward to is when we break her out—get her away from the LaBruzzos. She says September second will be a good day to make that move."

"Wait. No. That's four months away. Why? I was thinking next week. Four months no. No chance."

"She said that if we don't do this right, someone's going to get hurt. Giorgio has people watching her all the time. Hard people."

"What's happening September second that makes it a good day?"

"September first Mr. LaBruzzo is taking a trip to Italy a long cruise to, 'The Continent.' Dragging along a large contingent of thugs. He's leaving Giorgio in charge with limited security coverage. Lois says Giorgio is a fool, easily distracted."

"Huh. That might actually work. I'm just concerned about the added time she'll be exposed to...to that family."

"It's the way she wants it."

"Then I'm good with it."

Chapter Twenty-Nine

Current Day

S ylvia's letter took the wind out of Harvey. Sucked every bit of energy from his bones. The abject sadness was like nothing he had ever experienced. No wonder he waited so long to read it. Instinct had steered him away from it, and for good reason.

Two years had passed. Why had it taken so long for the Andrew Johnson to arrive? Only one possible solution. Oliver Buckingham—Slade had followed his own advice and said nothing under threat of death and torture. Good for Slade.

Andrew and his boss had found other bread crumbs leading to Harvey and the house in Riverside.

He stood and walked on wobbly legs into the sitting room /closet off the bed chamber, sat on the bench upholstered in a maroon silk Asian print with gold fringe on the edges. He stared into the wall-sized mirror. The reflection was always a shock. The mind, a lonesome beast that, out of self-protection, maintained the memory of a younger man. The old broken-down coffin-dodger looked nothing like what memory kept stored as an image. The strange person in the mirror added to the depression. "Thank you for telling me, Lois's." He said to himself. "I didn't know about the cancer. If I wasn't so self-possessed I might've spotted the symptoms, spotted you concealing the pain. I'm such a horse's ass. Truly. I let you down, and I'll never forgive myself."

Rita entered the room at the worst possible time. She took a seat, hip touching his, that unnatural body heat an odd kind of comfort. The reflection, the juxtaposition of beauty vs broken-down old never more poignant.

She reached for the letter loose in his hand.

"No." Jerked it away. "Please don't."

The idea of someone else reading something so painfully personal made him want to struggle to his feet, stumble into the kitchen, and burn the pages on the stove's blue gas flames. But at the same time not. These were Lois's last words to him. Some of her very last thoughts in this world.

Rita put a hand on his leg and rested her head on his frail, bony shoulder. "I know I came here under a false flag. That my intent was to fleece you, but I've come to like you, Harv. I've never met someone so kind and gentle."

"You don't know the real Harvey Usher. Trust me, if I told you about my past, you would run away screaming."

"Not a chance." She leaned over and kissed his cheek, her lips a soft caress. "I'm sorry."

"What are you sorry for?" She asked.

"I want to believe you. I do but…I…I—"

"You think you know my kind. That con artists are always on the make? Is that it? Well, I'm telling you the truth now. I do like you, and I'm sorry as hell that I was even involved in this caper to defraud you. I hope we can be friends after all this is over tomorrow morning."

"Is that right?"

"That's right."

The idea of a woman of Rita's criminal stature even sitting so close to Lois' words in the letter brought on a sour stomach and yet another emotional pang. Something that happened all too often of late.

He put a hand on top of hers, squeezed, and looked into her eyes. "True friends don't lie to each other."

She hesitated. "We *are* true friends, Harv. I promise that we are."

"You hesitated."

"I've never…I mean, I've never had a true friend before. I needed a moment.

Test me, please. Give me something to prove myself."

"Are you running a game right now?"

"No." She said it with a twinge of vehemence.

"Did you know about the gold? Did Andrew tell you about any gold?"

"No. I told you I was just trying to distract that Aussie Mike asshole, so I could get to that fireplace poker to do him in."

"So, no amount of gold would shake our friendship?"

"Yes, that's right. You're dead broke. Andrew told me as much. All you have available is the huge chunk of home equity."

He reached down with a free hand and depressed the button under the edge of the bench.

Rita whispered in awe. *"A switch under the bench. No wonder I—"*

In the reflection of the mirror, the wall of cubbies behind them, the one filled with shoes, slide aside to reveal the entrance to a small safe room, one with two comfortable stools and large enough for two people to wait out a threatening interloper. On the back wall of the safe room, stacked vertically, gleamed gold from the Suisse Air Transport heist. The numbers tumbled around in his head. Only a fourth of what it used to be, so, about 391 pounds. Small stacks really to equal 391 pounds. 16,256 ounces. But according to Sylvia, at two thousand dollars an ounce that equaled $32,512,00.

They had stopped spending the gold. Their connection to convert the ingots, stamped with a *Suisse Bank* logo, died in a robbery hold up of his pawn shop in the Belltown district of Riverside. The risk-to-gain no longer a viable option. Instead they crimped down spending and lived more frugally off the savings account, supplemented by selling off the expensive and sought-after antique furniture Sylvia had collected.

Harvey watched Rita's reflection, the way her eyes grew large, her beautiful lips forming an "O." The glint in her eyes was unmistakable. Greed and avarice are one of the seven deadly sins that, since time immemorial, have ruined men, states, countries, and the world.

Above the gold, two guns hung on nails, the ones used on Tommy Tee and Jimmy in the house on Daisy.

Rita stood up in a dazed state, turned to look straight into the saferoom without the mirror. Harvey leaned back, looking up, still watching her expression, waiting for what she had said about being true friends to become a reality. Waited for her to reiterate that promise. Needed her too in the worst way.

The gold reflected in Rita's eyes. Still agog, she uttered. "So, it's true, you are the Candyman."

Harvey shook his head. "Ah, shit."

Chapter Thirty

1968

Rising to start the day, every muscle screamed in pain. The hard labor from the night before wasn't a familiar occupation. First, lifting out of the hole in the floor the heavy ingots, lugging them through the house, through the backyard, through the house next door, and into the back of the truck.

He lingered in the shower, stayed under the hot jets until the water heater turned cold. He answered the knock at the door with wet hair and a damp shirt from drying off in a hurry, with no idea how long the visitor had been waiting. Abigail had grossly miscalculated the time needed to move the gold. They finished the entire load in less than five hours.

The titular Eugene Lujan stood on the stoop without expression. But cold, hard eyes said many a man died by his hand in a most brutal manner. A limo driver's status ranked below the family's accountant, yet an arrogant air said he thought otherwise. He grunted, turned, and headed for the limo.

Harvey, skip-hopped to catch up. "Where are we going?" His empty stomach churned with anxiety. Had they found him out? Did they have someone watching the empty safe house which was no longer of any use. The main security for the house was its anonymity, and now everyone statewide knew its location. Thanks to the Candyman.

Eugene didn't open the back door to the car, went around, and got in. Harvey stood outside, internal organs, ribs, and muscles quaking with fear, waiting for Eugene to get out and correct the error in protocol.

Slade, in one of his counseling sessions, said to always fake it, to show confidence no matter the situation. False confidence had gotten more than one fool out of a tight situation.

Time ticked by. Four or five minutes, or maybe it was twenty seconds. Sweat broke out on his forehead and ran into his eyes, stinging. An overactive imagination had Eugene exiting the car, coming around, grabbing him by the scruff, and banging his head against the car trunk until both eyeballs popped out.

But that didn't happen, which meant Eugene had specific orders, and if he hadn't yet, he wasn't going to bang a Ledger Man around.

Harvey got in. "Would you please turn up the air conditioner?"

The center divider whirred up. The air came on, but Eugene had activated the heater, hot air blew into the back. "Funny man. You're real funny." A fool's words muted by the bulletproof glass divider.

Not long into the drive, the destination became evident based on the turns and street names. They were not going to the office above the donut shop to perform the daily ritual of counting and logging in ill-gotten gains. They were instead headed to the LaBruzzo estate out in rural Hoboken. The burning question: where was Jackie the Nose? Why wasn't he in the limo picking up the Ledger Man, ensuring things didn't get out of hand. Controlling. Always controlling everything.

Eugene pulled up and parked in the turnabout in the front of the estate next to the glorious water fountain; two concrete cherubs with angel wings frozen mid-frolic with water shooting out of their flutes.

Eugene got out and, instead of going to the front door, walked to the side, headed to the pool area, Mr. LaBruzzo's "conference room," away from prying eyes and ears.

Harvey followed along.

In back, in the usual place at a patio table and chairs, sat Mr. LaBruzzo under the red and white CinZano umbrella. The black and dark crimson silk robe hung off the shoulders and chest. One hand held a diluted orange juice, probably spiked with vodka, in the other hand, the financial section of The New York Times. Weight loss made already wrinkled skin worse. Rheumy eyes watched everything with catlike awareness.

"Come. Come, Harvey, have a seat and let us have a nice, pleasant conversation."

Off to the side, over by the slump stone fence, sat Jackie the Nose, looking anxious, hands clutched tight in his lap, face glistening with sweat, and furtive eyes desperately trying to communicate important information across an expanse of bright green grass and concrete. Regulated to semi-seclusion. In a time-out, like a kid in Kindergarten. Only this wasn't a kid's game.

Scared to death, Harvey slowed but kept walking, trying to figure if suddenly bolting back to the side gate would allow more than three or four steps before getting gunned down like a dog. The entire setup looked exactly like what Slade described as a "Mousetrap." He was about to be mousetrapped.

They knew about The Candyman. Why else set the meeting like this? In a place with tall walls all around, with no easy way out and a stone-cold mankiller like Eugene Lujan standing by, hands crossed at his waist, waiting for the order to crush, kill, or destroy. Why else was Jackie on pins and needles with stress held incommunicado out of earshot of the patio table occupants? Mr. LaBruzzo believed The Ledger Man and Jackie the Nose conspired to steal all the gold. Mr. LaBruzzo would start with the sugar and go to the stick.

Harvey made it to the table and stood staring at Eugene's "waiting wolf," like demeanor.

"Sit. Sit, have some iced tea." LaBruzzo held up the glass pitcher, sweating with condensation, the humidity thick under the afternoon sun.

Harvey stood still. LaBruzzo nodded. Eugene moved in, pulled out the chair, and put a hand on Harvey's shoulder, the grip iron hard with inhuman strength. He guided him into the seat, pressing down.

"There," LaBruzzo said, "Now isn't that better getting into the shade and out of the sun? This heat can be murder. Am I right?"

Harvey nodded.

"Drink some iced tea, it'll cool you off."

The last time sitting at the table with Mr. LaBruzzo was in the parking lot of the park across the street from the hospital. The day of the kiss. The day Robin LaBruzzo tumbled off the back of that convertible changing many people's lives. Not for the better.

Harvey picked up the glass intending only to take a sip and instead slurped down half. The summer drink more an elixir tasting sour and yet sweet, spicy and earthy.

"Fine. Fine. Now let's have a nice little talk."

"With you is that even possible?" Where had those words come from. Had the Candy Man raised his ugly head? Suppress those thoughts or die a horrible death.

LaBruzzo gave a raspy chuckle and looked over at Eugene his trained dog. He said "Well, lookee here, our toothless little sloth has gown himself some balls, huh?"

Eugene dipped one shoulder ever so slightly in response, hands still crossed at his waist.

LaBruzzo expression shifted from amicable host to top tier predator shooting Harvey a withering glare. "Now we're going to talk about my gold."

"Er...ah, what gold is that?"

LaBruzzo sat back and stared.

Harvey squirmed inside his skin and hopped LaBruzzo didn't notice. But men like LaBruzzo noticed everything. They couldn't rise to the top of the heap with cunning and élan without being able to read everyone right down to their smallest tick or tell.

But could he differentiate a reaction from a lie over stark raving fear?

"You keep trying to look over at Jackie. Look right here." LaBruzzo said, "He can't do you any good. Not now. Only the truth can keep you from a beating like you've never experienced."

Eugene walked over and stood behind Harvey's chair. His presence made Harvey's skin roll and prickle.

"Tell me, where the hell's my gold?"

Harvey swallowed hard. The pause needed to form the lie and present it in a natural manner. "I know nothing of any *gold*." He put the emphasis on *gold* as bait.

Manfredi, in his book, wrote, *"The overtness of a lie is easy to detect. The best way to reveal the lie is to get the subject to proffer it first."*

"You said gold, like there's something else you want to say? Say it, boy, tell me."

Harvey let his eyes once again drift over toward Jackie the Nose, who couldn't hear a word of the conversation.

"Look at me. Look over here. I won't tell you—"

From behind a fist came down on Harvey's head with such force the sun's natural light turned oblong. Sharp pain shot up and down neck his and spine and the horizon wobbled.

"God damnit, Genie, don't cripple the son of bitch. That kinda thing's what got you set down the last time. Ya heavy-handed thug—bastard."

A strong hand on each shoulder straightened Harvey in the chair. The world still had not readjusted back to normal. Without prompting Genie took the pitcher of iced tea and poured it over Harvey's head.

The ice-cold was all at once shocking and chilling.

LaBruzzo leaned over. "Now, son, listen to me very carefully. I'm done playing tiddlywinks with you. I'm only going to ask you one more time. Wait, don't talk yet. Hear me out first." He held up a hand to keep any useless words from spilling out of the nearly-brained interrogation subject. "Think over your answer and remember I never ask a question I don't already have the answer to."

Harvey wanted to say, "That doesn't make a bit of sense. Why ask if you already know?" He hadn't read Manfredi who said, try to always ask a question with a little bit of truth built in. This makes your subject believe you already have the information.

Maybe LaBruzzo did already know everything.

"Okay, I'll tell you just…please don't hit me again."

LaBruzzo said nothing and glared.

"I'm scared." He moved his eyes askance toward Jackie the Nose.

247

Half an evil grin eased out of LaBruzzo's wrinkled lips. He whispered. "Why do you think that fat son of a bitch is sitting all the way over there. You don't have to be afraid. He won't get anywhere near you. Now tell me, does he have my gold?" The last part rose in decibels.

Over by the slump stone wall, Jackie struggled to stand with that walrus-like heavy girth. "Does *he* have my gold? I heard that. Don't you listen to that weasel-faced rat bastard. He's lying. Boss, you gotta believe me, not him."

LaBruzzo didn't take his eyes off Harvey's, pointed, and yelled. "Stay over there. Shut up and sit your fat ass down or I'll send Genie over to whisper in your ear."

Jackie, his eyes wider than normal, sweat pouring down his face, didn't sit down and continued to pace back and forth. The weight underfoot mashed a path in the brilliantly green grass.

Harvey nodded and whispered. "I swear to all that's holy, I know nothing about any gold but—" He paused for effect and again swallowed hard.

"But? Come on, spill it."

"He made me do it."

LaBruzzo reached out with one hand and grabbed Harvey around the throat.

The next words choked out. "If you go to the office, you know over The Hole in One and check out the tallest drawer on the right side. You'll find a false bottom where—"

LaBruzzo didn't need to hear anymore; he stood up too fast, bumping the table, and glared at Jackie the Nose across the expanse.

Jackie hurried over his right hand in his pocket. "No. No. No. I didn't hear what the little bastard told you, but I'm your lieutenant, and it's my word against his. He's a liar, pure and simple. Let me have him for an hour or two, and I'll get the truth out of him. He'll tell me all about the gold."

Eugene took off his black livery jacket, revealing a white long-sleeved shirt and black vest. He didn't have a gun. But when you're at the top of the food chain, like Eugene, you didn't need a weapon.

Jackie continued to rattle off a meager defense, waving his left hand in the air, the right still in his pocket. A threat not being taken seriously.

LaBruzzo straightened the silk robe that got bunched up and rumpled when jumping to his feet. "Jackie, I'm only going to ask you once, and you had better give me the got-damn truth the first time. You understand me?"

Eugene side-stepped until he faced off with Jackie. Six or eight feet between them.

LaBruzzo pointed off to the south. "If I go to that office right now, will I find a drawer with a false bottom that contains skimmed money. My money?"

Jackie violently shook his head from side to side, the fat waddling flinging sweat droplets that speckled the concrete pool deck underfoot. "No way. No how. This little prick is lying his ass off. You gotta believe me, boss. Just let me have a few minutes with him, I'll make him tell the truth."

"Is the drawer there, Jackie?"

Jackie the Nose suddenly realized no matter what he said, all was lost. He straightened his shoulders, raised his chin, and said, "You can kiss my fat, white ass if you believe him over me."

Everyone froze. No one breathed. No one talked to Mr. LaBruzzo that way.

Mr. LaBruzzo twitched his chin. The same as lighting a fuse to a bomb.

Eugene took a giant step toward Jackie. While Jackie yanked a gun from his pants pocket. He got it up and fired just as Eugene rose up on his left heel and with his right kicked Jackie square in the chest. The transference of such energy from the bullets sent shock waves through all that blubber. Jackie's body vibrated as he flew backward.

The gun fired once. And then a second time, seconds before the tub of lard splashed down in the pool, sending a tidal wave in both directions. Jackie sank. Bubbles rose. Under water, the gun fired four more times in muted whooshes. Jackie thrashed and struggled, and even with the massive buoyancy, the pure panic made it impossible to regain the surface.

Eugene stood at the pool's edge, watching without emotion as a man drowned.

No matter the kind of person, no one deserved to drown. A horrible way to die. Harvey stood, took two wobbly steps, and dove into the pool. The cold water, a shock to the nervous system. Jackie had already started to bob to the surface. Harvey took hold of him, an arm under his chin, and surfaced.

Jackie sputtered and coughed. Then threw up, the surrounding air filled with the sour reek of stomach acid, and semi-digested breakfast and lunch floated in a surface sheen.

Towering large over both of them stood Eugene Lujan holding a gun down by his leg. Where had he gotten the gun?

His white dress shirt at the shoulder turning a wet crimson from the bullet Jackie had thrown at him. Most men would've been down on the ground whimpering.

LaBruzzo sat at the patio table sipping a screwdriver. He raised a hand like a Roman emperor and turned a thumb down.

Eugene Lujan turned back, raised the pistol and shot Jackie six times in the upper torso. These bullets weren't made of candy and thumped hard into the gelatinous blubber. The air clouded with a blood mist. A blood slick mixed with recently expunged breakfast and lunch.

The shock from the abrupt violence caused Harvey to flounder. Pool water with the new additives slopped over into his mouth. He gagged and choked. Sputtered. Arms flailed but worked well enough to get back to the edge.

LaBruzzo stood, walked the two steps over to the pool edge, screwdriver in hand. Took a sip. He wore nothing underneath the robe. The result now grossly evident and hung-over Harvey, who couldn't help thinking, "Bald pet monkey."

"God Damn your soul Jackie for cheatin' on me. Look what you two bastards did to my pool." His eyes fell onto Harvey. "You rat bastard, get your ass outta my pool and get back to work."

Chapter Thirty-One

1968

The sun beat down on sopping clothes as Harvey walked down the long, tree-lined drive to the street. Shoes and socks slopped around, making blisters. Without the thick humidity, the shirt and pants would have dried a lot faster. He kept spitting and, with the back of his hand, wiped his mouth.

Jackie the Nose was gone, and Eugene Lujan was wounded; the theft of the gold in order to cause hate and discontent among the mob came to fruition much later than anticipated. And came very close to taking Harvey down as well.

At the street, he took a right and headed back to town. A car whisked by. Too late to raise a thumb. Hoboken was a mile and a half square that left no more than a mile or so to find a payphone. Another car barreled by with a roar. The walk turned into a trudge.

Thirty minutes later, at least it seemed like thirty minutes, he'd only made it halfway into town. Water had invaded the *Timex*, and now droplets hung suspended inside the crystal. He finally came upon a payphone at a Sunco Service station.

The taxi took more than twenty minutes to arrive, and another ten to get home. At least two hours had passed since the shooting, maybe more. Going to work at the office in rumpled and semi-damp clothes didn't sound at all appealing. What did sound appealing was a hot shower and the comfort and security of home. For decades to come the sound and feel of those bullets thumping into Jackie the Nose would taint memory and chase away sleep. Nothing would ever come close to the raw violence of that dreadful experience of holding someone in your arms while that person is gunned down. An event that somehow even eclipsed the shooting on Daisy.

Out in front of the house sat a brand-new Chevy Corvette, midnight blue with a T-top. The recently washed and waxed car twinkled and winked in the bright sun. Who did it belong to? Everyone worth worrying about was back at the LaBruzzo estate. Eugene Lujan would be busy for hours cleaning up the mess in the pool and making the trek out to the Meadowlands. But that trip would have to wait for the cover of darkness. For a moment, the conundrum in how Eugene would get Jackie from the pool into the car trunk presented in the form of a mathematical equation. Variables of mass, friction, and area all swirled around, refusing cohesion.

Inside the house, the temperature dropped at least ten degrees, and it felt marvelous to be out of the humidity.

Abigail stood up from the easy chair in the living room. Her big smile was something needed in the worst way after the morning's violent dip in the pool.

"Harvey, your clothes…your clothes look damp and rumpled."

"Yes, they are. What are you doing here? We agreed not to be seen together, it's too dangerous."

"Did you go swimming in your clothes?"

"Yes, I did. You didn't answer the question."

"I…ah. I need the fake passport and driver's license for Lois. You said you had a friend making them for the both of you?"

For the briefest moment, a wicked little thought flitted across a mind already full of a bleeding walrus-like body, one still too fresh to shove aside to answer an unfair question: were Abigail and Lois running off with the gold?

Then guilt sauntered in for even thinking that level of evil about two wonderful young women.

"I won't have them for two more weeks. Why?"

She rushed toward him and stopped just short. "Oh, Harvey, I have the best news."

The morning—early afternoon, rather, had already been too trying, so he backed up and plopped down in a second easy chair. "Tell me. Is it about Lois? Is it good news about Lois?"

"Yes. Yes, it is. I have her, Harv. I put her up at a motel not far from here until we can get her out of town."

He sat forward, the adrenaline shot into his heart sparked the soul. "What happened? How did you do it?"

"I didn't. Lois did it. She said Giorgio received a phone call, and he left the house with all his security people. In his haste, he didn't think to leave anyone behind to watch Lois."

The call had obviously come from his dad, telling Giorgio all about Jackie taking the plunge in the backyard pool and that Eugene Lujan needed help fishing him out.

"Lois simply went to the garage, got into Giorgio's—"

"1968 midnight blue Corvette?"

"Yes, that's right."

"Abigail, it's parked right outside."

"I won't be here long. When I leave, I'm driving right to Aberdeen to run that bastard's car off a cliff. Lois says he loves that car more than life itself." She stepped over to the chair, lifted a heavy purse, and returned with a pace slowing with each step. "Now, Harv, for the hard part."

"Ah, no. Not a hard part. I can't take much more today."

She knelt by the chair and put a hand on his knee. "I know you love Lois dearly. I know this because all that you have risked for her. She loves you just as much."

The ugly words came through a muddled fog. This wasn't happening. He waited for the worst word in the English language, waited for the "But" to drop.

Abigail continued. "I think it's because she's so ashamed about what's happened to her with Giorgio. What he did to her that first night." Tears filled Abigail's eyes. "That's why she made this decision. Harvey, she doesn't want to see you. At least not right now."

He swallowed hard. "I understand." Tears now burned *his* eyes. But he really didn't understand. Why? Not if she was free. Not if she really and truly loved him.

"No, wait. By your expression, I can see I'm screwing this all up royally. She said...Lois said that she loves you. Loves you forevermore. That's the way she said it, too. Forevermore, Harvey. She just wants time to get her feet back underneath her, that's all. She just needs some time. I'm going to take her somewhere to help forget all of this."

"Don't tell me where. I don't want to know. Giorgio will be looking for her and me. If he gets his hands on me, I don't want to tell under duress. The car out front has already been here too long. You took a big risk. You have to go. Right now."

"Wait. Just wait. One minute more. Lois insisted that I come in person to tell you. To make sure you understand. And I really do want to drive that car off a cliff." She took a heavy gold ingot from her purse. We're moving the gold, but we didn't want you to think we were ripping you off. This will hold you over until we can meet up."

A smart idea to move the gold.

But the odds of Harvey surviving after Lois disappeared were what— ninety to one? Ninety-nine to one? That sounded about right. He moved to the bookshelf and pulled out three Nero Wolf novels behind which he hid both guns, reloaded with hard candy. He came back over to her to give over the guns. "You have to go before it's too late." He tried to hand them to her.

She pushed them away. "Wait. I have to tell you how to find us. Once things cool down, call the Los Angeles Times and take out a personal ad that says, 'One if by sea, two if by land,' with a phone number or address where you can be reached. We'll be waiting."

"So, you're going to the West Coast? That's good. Get as far away as possible. Now you have to get going. Once they find Lois missing, this will be the first place they look."

"Too late, assholes."

Giorgio stepped from the hall that led to the back of the house. He'd breached a backdoor or window. He held a gun, black and lethal. The black hole at the end of the barrel was the same size as a train tunnel.

Giorgio came deeper into the room with Eugene Lujan at his side.

Giorgio, the man who married Lois. The man who returned to the hospital parking lot with claw marks on his neck and chest. A quiet rage burned bright, growing with intensity. Next to him, Abigail started to quiver, her face flushed red. She, too, fought the heated and blinding throes of rage.

Eugene wore the black livery jacket concealing the bullet wound to his shoulder. But the white shirt visible between the black vest and black pants was a sopping red. All the black made his ashen face even more gray. He clutched a long double-edged knife. Blood ran in rivulets over his hand and down the blade. One crimson droplet let go and spattered the floor. Then another.

Giorgio motioned with the gun, "Drop 'em. Now."

Abigail raised her hands, curled into claws, and let loose a long, low screech. She charged.

Eugene took a wavering step in front of Giorgio to protect him just as Giorgio fired. The knife caught Abigail below the sternum. Eugene took the bullet in the back from Giorgio. Abigail and Eugene tumbled to the floor in a writhing pile of arms and legs. Groans and pathetic squeaks of the dying.

Harvey screamed, advancing on the stunned Giorgio, firing one gun, then the other. The hard candy struck his face and neck again and again until he dropped flat on his back, unmoving.

Harvey dropped both empty guns and went to Abigail. On his knees, he shoved off the gurgling Eugene Lujan and pulled her shoulders onto his lap. Her mouth opened and closed. Opened and closed. A trickle of blood rolled from her mouth and down her chin.

He rocked back and forth. "No. No. No."

The light in her eyes faded.

And winked out.

Chapter Thirty-Two

Current Day

I nside the walk-in closet off the master bedroom, Rita stood up from the bench. On shaky legs, she walked on wobbly heels the short distance into the safe room. She picked up the top gold ingot from the stack that gleamed in the low light and marveled at it the same as a poor skinny kid would a chocolate bar.

"Rita, you just called me The Candyman. You knew all about my history before you started the scam. You're a liar. You've been playing me from the start."

She turned around and looked back. Something in her eyes had changed. Shifted. As obvious as the blue in the sky. Greed, the second deadly sin, had slithered in and stolen her soul right before his eyes. Maybe stole what was left of it anyway.

"Get over yourself, Harv. So, I knew. Big whoop. I wasn't lying about liking you. If I'd said I was madly in love...well, that would be a lie. But Harv, look at all this gold. We can run away and live like kings anywhere in the world."

"It's not that easy. Those bars are stamped with the bank logo. They're difficult to convert. And don't change the subject. Where did you find out about me, about my history?"

She again looked up from the gold ingot. "If you think I heard it from Andrew, you're mistaken. Andrew was telling me about the job here at this house and slipped. He called you Dortmund. Later, I got online and hunted for Harvey Dortmund. I found the newspaper articles: a young woman stabbed to death and a man shot in the back at your house. They found evidence of hard candy smashed against one wall and linked it to another murder house on Daisy Street. So, Little Mister, you better step down off that high horse of yours and help me with this gold. We gotta get outta here and I mean right now." She bent, picked up another gold ingot, and another. Three were almost too heavy for her arms to sustain.

He stood, came around the stool, bumped her out of the way, and took down the two guns that hung on nails. One with a short barrel, the other longer. The murder guns.

"What are you doing? We don't need those now. We got the—"

From the bedroom entrance, a deep baritone voice said, "Good, you saved us the trouble of tearing this place apart looking for it." Andrew Johnson waved a chrome-plated automatic. "Come on, step on outta there, the both of ya's"

Harvey reached out to the wall and pressed a button. The wall covering the safe room abruptly whirred shut.

"Hey. Hey. Open up right now or I'll start pumping rounds right through that thing." His muffled voice was barely audible.

Inside the room, darkness pure as pitch encompassed them. Rita whispered, "Can he shoot through this wall? Harvey can he shoo—"

"No, there's a thin steel plate that will stop all pistol and most rifle rounds. But we're still trapped like a couple of rats. He won't dare shoot. It wouldn't be smart. If he killed us, then how would we get the wall open?"

"I'll count to five. You don't come out, I'll shoot?"

"One."

Harvey reached in the dark looking for the switch on the wall and accidentally grabbed one of Rita's breasts.

"Hey, what are you doing? You're not looking for the switch to open the door, are you?"

"Two."

He found the light switch and flipped it on. A dull yellowness enveloped them, the bulb's low wattage.

"Three."

Harvey reached around her and picked up the phone receiver. He stuck a finger out to punch in 911.

She grabbed it. "What are you doing now?"

"Four."

"Calling the police."

She grabbed his hand. "You can't call the police, don't be ridiculous. Use your head. We'll all go to jail. They see all this gold and the bank stamp. They'll get you on four murders back in Jersey. And me for just being involved with you. Hell, they'll even think I'm married to you. Ain't that a big bite of an irony sandwich? They'll call it aiding and abetting after the fact."

"I don't care about prison. I'm more concerned about Lissette and Esther, what they've done to them while we were in here. What they will do to them if we don't come out? They're out there alone with that animal. I'm sorry about you going to jail, but there's nothing else we can—"

"Five."

Muted shots came from the other side, thudding into the shoes huddled in cubbies, the steel wall insert doing its job. Andrew only stopped long enough to reload.

He fired another full magazine.

Then nothing.

An odd quiet ensued. Had he left? Seconds ticked by.

She stared into his eyes, gritting teeth that made both jaw muscles bulge.

Andrew returned, evidenced by noise on the other side of the wall, a low murmur, someone crying. "You hear me in there? I got the old crow with me, and I'm going to pump a bullet into her head if you don't come out. Say something, ya old bitch."

"Harvey?" Esther said. "Don't come out. They're going to kill everyone no matter wha—"

A thump. Esther cried out.

He'd hit Esther.

"I'm going out and you can't stop me."

"All right, dammit. Just give me a minute to think."

"This time you have to the count of three. One."

"He'll do it. You know he will. We have to open the wall right now."

"Gimme that smaller gun."

"Two."

He handed it to her and yelled, "Okay, okay, give us one sec, we're trying to get the switch to work."

Rita pulled up her dress to reveal a long, sleek leg with a black lace garter belt toward the top. No one wore garter belts anymore. She stuck the gun on the left inside thigh.

"That's not going to hold, the gun's too heavy." She put her hand on his face and shoved him away. At the same time, hit the button to open the wall. As it opened, she grabbed the second gun from his hand and stuck it in the wide waist belt in the back.

"Ah, lookee here." He shoved Esther away, who fell to the ground. He reached in and grabbed a handful of Rita's beautiful red hair, yanking her out. "You were going to run off with all the gold, weren't you, Gloria?"

"Hey, hey, leave her alone." Harvey rushed out. Andrew backhanded him with the gun. The chrome is blurred a second before impact. Bright lights lit up the world. The next second, he lay on the floor with Esther trying to help him up. A trickle of blood ran from the corner of her mouth, and her bottom lip ballooned bright red and purple.

Andrew Johnson still had Rita by the hair, wrangling her. "Come on," he said, "get your asses out here." He herded them into the big living room where a crippled old man sat in a wheelchair.

"The gold's in there, boss. Not much left. At least a quarter of it."

The ugly man in the wheelchair who looked like he wore a flesh mask comprised of lumpy scar tissue said, "I don't give two shits about the gold. I told you what I'm here for."

Lissette lay on the floor curled up in a fetal position, her face covered in blood. She'd been brutally pistol-whipped.

Esther came down the two steps into the sunken living room and eased to the floor as if all the muscles in her body suddenly gave out.

"Is this him? Is this the bastard I've been looking for, for the last fifty years?"

Andrew, still holding onto Rita's hair like someone walking a dog, said, "That's him." He kicked Harvey in the hip and knocked him to the floor. Now, all three except Rita were on the floor. Rita continued to move and dodge, trying to keep Andrew from seeing the gun in her back belt.

The man in the wheelchair wheeled over closer to Harvey. "You know who I am?"

Harvey struggled to his feet, remembering something from long ago. When Jackie the Nose spoke about gunsels buried in The Meadowlands. Harvey said, "I thought you were dead and barking in hell."

Chapter Thirty-Three

Current Day

All of them in the living room stared at only one person, waiting for what came next, Giorgio drawing out the silence, knowing full well it's a form of torture and savoring it.

Finally, he spoke. "Where's Lois?"

No one answered.

With one hand, Andrew Johnson held onto Rita's hair and shook her again. "Hey! He grabbed the gun stuck in her back belt. Shoved her down and kicked her in the ribs. He put the six-inch .357 behind his narrow dress belt inside his pants and stood with his hands crossed at his waist, waiting for orders, waiting for Giorgio to give an order to beat and maim one or all of them.

Esther's small voice echoed in the near-empty room. "Sylvia passed away two years ago."

"Heh, heh. I knew that. I just wanted someone to say it. I outlived her. But that's a hell of a consolation prize, isn't it? She leaves me, steals a hundred million dollars on her way out the door, and all I get is the consolation prize."

Harvey couldn't conceal his abject hate for the man. "Consolation, that's a pretty big word coming out of Bronx PS 13." Giorgio had attended a blue-blazer prep school in New Jersey, but he caught the slight.

Giorgio pulled his right hand out from under the blanket that covered his legs. He pointed a small automatic at him. "You want to dig your hole a little deeper, Pal? We'll let you go last when we start the carving. You can watch these ladies get taken apart piece by piece." He started to cough a deep, phlegmy bellow that racked his body and flushed his face red.

Esther struggled to a sitting position. She raised her chin. "Sounds like that consolation prize is about to give up on you."

Giorgio stopped coughing, his eyes watery. He spat a wad of phlegm into a handkerchief already stiff with dried body fluids. "Something my dad taught me, God rest his soul, is that you have to nip rebellion in the bud as soon as it raises its ugly head." He nodded at Andrew Johnson.

Andrew took two long steps toward Esther, pulling out a switchblade. He flicked it open as he stood over Esther. He pulled back the blade as he leaned down.

"Wait," Harvey yelled.

Giorgio waved the little gun. "You, least of all, have no bargaining power. We already have the gold, and nothing you say will deter me from getting even for stealing my wife." He nodded again.

Andrew stabbed Esther in the stomach.

Esther had her hands up to ward him off. He held on to the knife hilt while staring into her eyes. A horrible little mewing sound came from her.

"You bastard." Harvey struggled to his feet.

Giorgio waved his little gun again. "Victor? Don't hurt him too bad. He needs to be around to see the show."

Andrew, whose real name was Victor, pulled the knife out of Esther and wiped the blade on her dress, the wet, bloody spot between her fingers growing by the second.

Harvey ran at Giorgio, intent on throttling him. Victor intercepted and kicked Harvey's legs out from under him before he made it halfway.

Lissette rolled over, her face bleeding and swollen. She'd taken the initial brunt of Victor's entry into the house, while Harvey and Rita played footsie in the closet. Lissette wasn't the kind to yell out, or they might've heard the attack all the way back in the closet. Lissette's eyes moved to the piece of rebar lying on the carpet from when she'd been disarmed.

Giorgio spotted her intent. "Don't do it. Don't."

Too late. Lissette rolled twice, coming to her feet like a circus acrobat. But it still wasn't enough. Giorgio tracked her with the gun and fired twice, the little gun kicked and spat fire, the noise oddly no more than a 'pop, pop.'

Lissette spun around, dropped, and was still.

Harvey said, "No. No. No." He crawled on hands and knees over to Esther, got under her, and pulled her into his lap.

Esther shifted from mewing to weeping, both her hands bloody from holding her stomach. "What about your son?" She said in between sobs, "You didn't ask about your son?"

The scared mask that was Giorgio's face turned to a scowl. "He's dead. Victor said..."

Esther shook her head, gasping. "No. You'd better ask him again."

Victor started to rush over.

Giorgio raised his hand. "Wait!"

Victor froze.

Esther's words finally penetrated Harvey's anger and grief, "Esther, what are you talking about? What son? I mean if he had a son he would be...Lois was married to him. You can't possibly mean—"

Was she talking about Lois? She couldn't be talking about Lois?

Then it all fell into place. In the letter, Lois said to ask Esther about the third item.

Esther, looking over at Giorgio, shook her head.

"Victor, what the hell is she talking about?"

"She's a liar. It's just like I said, your son was killed in a car accident five years ago."

Rita, lying on the floor, rose up on one arm, her other hand on the dress between her legs. "Two days ago, Victor stole my car and ran Eddie over, killing him."

"Victor!"

Victor shook his head. "No. Don't listen to them, they're lying. Can't you see they're just trying to drive a wedge between you and me? It's nothing but a simple-minded tactic."

Harvey's mouth worked all on its own. "Eddie Gurski was Lois's son?"

Esther moaned but got the words out. "I'm so sorry, Harvey. Lois was going to tell you in her letter. She said she'd tell you in—"

The little gun in Giorgio's hand spat fire. 'Pop. Pop. Pop.'

The bullets struck Victor. But he was a big man and already on the move, running toward Rita, who'd confirmed the truth. He drew the six-inch .357 from his waistband and fired again and again. The magnum was louder than the small gun, and the white smoke bellowed out, filling the room.

Rita screamed as bullets struck her. She rolled and flinched and jerked.

Giorgio continued to shoot bullets, striking Victor. He staggered. His gun clicked empty.

Giorgio's gun clicked empty.

Victor fell face-first on top of Rita.

The room turned quiet. Esther had gone still, her eyes tented, only the whites showing.

Giorgio sat in the wheelchair, breathing hard, eyes bulging in anger, face bloated.

Rita pushed Victor off, hands feeling all over her body, her expression stunned surprise.

"Candy!" Harvey yelled. "He shot you with candy. Shoot him! Shoot him!"

Rita caught on and pawed at her dress, trying to get to the gun strapped to the inside of her leg in the garter.

Giorgio's hands fumbled to pull the empty magazine from the gun and to get a fresh one loaded.

Harvey eased Esther off him and scrambled over to Rita and the dead Victor.

But Rita had the gun out and rolled up onto her knees. She fired at Giorgio. The hard candy struck him only twice in the chest. The other hit the wall in the entry hall.

Giorgio recovered faster than Rita had, both being shot with hard candy. He'd been shot before in the face in a similar manner. He chuckled as Rita's gun clicked empty. He casually stuck a fresh magazine in his gun and raised it, pointing it at Rita's chest no more than three feet away. "Kiss your ass good-bye, bitch."

Harvey rose up on his knees, Victor's chrome gun in his hand, and fired again and again until the gun clicked empty.

Giorgio's body jerked each time a lead bullet struck his chest and face. The first one would've been enough, but Harvey gave him the entire magazine, the full fifteen.

He eased down on one elbow and whispered to no one, something Slade had taught him, "If he's good for one, he's good for all six."

Chapter Thirty-Four

Current Day

Seven days after the shooting in the living room, Harvey Usher turned eighty-one. The Uber driver dropped him in front of RCH, Riverside Community Hospital. Bruised and sore, the walk from the drop off to the gift shop took twenty minutes, where he purchased two teddy bears.

The hospital was kind enough to move Esther and Lissette into the same room, a room always filled with flowers. Some of them are fresh-cut roses from Sylvia's rose garden. But most from a florist. Harvey paid the florist to bring more when needed and to cart off the others before wilt set in.

The night of the shooting, Rita helped get both Lissette and Esther into the Tahoe. Rita closed the Tahoe door, turned, and said, "I'll stay behind and get this mess cleaned up."

"I don't know if I can drive. I haven't driven in—"

She kissed him on the lips and hugged him. "I'm confident you can do it. You just saved us all, Harvey. Thank you. I'll never forget it. Now get going, they're both hurt pretty bad and need to get there fast."

What else could he do?

He spent the night in the hospital waiting room. Paced for several hours until body and soul screamed out for rest. He sat down in the comfortable chair in the surgical waiting area and slept for ten hours. No one disturbed him. No one thought to wake him to give patient status. Why would they? He wasn't family. He didn't have anyone left. Not after Sylvia passed. She'd been 'Sylvia' longer than 'Lois.' She'd stay Sylvia.

That next day, when he struggled up out of the chair and made it to the nurse's station, the kind nurse said both patients made it through surgery and were in the ICU. "Neither are visitors allowed at this time." He nodded, turned, and twenty minutes later caught an Uber home.

Inside the house, the living room was immaculate, the same as if no one had been stabbed or shot. For a brief moment, he thought maybe it hadn't happened and it had all been a bad dream. He wandered into the master bedroom to lie down in a familiar place and sleep for an age, when he abruptly changed direction and walked into the closet/sitting room. The wall was closed. His hand searched for the button under the edge of the bench. He took in a deep breath and held it. He pushed the button. The wall slid open. All the gold was gone. Of course, it was.

He slept all through the night and got up to make breakfast before heading to the hospital. On the dining room table, he found bank papers; a mortgage taken out on the house for a million, five hundred thousand. Signed by his wife of two years. The monthly payment listed was $5672.35. No money remained to make that payment. The house would go back to the bank in six or eight months, leaving a poor fool to live in a cardboard refrigerator box under a bridge. Like the troll waiting to eat the three Billie Goats Gruff.

But the loss of money didn't mean as much as the deceit, a black emotion that hung in the back of his throat, unable to swallow down.

He entered the hospital room carrying the two teddy bears. Esther sat up in bed with a tray containing green Jell-O and chocolate pudding. The knife punctured the intestines and stomach. She almost didn't make.

"Hello, Harv." She set the spoon filled with jiggly green down on the tray. She still looked gaunt and pale. Her skin was papery thin, exposing a myriad of blue veins. Even so she looked the best in the last seven days.

Over to the right, machines controlled Lissette's breathing and monitored her vitals. She was in a coma with a fifty-fifty chance of ever coming out of it.

Harvey stood next to Esther's bed and held her hand.

She said, "You finally ready to talk about it?"

He nodded.

She said, "Sylvia wanted to tell you about Eddie, but every time she started to, she couldn't."

"Why? We didn't have any secrets."

"She loved Eddie dearly and worried Giorgio would eventually find him. Sylvia was sure that any day Giorgio would discover you and her. He'd torture both of you until you told him. If you didn't know, you couldn't tell. That was her skewed way of thinking because she knew where Eddie lived."

Harvey tried to comprehend the enormity of the secret, how it must've weighed heavily on Sylvia every waking hour and even in her dreams. Studies have shown that stress can cause cancer. Had this secret been the cause of her demise?

Sylvia must've used Esther as a conduit to Eddie, someone to tell her everything about Eddie's day in school, at home, on birthdays, holidays. Sylvia emotionally broken living away from her son.

Harvey said, "Eddie's gone now. What about Maribelle?"

"She's got no one else. No family. I've made some calls. Maribelle will be fine as long as…as Lissette is still alive."

Harvey glanced over to Lissette's bed, then back. "We need to find a lawyer who, for a price, will post date a forged living will, giving you and I custody. So, we can find her a proper home and not leave it up to the state."

Tears welled in Esther's eyes. She squeezed his hand. "I was hoping you'd say that. Where are we going to get the money?"

"Don't you worry about that. I've got some equity left in the house. I'll sell it. There should be plenty for what we need."

"Thank you, Harv. Oh, a FedEx package came for you. It's over on the counter there next to the balloon bouquet."

"A package?"

He went over and picked it up. It wasn't a package at all but one of those thin cardboard envelopes that contained business papers or a letter. He pulled the tab and zippered it open.

Inside were two regular business envelopes, one with his name, "Harvey Usher."

He opened the one with his name and found a letter:

My Dearest Harvey:

I'm sorry to have left you in a lurch, but the cops could've come through the door at any second. A pressure I wasn't at all accustomed to. I cleaned everything, but don't trust it, not with the forensics they have nowadays, you just never know. Sell that damn house and get the hell away from it. You should easily get another million out of it.

I did a little better selling the gold than I thought I would. Enclosed is a cashier's check for six million. Half of the gold. I'm keeping the equity I stole from your house. I figured I earned it.

If you ever travel to Lisbon, look me up, lover, and we'll paint the town.

Rita

P.S. I lied about just liking you. Harvey, I will love you forevermore.

Acknowledgments

I would like to thank all the folks at Level Best Books for their help in bringing this project to fruition. I couldn't have done it without them.

About the Author

During his career in law enforcement, best-selling author David Putnam has worked in narcotics, violent crimes, criminal intelligence, hostage rescue, SWAT, and internal affairs, to name just a few. He is the recipient of many awards and commendations for heroism. He has three book series: The Bruno Johnson series, The Dave Beckett series, and the Imogene Taylor series. *The Obsessions of Harvey Usher* is a standalone.

AUTHOR WEBSITE:
  www.DavidPutnamBooks.com

SOCIAL MEDIA HANDLES:
  David@DavidPutnamBooks.com
  Facebook.com/DavidPutnamBooks
  Instagram.com/DavidPutnamBooks
  Goodreads.com/ DavidPutnam

Also by David Putnam

Bruno Johnson Series:
The Disposables (2014)
The Replacements (2014)
The Squandered (2016)
The Vanquished (2017)
The Innocents (2018)
The Reckless (2019)
The Heartless (2020)
The Ruthless (2021)
The Sinister (2022)
The Scorned (2023)
The Diabolical (2024)

The Dave Beckett Series:
A Fearsome Moonlight Black
A Lonesome Blood Red Sun

The Imogene Taylor Series:
The Blind Devotion of Imogene
Imogene's Grand Fiasco

www.ingramcontent.com/pod-product-compliance
Lightning Source LLC
Chambersburg PA
CBHW020408110726
47899CB00006B/1906